THE MIDSEASON FAKEOUT

WARNER UNIVERSITY BULLDOGS
BOOK 2

E. M. MOORE

Manufactured in the United States of America
First Edition December 2023

Edited by Chinah Mercer of The Editor & the Quill, LLC

Cover by 2nd Life Designs

Huge thanks to my beta reader, Jennifer!

Game On

Foul Line

At the Buzzer

Rockstars of Hollywood Hill

Rock On

Spring Hill Blue Series

Free Fall

Catch Me

Ravana Clan Vampires Series

Chosen By Darkness

Into the Darkness

Falling For Darkness

Surrender To Darkness

Coveted by the Dark

Thirst For Her

Ache For Her

Order of the Akasha Series

Stripped (Prequel)

Summoned By Magic

Tempted By Magic

Ravished By Magic

Indulged By Magic

Enraged By Magic

Safe Haven Academy Series

A Sky So Dark

A Dawn So Quiet

1

AIDAN

EVEN WITH MY EYES CLOSED, my traitorous brain keeps showing me the game clock count down to zero in the fourth quarter. Watching it is a slow, painful death because I know what's going to happen. And when it does, I still reel from the hollow ache in my heart. The despair that grips me in places I didn't even know could feel at all.

The worst part about the loss? My ass hurt from riding the bench. I wasn't sweaty. I wasn't even wearing the Bulldog-blue uniform. I couldn't help save anything.

An overwhelming pang of disappointment rings through me again when the memory of the buzzer sounds in my head like a morbid knell.

Our first L of the season. Our first L at home *all* year.

I was wrong about the worst part, though. What

hurt more was seeing the dejected faces of my team as they jogged off the field. Most wouldn't even look at me. Some did, and judging by the accusing glares they sent my way, not looking at me would've been better. For me, at least.

It was West who broke the mold and walked up to me, gave me a short nod and knuckles. Sweat poured down his face. Hair plastered to his forehead like he'd been in a war, but even The Hulk couldn't pull this one out.

"Do you see now?" His earlier words reverberate through me while I sit at my usual booth at the diner, my leg jumping up and down. I'd called for an emergency offensive meeting at Richie's, but none of the guys are here yet. I don't even know if they'll show, but that's old insecurities talking. Hopefully.

The waitress at the counter peers over at me, and I quickly look away, reminding myself that all the guys had to hit the showers after the game. That's why I'm still sitting alone. Everything's fine. Everything's good.

They'll be here.

I drag my fingers through my hair. The last few months have been a whirlwind. I was too far into it until there I was, a girl on each arm, beers dangling from both fingertips. Everyone wanted a piece of QB1, and I gave it to them like forfeiting pieces of my soul. Gave so much of myself away, I didn't have any parts left for football.

Asking myself for the hundredth time how I got so off track isn't going to help. That's not the issue now. It's getting back on track before Coach Thompson kicks me from the team permanently, and I have to go home a failure, a feeling I know all too well.

My stomach tightens as I have to bat away thought after thought.

Football is the only reason you're lovable, and you've failed at that.

You're discardable.

Trash.

They're not going to respect you now. They're going to drop you.

The bell above the door rings, and my head snaps around to see West and Kenna walk in. I breathe out a sigh of relief as he gives her a kiss on the forehead, and she strides toward a booth in the corner. My roommate blocks most of my view until he slides into the booth across from me. "Well, that was—"

"Fucking horrible?" My fingertips buzz with restrained energy as I peer behind me to see if anyone else is coming. I can't even begin to describe how shitty it felt to ride the bench while my team was struggling. West eyes me, and I snap my mouth shut. "I mean it was horrible for me. You guys did everything you could. Everything," I assure him.

"TT's too young. Inexperienced. He was scared more than anything."

My fingers clench and unclench. The backup QB did look a little pale, but I'd been too busy glaring at him all night to really notice. He was in my spot, even though the fault was totally mine. "I fucked up," I say, more to myself than to West. Misguided anger doesn't do me any good. TT stepped into my shoes when I wasn't good enough. I shouldn't be pissed at him. I should be thanking him.

"Well, I guess you know now that showing up late to practice and acting like a pompous ass will get you benched."

I drop my head low. QB1 at Warner University holds celebrity status on and off campus. Anything I want, I can get. I didn't understand that when I was backup for Reid Parker because he was a good dude. He didn't party. He didn't sleep around. He had his girlfriend, his close friends, and that was it. His goals were in play all the time. He never lost sight.

Mine got buried in a fog of alcohol, women's perfume, and the toxic magnetism of being the "it" guy.

As stupid as it sounds, everyone wanted me at their event. All the sororities, all the fraternities, local galas. They took pride in knowing I showed up.

They all wanted me, and when you grew up the way I did, it was a siren's call I couldn't turn down.

"Hey," West's even-keeled voice says, tugging me out of my thoughts. "What's done is done. You can turn this around."

I wish I was that confident. "Coach is pissed." I think I can still feel the spittle on my cheek from when he chewed me out, ending in him telling me I was sitting today's game out while I stood in horror, sure I was on some other planet. *I thought I was everyone's favorite person right now.*

West chuckles, and I glance at him. He's a changed man since Kenna. He talks more. He seems looser, more carefree. To think he overcame everything with the bad press and his dad...

If he can do it, so can I. Coach pulling me from the game was a wake-up call.

"You show him respect, he'll give respect back to you. He's not petty, man."

I know all this, it's just the embarrassment of having to crawl back to where I was.

The bell over the door rings again, and I peek behind me to see an older couple walk in. Turning back around, I slump deeper into the booth, my heart hanging heavy.

"They'll be here," West assures me. "They're not petty either."

I wouldn't blame them if they didn't show. We were headed for an undefeated season. What happened out there today was like watching a train wreck. The crowd was as quiet as I had ever heard them in our own stadium. At times, you could hear a pin drop. Observing the whole thing made me sick.

And not being able to do anything about it? That was like digging my own grave.

"Yo, QB1!"

I nearly jump, my gaze shooting up. A man behind the counter with a grease-stained apron waves at me. "You sick or what? We missed you at the game tonight. We could've used that magic arm."

My stomach tumbles over. I sit there, unable to form words. Finally, West turns around. "Don't you worry. He'll be back in no time."

I blink at West. Since when does he talk for me? Somehow, we've switched places, and it doesn't feel great. "Thanks," I mutter as the guy gives us a smiling salute and walks back through the kitchen doors, yelling "Go Blue!"

That chant usually sets a fire through me, but now, it's only a reminder of my fuckups. Behind me, the welcome bell rings again, and I twist in my seat to find Zo and Colt saunter in. Both of them look grim, and it's like a hammer driving a nail into my chest.

They pull up chairs to the end of the table while Cade enters. He forces me to move inside, and I rest my back against the cold, damp windows so I can see my team finally coming in. These guys put their trust in me on the field all the time. I'm the play-caller. I'm their leader. I'm the damn QB1, and I let them down.

The rest of the starting lineup arrives. Some sit in the

booth behind us, and some sit behind West and Jackson. Others have dragged up chairs like Zo and Colt until it looks like our huddle out on the field. I'm surrounded by my team who've been more like my family than—

I give myself a shake, avoiding that particular dark rabbit hole.

Instead, I focus on them. Nerves skate through me as they watch and wait.

"Listen," I push out. "I fucked up." I open my hands wide. "I let you all down, and I hope you realize that I get that. I'm pissed at myself, and I take full responsibility for tonight's loss. It's not on you guys, it's on me."

"No shit," Cade snarks. He gives me a teasing smile, but there's none of his usual easy air about him. For fifth year seniors like Cade, this was his final chance to go out with a bang—his last attempt at an undefeated season. And I'm the one who messed that up for him.

"We just want to know where your head's at now," Zo says.

"No more late to practices, I can guarantee you that," I tell him, voice firm.

"And the partying?"

"What parties?" I shrug, already done with them. They were messing with me anyway. The alcohol made me feel like shit. They screwed with my sleep

7

schedule. The girls were fun but didn't fill the part of me I thought they would.

Honestly, I don't know what I was thinking.

The guys start to look up. They give me nods as I stare at each and every one of them. "I'm sorry." I reach my hand up and hold it over my heart. "It won't happen again."

Promises to football brothers are set in stone. I have no intention of ever going back to the guy who sought to be accepted by people who don't matter. These guys? They're the ones who matter.

At that, the conversation turns. Colt calls over the waitress, and everything goes back to normal. For me, though, guilt still hovers. Until I bring this back around, I won't feel better. I need to nail the next practices, so Coach starts me again, and the game coming up is a must-win. If we don't, the team will lose their faith in me. And once I lose their trust, I'm out, or as good as.

Goodbye NFL dream.

Goodbye being accepted.

My stomach churns some more, and I order a water and then nurse it for the rest of the night.

A half hour goes by, and West kicks me under the table. My gaze snaps from my water glass to him. He tilts his head, and I shrug.

All around me, the guys discuss the game. They talk about girls. They even talk about classes, but it's like this life is slipping away from me. Every time they tell a story from tonight, a hammer drives the *outcast* nail in a little deeper. I don't have anything to add. I didn't see the D-lineman up close to notice his snaggle-tooth nor the huge-ass booger hanging from his nose.

I can tell them what it's like to ride the bench, though.

By the time our group breaks up, I feel further apart from them than ever.

"You okay?" Cade asks as he scoots out of the booth.

I shrug. "Just feel like shit about everything."

"The past is the past." He swallows, gaze falling away from me and landing on the floor. "There's nothing you can do about it." Perking back up, he says, "Reid would say: 'in the grand scheme of things, one game don't mean shit.'"

He emphasizes each word and slaps me on the back when I stand. "Yeah, man, I know."

"Practice, bright and early. I'm sure there will be more lines in your future."

My legs ache just thinking about it. Coach has had me running lines for the last three practices. I've been running lines so much I was surprised he didn't have me running them during the game itself. Give everyone a reason to talk about why I wasn't playing. I'm sure they're already speculating. The loss will only make their hypotheses worse.

"Don't I know it." I chuckle for Cade's benefit, and then he's out, leaving me, West, and Kenna.

West places his hand on my shoulder. "Unless you need to talk, I was going to spend the night at Kenna's."

"I'm good," I tell him. I'd rather be by myself tonight anyway. You know, really make myself feel like shit.

West stares at me a little longer, like he's trying to make sure I'm telling the truth. Eventually, I walk out behind them, and Kenna gives me a small wave before they climb into the Hulkmobile and I get in my Charger, a gift from my parents when I turned sixteen. Well, my adoptive parents. If my birth mom even remembers me on my birthday—or any other time for that matter—she never reaches out.

The drive to campus is short, made shorter because my mind is too preoccupied. I step out, shutting the door behind me and locking it before walking toward my dorm. There's a chill in the air, so I pick up the pace.

A girl squeals, the sound like nails on a chalkboard. "Aidan Michaels! Why weren't you playing?" It's Friday night, so of course there are drunk students everywhere. Without waiting for me to answer, she and her friend start giggling and talking in hushed whispers. I hear the words *he's a whole-ass snack* and smirk despite being annoyed. Before, that would've been enough of an invitation to waltz over and put the charm on her. One of them would've been in my room within half an hour. Or we'd end up going to some party where we'd find ourselves in an upstairs bedroom. Or, hell, there was an instance in a dark conference room at one of the nicer hotels in town during a community event.

That Aidan had a lot of fun, but he didn't have his eye on the prize, and it was unfulfilling as hell.

I keep my head down and walk on, ignoring both of them. When I come around the side of the building, I spot two figures waiting at the front entrance. I groan inwardly. One's a girl—a beautiful one at that. And the other is...

Oh shit.

"What the..." I start.

"Hey, bro!" Darrin calls out. He walks forward, and the girl walks up with him. I give him a short hug with a handshake, my gaze sliding over the girl briefly. She's even prettier up close.

Lucky bastard.

"What's up? What are you doing here?" I ask when we step away.

The girl comes up then. She throws her arms around me, and I nearly stumble. Placing my hands on her hips, I try to push her away, but she has a viselike grip on me. "Please go with whatever I say," she whispers in my ear.

I finally get her off me, and she stands before me,

hands on my arms. Now that she's so close, I can't believe I didn't recognize her. This isn't one of Darrin's girlfriends, it's his younger sister, Bailey. She flutters her lashes at me, a stricken look on her face. Her hair is in waves down to her shoulders, spun like gold and kissed with honey. In the air between us, her perfume still lingers, its blend of provocative flowers nearly drawing me closer. I haven't seen her in a few years, and she's...*gorgeous*.

Darrin sighs. "Dude, you don't need to act. I know you guys are seeing each other."

Seeing each other?

"I'm sorry, what?" I ask, my gaze dropping to Bailey in confusion. Her full lips mouth a silent *"Please?"* Her perfectly manicured hands come up in a prayer position while she gives me doe eyes.

I don't know what this is about, but my hero complex rears its head. I can never stand to see someone in trouble. Especially not someone like Bailey.

"It's okay," Darrin forces out. "I only hate you a little for not telling me first."

My mind whirring, I stand there speechless. I wish I knew what was going on. And how the hell Bailey grew up looking that fine in a simple sweater, her chest filling it out perfectly. The color on her lips matches. She looks like she stepped out of a beauty magazine.

Bailey moves next to me and grabs my hand. "Darrin, can you give us a few minutes? I didn't tell him you knew, so he's probably in shock. And he, you know, probably wants to talk...alone."

Her tone implies more than just talking. My brain is screaming *no, no, no. That's not what we do with our best friend's sister.* But my body says something completely different.

Where the hell did all that resolve about swearing off of girls just go?

"As long as you don't ever say it like that again." Darrin gives us both a disgusted look, then peers down at our joined hands, shaking himself like he got a chill.

He walks off in the opposite direction, and my mouth nearly comes unhinged when he disappears from view. I turn to Bailey. "What the fuck was that?"

"I have a teeny, tiny favor to ask you."

She grins at me, hopeful, and I already know I can't say no.

Lucky me, the universe drops the perfect representation of my spank bank right in front of me.

I shake my head. *Good thing she's off-limits because staying away from her might be a problem.*

2

BAILEY

SEEING Aidan again sends goose bumps through my whole body.

He leads me up the stairs to his dorm room. I have no idea how I'm going to explain to him that us dating just kind of popped out in front of everyone, and now I need him to agree. For my own sanity. For my own happiness. My whole future is at risk.

...Maybe. I've been known to be dramatic.

While I walk next to him, I have the perfect opportunity to take him in after not seeing him for years.

Damn.

His forearms got bigger. More muscular, like a man's arm, not the boy's arms I'm used to seeing on him. Nerves pulse through me, and I'm suddenly super intimidated. He's taller than I remembered, towering over me now. I'm like a little girl running to catch up to him—but maybe that's because I'm too busy ogling him to worry about keeping pace.

Finally, my toes in these stupid boots get a reprieve when we reach his room. He pushes the door open, and I blink at my surroundings. His dorm is smaller than I imagined it would be. Two beds are on opposite sides of the room, pushed against the walls. The bed on the right has a desk next to it, while the bed on the left has a desk at the foot of it. Comparatively, this room is so much worse than the alternative place that I refuse to go to, but somehow, it's better. It feels cozy. Real.

So, this is where normal kids go to school?

I'm impressed. Like super-duper impressed, and I can't get the gooey smile off my face. I itch to touch all the things. From the pint-size refrigerator to the sports posters hanging on the walls. This is so...college.

Aidan clears his throat, and I turn to find him staring at me. I suck in a breath. His blue eyes are like topaz fire. His brown hair shines with a golden hue. Unfortunately, his voice isn't laced in awe, mimicking the current feelings zipping through me. "Please tell me why I just lied to my best friend out there." He points in the direction of what I'm guessing is the entrance to the dorm, but really, I'm lost. I was so preoccupied checking out his new muscular build that I couldn't get out of this dorm if I tried.

"Don't be mad."

His eyes widen, clouding over in a thunderous haze.

"I said don't be mad."

He laughs incredulously. "Bailey, give me something to go on here. I don't understand why your brother thinks we're together. Like, together, together."

I rub up and down my arms, trying to smooth down the goose bumps that'd sprung up when he said *together*. "That's because I told him we were." I look away so I don't have to see his face when I tell him the next part. "And Mom and Dad, too."

"You told— You *what?*"

My eyes shudder for a moment, but then I walk forward. "Okay, please, please hear me out. You know how my mom and dad are. They were talking about sending me to this fancy private college and suddenly, I could see my whole life laid out before me. Marry some guy I meet at college. He'll probably work for my dad. He'll probably be shit in the bedroom. I'll pop out kids to make my parents happy. We'll go on one vacation a year that lasts two weeks, and the other fifty weeks, I'll be wishing we were on vacation because at least I get a change of scenery and a chance to look at pool boys." I take a deep breath, my heart hammering while I wait for his response.

The look he gives me would be funny if I wasn't pouring my heart out to him here. His eyebrows scrunch adorably, mouth hanging open. *God, he's got kissable lips.* I've always thought so, but I was just Bails, the younger sister always around like an unwanted toy.

And now I'm asking him to pretend to date me.

This is so not going well.

He runs his hands through his hair. "I think you're losing it. I didn't understand any of that. Somehow, where you go to college means you'll have a miserable life, which I don't even understand because you're not in college yet."

I grimace. "I actually skipped a grade." I shake a nonexistent pom-pom.

He rolls his eyes. "Of course you did."

Sealing my lips shut, I bite my tongue. People don't understand how much that bothers me, especially others my own age. How do I even begin to explain that I have this overwhelming urge to make my parents proud...in everything? Even when it's detrimental to myself.

He sits down on his bed. I knew the right was his side. It's a little messy, but not bad. The TV is turned toward his bed, and there's a football video game paused, something he and Darrin used to play nearly all day when Aidan would visit.

Leaning over his thighs, he peeks up at me, his gaze drifting down my front and back up quickly. A thrill shoots through me. That might have been the first time

Aidan Michaels has ever checked me out. If that's what it was.

I still consider it a personal victory.

It's no wonder his name popped out when I was trying to convince my parents not to send me to Carnegie University. Sure, it's a great school, but I wouldn't be meeting anyone different. I wouldn't be experiencing new things. I live in a posh bubble, and I can't escape it.

I'm going fucking mad.

"Let's start from the beginning," Aidan instructs. "And I promise I won't get angry."

I move toward the bed and sit next to him, frowning a little when he puts some distance between us. Distracted by all the new things in this room, I bounce up and down on the mattress. Not bad. It's definitely no plush luxury brand, but I could deal. Mom made it sound like kids at other colleges sleep on army cots or some shit.

"What are you doing?" Aidan asks, jumping to his feet.

"Nothing," I say hurriedly. "Just...looking at things." I take a deep breath. "Sorry, I've never been in a dorm room before. But moving on, you know how my parents are with me. The piano recitals, and the dance classes, and—"

"You like all those things."

I give him a withering look. "—the pressure. Oh my

18

God, the pressure. I need a break, Aidan. It's like being in a cage."

"Yeah, a diamond-encrusted cage."

My head snaps back, and I clamp my jaw shut again. I'd suspected that's what Aidan thought of me. It's probably what everyone thinks of me. I'm my mother's mini-me. Louis Vuitton's and designer clothes. Straight A's.

My mother is the stud, and I'm the prized mare to be shown around with ribbons draping my neck.

"Aidan..." Emotion clogs my throat before I can compose myself. "You must have noticed my parents never let me do anything. You and Darrin would go out. I had to stay home. You and Darrin would get to do all these fun things, and I had to practice and study and be the *good little girl*."

He shakes his head. "You were too young to go out with us."

"I'm only a year and a half younger than you," I snap. "Get over it."

He holds up his hands. "Whoa."

I barely let him take another breath. "Even when I got older, they still wouldn't let me do anything. I'm like the mannequin in a store—you can look but you can't touch. If I go to Carnegie, everything will stay the same. *Everything*. I need space. I need freedom."

He scratches at the little bit of stubble that lines his jaw, and I find myself wondering if it's always there now, or if he just didn't shave today. When he speaks, though, I meet his gaze. "I'm sorry, Bailey. I didn't realize you were...unhappy. I thought you liked being the princess."

"How could I have shown otherwise? A princess throwing a fit looks like a stuck-up bitch."

He nods. "Fair enough. Really, I'm sorry. I didn't even know you wanted to come out with us. If I did..."

This is what I love about Aidan. Always so quick to understand and empathize. "So, then, you understand why I'm here?" I ask hopefully.

"I get that you want to be your own person. I don't understand why you need me to do that."

Well, that's a story within another story. "So, here's the thing. Darrin's been talking about transferring here for a year or so, and my parents were all on board as sort of a fun reprieve before he returned to 'real college.' I said I wanted to, too, but it was an immediate no, which so isn't fair." I peer at Aidan for confirmation, but he still looks confused. "They told me Darrin had a reason for wanting to go here and I didn't. You and I dating kind of popped out after that. You know, as the reason why I would want to go here."

"And they believed that? That was enough for them?"

I wish. My parents were taken aback when I told them I was dating Aidan. They love him, they do, but they think I should marry a CEO or something, not an

NFL prospect. I was ashamed to overhear my dad tell my mom to let my "little flirtation" run its course. That I'll be pleading to go to Carnegie in no time.

Telling Aidan that part would only stir the pot, so I keep it to myself. "It was," I lie. "They were happy for us. Plus, you were Darrin's only reason, too."

"Except there's not an *us*," Aidan interjects. "And, someday, we're going to have to break up."

"Ouch." Why did that hurt so much? Oh, I know. Because I've been harboring a crush on my brother's best friend for a while.

Aidan sits next to me, knocking his knee against mine, teasing. "That's kind of inevitable when your relationship is fake."

A jolt of sorrow pings through me, but then my heart jumps. Peering at him hopefully, I ask, "Does that mean you'll do it?"

He slides back onto his bed, leaning against the wall. "Why not? What do we have to do? Take a couple pictures every once in a while to send to your parents? Easy. I can pretend."

Not realizing he's kicked me where it hurts, he keeps going on and on about how easy it will be to fake this. I flick his leg. "Did you not hear the part about Darrin transferring here? We can't just take a few photos. It has to be real."

His eyes bug out of his head. "So, he is transferring here? When?" The pure excitement on his face makes me smile...and only leaves me with a small hole realizing I'm not that person for someone.

"Like, this next semester. Along with me... I hope." Raising my brows, I watch while he takes everything in.

"So..."

"This is going to be full-on pretending. Darrin will know if it's a lie, and he has the biggest mouth. He'll tell my parents for sure."

"Well, that changes things."

My heart sinks. "It does?"

"I mean, what are we talking about doing here, Bails? How far are we going to take this?"

My heart starts to take off again. The fact that he's even considering it means I still have a chance. If Aidan doesn't bite, I'm going to have to go back home with my tail between my legs, and that would crush me. I already love it here. I saw drunk people and a dorm room.

I swallow. "Well, what would you do with an actual girlfriend? We can do that."

He runs his hand down his face, staring at me for a few long moments. Outside, tires squeal in the parking lot, and he peers out the window briefly before saying, "Okay, let's do it."

I gasp and attempt to hug him, but he puts up a finger, stopping me with my hands straddling his thighs. I'm bent over him, frozen, acutely aware of how close we are and what this position looks like. His next words throw me back into reality, though.

"I want to let you know my intentions aren't unselfish."

Sitting back on my calves, I steel myself for another pang of hurt. "Okay..."

He takes a deep breath, his face morphing from relaxed to miserable. "I fucked up. I don't know if you guys saw that I didn't play in tonight's game?"

I nod. Darrin and I were there, actually. We were going to surprise him at the stadium, but he was up and out of there so quickly, and we didn't know where he went afterward. We'd been waiting for him outside his dorm complex ever since.

He brushes against his pants absentmindedly. "I let QB1 go to my head. There was too much partying. Too many girls."

Too many girls? Jealousy rages inside. That sounds like he was with a lot, yet he was second-guessing even wanting to *fake* date me.

Talk about a sucker punch to the old confidence.

"If you're my 'girlfriend'," he says, using air quotes, "then they won't be around me all the time."

"Who's *they*?" I ask, confused.

"Mainly jersey chasers, but there's a whole slew of girls here. It's crazy."

"So, I'll be, like, your girl repellent?"

He smiles, blue eyes warming up. "Exactly."

As much as his words hurt, he's agreeing to what I asked and he's being upfront with me about it. "Sounds like a win-win," I tell him, even though I'm not totally feeling it. I don't know what I thought would happen when I came up with the idea, but I was a bit hopeful he'd see me and be at least a little interested. I've grown up a lot since I last saw him.

He sighs in relief, then holds up his hand to give me a high five. I follow through, and the look he sends me makes my heart flip.

Aidan's phone rings, and I jump, the harsh sound yanking me out of the moment, but he just casually reaches for it like nothing happened.

He chuckles, turning the device toward me so I can see who's calling him. *Darrin* fills the screen.

A huge smile takes over his face and he winks at me, and I already know something smartass is going to come out of his mouth. "Dude," he answers, "I thought we had a pact that we don't cockblock?"

My mouth unhinges as a strikingly hot sensation races toward my thighs at the thought.

I can't hear what Darrin says in response, but Aidan laughs. "Kidding, man. Get your ass up here. I'm in 327. Take the stairs on the left."

He ends the call and continues to grin. "This could be fun. Are you guys staying on campus?"

I shake my head. "Please, Mom and Dad wouldn't go that far. They rented us a house close by."

"Sweet." He shrugs. "He's still nearby. I mean, you'll both be nearby."

I try not to take that personally. "Yeah, except I have to share with him." I roll my eyes.

"Good thing you don't need real privacy," he says, jabbing me with his elbow while he slides off the bed.

I frown. I was hoping for exactly that, actually. This isn't a plot to get Aidan to date me, but I was hopeful it could be a happy side effect. "You know, you should probably sleep over sometimes to make it look good," I add, sure that's what a couple in a real relationship would do without parental supervision.

He turns toward me, face pale, but he doesn't get a chance to respond before Darrin barges into the room. Glaring at the two of us, he then scans the room like he can detect what we were actually doing in here. Nothing as damning as he thinks. Unfortunately.

"You asshole," he growls, then punches Aidan in the shoulder.

"Not the goods, man," Aidan replies, working his arm out. "I was only messing with you. Like I'd actually talk about your sister with you. I'm glad you're here. This is awesome." He pauses for a moment. "And Bails, too." He holds out his hand for me to take. "It's good to finally see her."

His eyes are like homing beacons. Being this close to Aidan's bubble has me crushing on him all over again.

I stand on wobbly legs and hold out my hand. He immediately closes his around mine and tugs me into his side, draping his arm along my shoulders, crushing me to him.

Across from us, Darrin shakes his head. "I don't see it."

"What?" I ask defensively.

"You and him. My best friend. It doesn't make sense."

My insides twist. This is what everyone is going to think. What is Aidan, starting quarterback, doing with *that* girl? I'm nothing like the type of girl I've seen him go for. I don't have model-long legs. I'm not bare-my-midriff skinny. In fact, I'm a little on the short side with wider hips and a bubble butt.

"Which is why we didn't tell you," Aidan snaps.

My body freezes. I don't understand why he's mad. Like really mad. That wasn't pretend.

I peer up, and his eyes are guarded. They're no longer looking over at Darrin, they're staring off into space, his fingers flexing against my skin.

"Dude, we're cool," Darrin says. "I was just surprised. I won't say anything about it again. But I'm warning you two right now, if you break up, I'm not taking sides. That's my sister, and you're like my brother."

"That's kind of gross," I answer, and Aidan says "gross" at the same time.

He pulls me in close, like we're actually a couple thinking how cute it is that we end each other's sentences.

Darrin makes a retching sound. In return, Aidan and I glare at him.

He laughs. "Last one, I swear. I'm getting there."

All I know is, unlike my brother's feelings on the matter, I really like being plastered to Aidan's side, and my body does, too.

Pretending won't be that hard for me at all. In fact, I'll probably have to rein myself in.

3

AIDAN

THE FAMILIAR SOUNDS of my video game fill the room, but my gaze keeps traveling to Bailey, which means Darrin is owning my ass. He intercepts my pass and laughs like the competitive fucker he is.

"Yeah, yeah," I grunt, my eyes flicking toward his little sister who isn't so little anymore. She's sitting on the chair at my desk, staring at her polished nails, frowning.

Uneasiness creeps over me. Suddenly hot and cold at the same time, I wipe my brow. We're not doing a good job of pretending at the moment. I'm usually great with the ladies, but this feels different. I don't know how to act.

The way she'd stared at me with those tortured honey brown eyes, I couldn't say no. Luckily, I'm not in any danger of falling into a complicated relationship with her. She's Darrin's sister. It's Bro Code 101 that you don't actually date them. Not to mention that she was never actually on my radar. She's too proper. Darrin and I would be eating at the table, and she'd come in, back ramrod straight and smiling like a porcelain doll. She'd wear fancy dresses on a Saturday. And dresses in the evenings when most girls put up their hair and put on sweats. I don't know, she seems too far out there. Stuck-up, even.

Darrin snaps his fingers. "Dude, waiting on you."

I peer at the screen and pick my play, run it briefly before glancing back at Bailey. She's dressed in a pair of tight jeans with heeled boots squeezing her calves. Her sweater looks soft, like cashmere, and her hair is perfectly styled.

Honestly, I don't know how her parents even agreed to this. Not only does she look out of my league, I always got the impression that though I was accepted at their house, I was never really one of them. They were rich, and Bailey? She screams high maintenance. I don't have the time for that. However, what won me over is that we could be good for each other. She can go out and explore college life like she wants, and she can be my jersey-chaser repellent so I can focus on football, which is exactly where my head needs to be at.

I return my focus back to the video game and kick Darrin. "You play better ball in the game than in real life."

He flips me off, and I grin.

"You still want to play?" I ask. He was always good, but he never took it to the next level.

He shrugs. "I could make the Bulldogs. Seems like they let anyone on."

His jab rolls right off me, and I laugh. His gaze, though, turns toward his sister and then back to me. When he sees me staring, he looks away quickly.

Was Bailey right? Will he notice if this isn't real?

If I want her to do her part for me, I have to do my part for her.

When Darrin isn't looking, I poke Bailey in the leg, then nod my head to call her over.

She points next to me and mouths, *On the bed?*

I nod, making room for her. She takes a quick glance at her brother and then stands, sliding toward me hesitantly.

I roll my eyes, tugging her closer until she's practically on top of me. "Come on. Don't be afraid. Darrin knows now." The lie comes out easily, and it's surprising. It's kind of fun. Who wouldn't want to pretend they had this beautiful, smart girlfriend? I mean, high maintenance or not, that doesn't take anything away from her looks.

She settles next to me, her perfume wafting around us, and I breathe in deep for a moment. Honestly, she smells like a dream.

Darrin peeks over but doesn't pretend to throw up this time. "How did you guys get together, anyway?"

Bailey freezes next to me. I can only take that as she actually hasn't come up with our perfect story yet.

Again, the fib comes easily. "Bails must have gotten my number off your phone. She professed her undying love for me in a text. Seems like she'd been crushing on me the whole time we've been friends. A little creepy actually."

I nudge her with my elbow, and her mouth falls open. Hey, she didn't say not to tease her through this whole thing.

With his eyes glued to the screen, Darrin states, "I saw how she's always looked at you."

Now it's my turn to freeze and peer over at her. Her cheeks turn pink, and she won't look at me, even though she must feel my gaze burning through her. "Is that so?" I ask, my voice coming out low and gravelly.

Her mouth shuts, then opens again. I rib her again, and she finally looks at me. Her face is so open, and I can see it written there. What Darrin said is true.

Darrin laughs. "It was pathetic. She was like a puppy, and you didn't even notice."

I stare at her, dumbfounded and...something else. Confusion. I had no idea. "Well, I notice now," I tell him, because that's what the perfect boyfriend would say. He would save her from her older brother's teasing.

Her chest rises with a breath, and her gaze drops to my lips.

Mine drops to hers, too. They're like soft pillows tinted pink.

What am I doing again?

That's right. Pretending.

I maneuver my arm around her, making her move close enough so I can still use my controller with both hands. "Her confession was too cute," I add with a smile.

"Did she tell you she wanted to ask you to her prom?"

Bailey grabs one of my pillows and throws it at her brother. "Would you shut up?"

Darrin laughs disinterestedly. "I told her she couldn't, and she was so mad."

I pull Bailey back into my chest, but she's stiff, glaring at her brother like she could choke him.

I never really paid attention to their dynamic before, only that they didn't spend a lot of time together. At least not when I was there. But this? This is fun. I get that family feeling. Sure, she's mad now, but that's her brother. She'll be over it soon.

At least, that's how functional families work. Or so I'm told.

But that's something to unpack for another day. Now, I'm genuinely curious about Bailey's feelings for me. I lick my lips and reach for the remote. Turning the volume up, I don't do anything for a moment, but then I tug Bailey's hair back and move it around her ear. My mouth is a little dry when I whisper, "You wanted to go to prom with me?"

She doesn't answer, but I can see her face getting redder and redder.

"It's okay," I tell her, wondering if she still has a thing for me. Most likely not. No way would she want to torture herself by making this fake date plan. It was probably a childhood crush.

The longer she's cuddled next to me, the more she relaxes. I find myself rubbing her leg when I can, and when I notice it, I chalk it up to keeping up the pretense we're selling. I certainly know what to do when a beautiful girl is almost in my lap. In contrast, though she's relaxed, Bailey doesn't move at all. I have to look close to see if she's even breathing.

At the end of the game, Darrin throws his hands in the air triumphantly. "Take that, Hot Shot!"

"Those who can't actually play do it on the screen."

"You're just jealous."

A knock sounds on the door.

I peer over at it, and then at the clock on my desk. It's eleven o'clock at night. *Shit*. I should actually be in bed in preparation for practice tomorrow. I shake my head at myself.

Bailey moves over so I can get up. I walk across the room and check the peephole.

Fuck me. I recognize who it is instantly. A blonde-headed jersey chaser that I hooked up with last week after a party. She's wearing a robe, smiling innocently.

I turn toward Bailey with what must be a stricken face. Fear ramps up. If Darrin finds out I hooked up with this girl, she could spoil this whole thing for Bailey...and me.

In a split second, I have to make a decision. "Hey, babe," I say to her. Bailey doesn't even look up at first, so I walk toward the bed as the knock comes again. That gets her attention, and she peeks up at me, surprised to see me so close. "Remember when I told you about the girls who wouldn't leave me alone?" I widen my eyes to show her the urgency of the matter. "One of them is at the door right now."

"Oh? Oh..." she says, standing up. "Maybe I should answer the door, then?"

I give her a smile, urging her on. "Perfect."

She straightens her shoulders and brushes past me, leaving her delectable scent in her wake. When she opens the door, I see the jersey chaser in front of her, and I study the both of them. If Bailey wasn't Darrin's sister and she wanted to crawl into my bed, I would let her. She's stunning, and she actually has a personality, rather than the football-player-obsessed one all the girls like to use with me. That one is good for stroking my ego, which it did. A lot. Too many times, apparently.

"Hey, can I help you?" Bailey asks. She runs her gaze up and down the girl in front of her, and her shoulders stiffen. It's apparent what this girl is here for. Her robe is tied loosely, leaving a hefty amount of cleavage to be seen.

"Who are you?" the girl snaps.

"Bailey. Aidan's girlfriend. Are you here to see him?"

The jersey chaser's mouth drops, then she shuts it again. Over top of Bailey, I see her looking for me, so I stride forward, throwing my arm around Bails. Like a pro, she cuddles into my side, placing her hand on my abs in a possessive way.

"I just got in from out of town," Bailey says politely. "We're both so happy I've decided to go here." Peering up at me, she finds me already looking down at her. "Now we can spend so much more time together."

Her words and the way she stares at me adoringly hit me in a way they shouldn't.

She's good at lying, I'll give her that.

"You have a girlfriend?" the girl asks, ignoring Bailey completely, clearly put out.

Bailey hasn't taken her eyes off me, and I haven't with her either. Her stare drops to my mouth, as if in warning of what she's going to do next. My heart stammers, and I say "Yes" at the same time Bailey lifts onto her toes and kisses me.

My stomach clenches.

She pauses a moment, like she's wondering if this is okay, leaving me enough time to take over. I cup her cheek on instinct, and my lips move against hers, slow at first, then fervently as she kisses me back.

Holy shit. She opens her mouth in invitation, and I dive right in, a groan spilling from my throat. My lips buzz in excitement, and I get lost in the feeling of the two of us connecting. *I could do this forever*, I think, until Darrin clears his throat.

"Alright already. Tell the girl to get lost."

I pull away, almost surprised to see it's Bailey looking back at me, her lips plump from being ravaged by my own. Her honey eyes stare openly at me, like she's as surprised as I am. She made me feel that way, and it's evident I made her feel something too.

I swallow thickly, my throat as dry as the desert while I try to come to terms with what just happened, which I guess is that Bailey is an excellent kisser. So, there's that. Yet, she also stirred something inside me too. Something I've been missing.

But she's not for me, I remind myself.

No one will be. Not until after I get my shit together in football. Bailey doesn't deserve to be treated the way I've been treating girls. She's different.

Bailey puts some distance between us first and smiles at the girl. "Aidan's going to be too busy to hang out for the foreseeable future, 'kay? Thanks, bye." Then she shuts the door in her face.

I stand there frozen, trying to get my mind and my body on the same page.

Darrin stares at us. "You guys are lucky the door was in the way for most of that. Can we make a rule that you two don't kiss in front of me?"

Bailey takes a steadying breath. "You should get over it. Apparently, I have to stake my claim while here on campus."

Darrin laughs. "If I know Aidan, you won't need to. He's too invested in football."

His words make my stomach turn over. I really haven't been acting myself. It's disgusting, actually.

Without responding to her brother, Bailey asks me, "Do they do that often?"

I shrug. "Sometimes."

"You can stay at our place if you need quiet," she says, lids fluttering.

It seems like there's an underlying tone in that sentence.

Darrin shoots up from the bed. "I swear to God, if I hear you guys, I will yeet myself off a bridge. First, I will stick a Q-tip so far into my ear that it permanently punctures my eardrum, then I will wander around aimlessly until I find a bridge tall enough to jump from to do some real damage."

I peer over at my friend. "I would never—" I stop there because just a minute ago, I would've said that there was no chance in hell that his sister and I would ever kiss, but here I was, devouring her face right in front of him.

I was transfixed. Everything else in the outside world melted away until it was only the two of us. I swear, it was magic.

"Sure, sure. I'm going to go," Darrin declares, getting up from the bed.

"Me too," Bailey pipes up. "Aidan has practice tomorrow, so he should get some sleep."

Darrin walks by me awkwardly, and I sigh. "I'm sorry," I call out.

"I'll get used to it." But there's a hint of disappointment in his voice.

Bailey starts to turn, too, but I hold back on her arm. "We should talk about that kiss," I hiss.

She had to have felt the same thing I did, but we both know we can't go there. Right?

She peeks at my lips. "It was perfect," she says, her gaze meeting mine. After a deep breath, she says, "I think it worked in getting her to stay away from you. You'll probably be in the clear for tonight. No random girls showing up at your room in nothing but a robe. Super classy, by the way."

She turns and follows her brother, and I'm left with the feeling that I should apologize for something that happened before our fake relationship.

That was all a little too real, though. I take a deep breath, letting them both go. Everything will be better tomorrow when I show up to practice on time, run drills, and forget the feel of Bailey's lips on mine.

I shake my head. Not only is the relationship not real, but no girl is worth losing my best friend—and football—over. It's probably better that we don't discuss the kiss.

Sleep it is, then.

4

BAILEY

Come to my practice.

FIVE MINUTES LATER...

At least the end. About noon.

Ten minutes later...

There are always girls hanging out
there, so I need my fakey-poo.

Fakey-poo? Please tell me that's not going to be a thing.

With the whirlwind of moving in yesterday and then staying up late to see Aidan, it's already 10:30 a.m. Sleep still clings to my eyes, and I stretch in bed before throwing the covers off me. Good thing we actually exchanged numbers yesterday because I most definitely did not text him my undying love. Though, I had to pretend I didn't already have his number because I actually did grab it off my brother's phone years ago. At least now my number lives in his phone, and apparently, he's not afraid of using it.

A quick shower later, and I'm standing in front of my closet. Plenty of nice clothes fill it, but it's Saturday. Isn't Saturday a time for lounging? My mom would never let me wear something casual out in public, but she's not here. She won't know what I wore this morning to go watch my fake boyfriend's football practice. Right?

Right.

I grab a pair of leggings and a long-sleeved Henley-like shirt that I usually sleep in. I unclasp the buttons on the lilac purple shirt so it gives me a bit of a V-neck.

Hair will go up into a messy bun, not curled. Hell, I might as well go all in. Make a statement. I'm going with minimum makeup, too.

My stomach churns with butterflies while I meticulously put my ensemble together. Twisting to the side and back again, I stare at my reflection in the floor-length mirror. I look...perfectly normal.

I love it.

I walk out into the shared kitchen with some extra pep in my step and find Darrin already there, eating a bowl of cereal. "How did you get this?" I point at the Count Chocula box on the table in front of him.

"DoorDash," he says around a mouthful.

I roll my eyes, and he finally peers up at me because a knit forms between his brows. I stare back. "What?"

"Why are you wearing that?"

I smile to myself. "Because it's comfortable."

"You never wear that."

"Well, I do now." I pat him on the head and grab the Froot Loops he must've added to his order for me and pour myself a bowl. It's been forever since I've had Froot Loops, and I take a moment to smell the sugary goodness before diving in, leaning against the counter.

The house Mom and Dad rented us is fairly large. My bedroom is downstairs while Darrin has the entire upstairs at his disposal. He turned one of the extra rooms into a living room of his own, and he also has his own bathroom up there, too. The only space we really have to share is the kitchen, and I've already told him that I'm not cleaning up after his ass.

Instead of moving us in, our parents hired professional movers to help settle us in before classes start on Monday, which was fine by me. The sooner I got space from them, the better.

"What are you doing today?" Darrin asks, watching me over his bowl.

I study him a moment before an awful thought flits through my head. "Don't."

"What?" he asks. "I just asked what you were up to today. Is that a crime?"

I squeeze the spoon in my hand. "I swear to God, Darrin, if Mom and Dad told you to watch me, or something even more mortifying, I'm not having it."

"What?" he asks with a little too much surprise. He knows he's, like, the worst liar. He starts to laugh and sets his bowl down on the table. "Of course they asked me to look after you."

I set my own bowl down. "Darrin, I need space. That's the whole reason I'm here. I can take care of myself. Isn't that what college is about? Learning how to go off on our own. Don't you want to live your life without having to see if I'm okay?"

"One, I thought the whole reason you were here was because of Aidan? And two, I don't want to have to worry about you, but Dad said if anything happens to you, it's on me."

My head falls back, and I groan. "Obviously, I'm here because of Aidan. I want Aidan and space. So let's make a deal." I walk up to him and stick out my pinkie. "You leave me alone and I'll leave you alone. I promise that if I get myself in a tricky situation that I'll come right to you. If I need you, I will definitely tell you."

He eyes my pinkie, then me. "You can't get in trouble."

"What am I going to do?" I scoff. My list of things I

want to experience here is fairly innocuous. It's probably boring to most people.

He shrugs. "Get pregnant."

I nearly choke. "What? And how are you going to stop that from happening? Follow me everywhere to make sure I'm not having sex?"

He points at me. "Don't think I'm not going to have a talk with Aidan about that."

Just shoot me now.

I grab his pinkie forcefully with my own. "We are roommates, but you are not my bodyguard. Understood?"

He clamps his mouth shut.

"And unless you want me to ask every single girl you talk to if she's going to have sex with you, don't even give my sex life another thought." My face flushes. Of course my brain would take this moment to think about Aidan and me—and it's a damn good visual, too. "And I'm not a child. I know how to prevent pregnancy. You don't have to worry about me. Promise."

We shake on it and both go back to eating, but Darrin keeps eyeing me all the same. It's going to take a while for him to relax. Our parents must have given him a strict rundown of what I was allowed to do, but I don't plan on following any of their rules.

It's time for *my* rules.

After eating, I rinse my bowl out and place it in the

sink. "I'm going to go walk around. Get a feel for campus," I tell Darrin. He jumps up from his chair, and I spin to pin him in place with my hard stare. "Alone."

He sighs. "You got your cell phone on you?"

I nod.

"Send me updates."

I give my big brother a hug. "I love you, but no. I'll see you when I see you. Let me know if you want to have lunch or dinner together."

Turning away feels good, and I'm almost at the door when he says, "Please don't make me regret this. Actually, better thought: Please don't make me regret trusting you."

Grabbing my jacket, I spin and blow him a kiss. "Thanks, big bro."

"Yeah, yeah."

The air has a bit of a chill, but not too bad. I end up walking with my jacket in my hands. The sounds of freedom are everywhere. Cars driving by. College kids talking in groups, laughing, screaming. The wind rustles through the trees and teases the hairs poking out of my messy bun, and it's like the perfect symphony of autonomy.

I studied the map of campus earlier, so I head toward the football area, which runs along a trail. Whistles pierce the air, and as I get even closer, I can hear pads colliding. The sound is familiar enough.

Darrin played football in high school. He was good, and I loved going to his games when I wasn't scheduled to do my own things, but sitting next to my parents in the stands is different than sitting with friends and enjoying the atmosphere. Even out in public, it felt like I was in a cage.

My feet pick up the pace all on their own, and I round the bend and find a fence surrounding a practice field. I hike up the hill and search for Aidan. It doesn't take me long to pick him out. He's devastatingly handsome, his face in concentration mode as he drops back to throw the ball. A yellow pinny covers his practice jersey—without any pads, so his full, muscular figure is in view.

He's downright gorgeous.

On the other side of the fence, I notice a small section of bleachers and spot a few girls sitting there. Those must be the ones Aidan was talking about—the jersey chasers. I head that way, dragging my fingers along the chain-link. All the while, I keep my stare on Aidan and try not to think about the electrifying kiss we shared last night.

Instead, I focus on our agreement. A fake relationship that just so happens to come at the best time for both of us. I feel bad that he's had a rough time. Darrin and I always kept up with his games. We watched them on TV, and I would get jealous when Darrin would text him afterward, congratulating him on his win. I guess his getting benched goes to show that even the good ones can flounder a little. I bet it's hard being almost famous.

Finally, I get to the metal bleachers and climb up them. The girls peer over at me, and I smile. The girl from last night catches my eye. She's sandwiched between two others, and she grabs their arms when she sees me and immediately starts whispering.

Guess I haven't found my tribe yet.

I take a seat away from them and watch Aidan throw a few more passes, then jog to the sidelines. He reaches for a water and gulps it down. Despite the chill in the air, he's sweating profusely.

The girls on the other side of the bleachers call his name and wave. He ignores them, turning his back. I have to hide a smile, but I don't dare glance over to see their faces at the absolute rebuff he just gave them.

I want him to know I'm here, but I'm not about to call out like they did.

A few minutes later, he turns back around to set his water bottle down. Straightening in my seat, I wait to see if he looks up. He does, slowly, almost like he knew I was here.

I give him a small wave, and his shoulders immediately relax. Then, in complete Aidan form, his lips split into a cocky grin. He points at me, then makes a heart with his hands.

I chuckle because I've seen him and Darrin do that

when they're playing a game and one of them completely wastes the other. It's like a sarcastic *I love you, bro.*

Someone calls his name, so I don't get a chance to respond before he turns his attention back to football, jogging over to a middle-aged man with a clipboard. I recognize him from TV, too. Coach Thompson. He's a big deal in the college football scene, and for that matter, so is Warner University. ESPN always shows their games, and the commentators love talking about Aidan.

I can't hear what the coach is saying, but the group of girls has started talking louder.

"I don't know," one of them says. "She doesn't look like his type."

"Not at all," answers another, and I can't help but think they want me to hear.

"Do you think he was with her when he was, you know..."

"In your bed?" the girl calls out loudly.

My stomach churns. It hadn't even occurred to me that Aidan might have a girlfriend when I told the lie. Though that's obviously not what any of these girls are. Still, at least one of them has more experience with him than I do.

"Actually, it was his bed."

Noted. Never getting in that bed. That's disgusting.

Well, what am I here for? Definitely not to listen to this. I'm supposed to be his girlfriend, and if they think they're going to stake their claim... That's not going to happen.

I stand and walk toward them. They were all looking at me anyway, so they watch as I casually glide their way. "Hey, ladies," I say with a smile I don't feel. "I couldn't help but overhear. Just so everyone is clear, Aidan and I are together. No, we weren't together if or when one of you was actually with him. His past is his past, but I do want to warn you that he doesn't cheat, so you should set your sights on another player because that boy is off the market."

"How did you do it?" the one with the robe asks. She looks me up and down like she doesn't see much.

I push my insecurities aside and wink at her. "Now that's a secret." I give them a small wave while I'm still keeping it together. "It was nice talking to you."

Turning, I go straight back to where I was sitting, but find Aidan again in my peripheral. He happens to be staring at me, and he tilts his head like he's wondering if I'm okay. I give him a sly thumbs up before Coach Thompson blows his whistle and gathers up the players.

Practice ends a few minutes later. Aidan jogs right past the other girls who waited at the fence for him. Before he even gets to me, I mouth, *Kiss me.*

"You read my mind," he says, then he lays it on me,

49

cupping the back of my head. His upper lip is sweaty, giving our kiss a hint of salty flavor, but it's barely noticeable because Aidan kisses like a god. My inner thighs burn. He knows exactly how to work my lips, priming me for something more—

I tamp that thought down. Aidan is *not* for me. He clearly doesn't want a girlfriend right now, which is weird to think when his tongue is stroking my lips, sending me into a frenzy... But I have to stuff all these feelings away.

Aidan and I need each other, but we don't need one another in *that* way.

5

AIDAN

"WAIT FOR ME." I make Bailey promise before grabbing a handful of her ass.

Her eyes go wide, squealing a bit. Damn, it's too easy to pretend with her. She giggles, her cheeks turning red. I lean forward to whisper in her ear. I'm sure as far as the jersey chasers are concerned, they probably think I'm saying something super sexy. Instead, I apologize. "I'm sorry. I should've asked. Maybe we need, um, parameters?"

"It's fine," she says quickly, gripping my practice jersey in her hands. "That's what a boyfriend would do, right?"

I don't know about that, but that's what *I* do. Public affection is kind of my jam when I'm seeing a girl. No one has been that close to me here, though. The girls I hooked up with were a moment of... Well, of pure enjoyment.

This close, the scent of flowers wafts up from Bailey's hair, and I take a deep breath but don't smell her perfume from yesterday. Not that I should be noticing those things.

I pull away before I lose my head, letting my hands linger on her waist. "Give me about fifteen?"

She nods, glancing toward the girls ogling us from the fence. I make a note to ask her about what I saw during practice because it looked like the jersey chasers' claws were out.

"You know what? Follow me," I tell her. "You get the player's girlfriend treatment."

We walk in front of the others, and I peek at the one I had a fling with a week or so ago. I don't know what I was thinking. She's good looking, that much is true, but she's spiteful. The stare down she's giving Bailey makes my hackles go up. I didn't anticipate this part, though I'm not sure why. I want Bailey to be more like my electric fence, not a target for bullying.

As soon as we clear them, she asks, "What's the player's girlfriend treatment?"

I shrug. "No idea. I just wanted it to sound good."

She chuckles. "So, you haven't had a girlfriend here yet, Aidan? I find that hard to believe."

"Girls are distracting, and this is a big year for me."

Her face scrunches like she's trying to figure me out. "But the girls you—"

"I know," I sigh, shaking my head. Honestly, I don't

really have an excuse, I just lost myself for a little while. "I guess I thought hooking up was less distracting, but I think it was more. The whole being the "it boy" thing was like an avalanche. It started out small and then everything kept getting bigger and bigger, and so did the ramifications." I shudder to even think about it. It felt good having all those people want to be around me, but it was only a mirage. It ruined everything in the end.

I'm not going there again. Playing QB1 for Warner was on my dream board. Next up, winning as many championships as I can before getting drafted to play professionally, and I can't win championships riding the bench.

We approach the locker room door, and Bailey hangs back. "Did you really want me to wait for you? Or was that for show?"

She peers at the ground, and an uncomfortable sensation pricks at me. I step toward her. "No, I really wanted you to. A few of us usually go get something to eat after practice. Sometimes the girls come along, so it's best if you're there. I mean, if you want to, that is."

Squaring her shoulders, she says, "That's what I'm here for."

She meets my gaze, and her beautiful honey-brown eyes make me take a step back and look at her. Her makeup is more subdued this morning. I hadn't even noticed that she's not dressed as fancy as she was yesterday. She's wearing leggings that hug her curves and a long-sleeved shirt instead of heeled boots and jeans. I stare appreciatively. No wonder my hand instinctively cupped her there. Her ass is—

Not mine. I need to remember that.

It's not mine, nor do I want it to be. Taking a deep breath, I remind myself that I have plans. I have goals. "I swear, I can do something for you next," I tell her. "You know, to keep up my end of the bargain."

She shakes her head with a small grin. "You are already. I can't remember the last time I've actually been out with a group of people my own age that wasn't prearranged by my parents, like we still need playdates or something."

She laughs it off, but shock rings through me. She can't be—"Are you serious?"

"Very," she says, nodding.

I guess I don't actually know Bailey well at all. She and Darrin seem to have had a different upbringing by the same parents, which doesn't make any sense to me at all. "Well, I will make sure this is the best friend get-together you've ever had."

She rolls her eyes. "Just take a shower or something. You're sweaty."

At this point, I'm the last guy in the locker room. My teammates are probably already discussing where we're going. I wipe at my forehead, drying my fingers on the hem of my practice jersey. "Since you asked so nicely…" I tread backward, almost disappearing inside before I stick my head back out. "Meet us at the front of the building."

"You now have ten minutes," she says, tapping her wrist like she's keeping time.

"Damn. Taskmaster."

"Just get ready," she demands, giving me a playful shove.

I laugh. Spinning and walking down the corridor that leads to the football locker room, I take in the sounds of my team. Everyone's talking and ribbing on each other. In the back, the showerheads are turned on full blast. West is already freshly showered and at his locker when I walk up to open my own.

"Who's that?" he asks, nodding toward the practice field.

I act coy. "Who?"

He gives me a look and lowers his voice. "The girl you were kissing."

"Ohhh."

The wary vibes West is giving off tells me this isn't a talk to hit me up for information about Bailey. No, I promised them I was done with partying last night, so I can imagine what this looks like.

"It's not like that," I confide, moving closer. "She's not a fling kind of thing."

"So you're serious with her?" he asks doubtfully.

More sweat gathers on my forehead, and I wipe it

away. "Not exactly." I can't lie for shit, and West is West. He knows everything about me, so I might as well tell him what Bails and I are up to so he doesn't think I'm already going back on my word. "That's Bailey. Remember me telling you about my friend Darrin? That's his sister."

"Okay..."

I lower my voice. "We decided to pretend. To date," I clarify. "If she's my girlfriend, the other girls will steer clear, and she—" I clam up. It's not up to me to tell West Bails's business. "She has her reasons, too." I clap him on the back and smile. "This is good news. I can completely focus on football moving forward." He's quiet, so I reach into my locker to grab my clothes and towel. I close the locker door to find him still staring at me worriedly. "Isn't this a genius idea?"

His look says he thinks it's a terrible idea actually. "I— No."

"Don't you see?" I tell him excitedly. "She's like my jersey-chaser repellent. She's going to be there, and they won't be. Plus, there's absolutely no chance of me getting serious with her."

"You're not attracted to her?"

A picture of her flits through my mind, and I am. I'm definitely attracted to her, but I'm not telling West that. I shrug to throw him off the scent. "She's my best friend's little sister." I never thought about her that way before, so there's no indication that I would act on

56

being attracted to her now. "You don't actually catch feelings for your best friend's little sister."

Nope, she's just the perfect barrier I need between the outside world and my future goals.

"You didn't kiss her like she was your best friend's little sister."

I sneak past him. "It's called pretending, dude. Don't you worry." I walk backward so I can still look at him. "We meeting up anywhere?"

"Yeah, Richie's."

"Cool. Bailey's coming."

He gives me a wave so I know he's heard me, and then I work my way to the back to take a shower. I probably only have five minutes left now, so I quickly wash up and change. They stick to me as I style my hair, grab my wallet out of the locker, and head out.

Some of my defensive teammates are having a meeting, so I wave as I exit out the front. When I get outside, I immediately look for Bailey and find her next to the parking lot, standing under a nearly bare tree. From this vantage point, I can say I definitely agree with her choice of outfit today. She looks normal. The way she fits in with the other girls here after only a day is crazy. No one would know that her family is stinking rich and that she's basically been raised in a bubble.

She walks her fingers up the tree and tilts her head back to look up the trunk. The sun's rays catch on her hair, casting it in a faint halo of gold. "Hey, Angel," I greet her.

Spinning, she checks our surroundings and then gives me a confused look. "There's no one here to pretend for."

"Don't you think it would be hard to turn it on and off?" I rush out. The truth is, *Angel* just kind of popped out. It felt fitting in the moment where she was backlit by the sun.

So we don't get stuck on the subject, I ask, "What do you think of your new nickname?"

She shrugs. "It's good, I guess."

I wave her toward my car. "Do you have one for me?" Opening the passenger door for her, I tilt my head in thought. "Something masculine." She gets in, and I move around the car to the driver's side. "Adonis?" I throw out there.

She scrunches up her face as I get in. "That's a mouthful with a healthy dose of weird."

"Hotcakes?"

She giggles. "Like McDonald's?"

The engine roars as I start the car. "Fine. Whatcha got?"

"Babe?" she offers.

"Boring," I chime while maneuvering through the parking lot and pointing the car toward Richie's. "Stud?"

She waffles back and forth. "Contender. Possibly. Though a little self-satisfying if you ask me."

"Well, what did you call your last boyfriend?"

Shifting in the seat, she avoids my gaze. "Just, you know, his name."

"Wow, you really are lame," I tease.

Her mouth drops. "Maybe you're too out there. Would people actually buy it if I walk around calling you *stud*?"

"I mean, I am, so..."

She reaches over to hit me playfully. "Maybe QB1?"

"But everyone calls me that. It needs to be special."

"I don't know," she says, clearly frustrated. "I like timeless, so maybe just *babe*. It's an oldie but goodie."

"Meh," I grouse. I don't love it, but I don't hate it either. It's what everyone else uses.

"Forget it," she says. "I'll just call you Aidan. Problem solved." She peers over at me, her eyes latching to mine. "Just Aidan. I love your name."

Her words wash over me like a comforting ray of sunshine after a rainstorm. *Just* Aidan. "If you insist," I tell her, trying to keep my tone light even though my stomach has tightened. I realize it's a weird thing to get emotional about, but I had to fight for my name once, so it's a big deal to me. "What's Darrin up to?" I ask quickly to change the subject.

Her shoulders drop, obviously less thrilled by the topic shift. "I don't know. I left him in the kitchen eating a bowl of cereal and warning me not to get pregnant."

I gasp so hard I choke. My fingers tighten against the wheel. "You're serious? Your brother thinks I'm going to knock you up?"

"He thinks there's a chance since we're having sex. I mean, he assumes we're having sex," she clarifies. "Of course he does. That's obviously what you do in college."

She waves at me like I'm a prime example, and the contents of my breakfast churn in my gut. We've been fake dating for less than twenty-four hours, so I haven't had the chance to think about all the ramifications. I'll have to have a talk with Darrin, but more importantly, does she really think that's all you do in college? "Is that on your list of things to do now that you're free?" I ask, feeling big brotherly, like maybe I should give her the talk too. "Not with me—obviously—but, I mean, if you're going to, you should be safe, and you'll have to figure out how to do it on the down-low or else it'll look like you're cheating on me."

She rolls her eyes. "I'm not going to fake cheat on you."

For a moment, I feel like an ass when she turns away to look out the window. Maybe that's exactly what she wants to do, and I can't really tell her not to. That's not fair. We're not actually dating. "You could find someone who doesn't go to this school? Or, you know, if you do find someone and we have to break up, we will. Don't feel pressured to stick this out if something better comes along."

She turns toward me, fire in her eyes. "Listen, we don't need to talk about sex. I'm good."

"Okay, I was just saying—"

"Sex is the least of my concerns right now," she grinds out.

"Whoa, okay," I concede. "I'll talk to your brother and tell him he doesn't have to worry about it. That we're being safe."

She gives me a look. "He can't know we're pretending, Aidan. He's as protective as my parents are, so if you do talk to him, you better make it good."

I hate lying to Darrin, but he'll never find out this was all fake. This relationship will run its course, we'll break up, and that will be the end of it. I'll still have my relationship with Darrin, and Bailey and I will be fake exes for the rest of our lives.

When I put it like that, it sounds like a long-term commitment. But it's a commitment that could potentially set me up forever, and Bailey deserves her independence, too.

I reach out my fist to her. "We got this."

She touches her knuckles to mine, and the skin where we connect heats.

I pull away immediately, clenching my jaw. I rub

the back of my neck. "You should take a picture of me and send it to your parents. But only if you get my good side."

She shakes her head as she takes out her cell phone. "What are you talking about? You don't have a bad side."

"Aww. Thanks, Bails."

She holds her phone in the air. I smirk, driving one-handed, and glance over at the camera. She snaps the picture and stares at the screen. "*Just* Aidan," she murmurs.

"What?"

She chuckles. "Sorry, this just looks like the most Aidan picture ever."

Turning the phone toward me, she shows me the pic. To me, I look normal. "What do you mean?"

She peers down at the screen, dragging her fingertip across my jawline. "The smirk. The confidence. Your whole personality. It all comes through here."

I concentrate back on the road. She taps her screen and then sets the phone on her lap.

"Sent?"

"Sent."

I'm not sure where the shift in the car comes from, but it's suddenly filled with tension as I pull into Richie's. After parking, I face her. "Are you ready for this? It's our first big test."

"Ready," she states confidently, nodding so that her messy bun flops.

"Should we go over parameters so I don't scare you again? Like with the ass grab?"

"No parameters. We'll act normal."

Yeah, normal. Except there's nothing normal about dating my friend's little sister, and there's especially nothing normal about faking that relationship.

But, hey, what could go wrong?

6

BAILEY

LAUGHTER and the smell of grease fills the diner Aidan takes me to. My skin buzzes as I soak up the atmosphere. The football team takes up the left side of the diner, the rest of the public on the right. We sit at a circular table with other players, and luckily, I get sat next to another player's girlfriend, who introduces herself as Kenna.

Immediately, we get along, and soon, with Aidan's comforting arm around my shoulders, it feels like I belong.

Aidan's teammates are rowdy, drawing the attention of the other patrons, but no one says anything. In fact, they all smile over at us, and more than a few times, they come up to the table to tell the team what a hard loss yesterday was and to keep their chins up.

Their words seem to impact Aidan the most. He keeps flexing his arm around me, and instinctively, I get closer each time he does. Like somehow, I could be his shield.

Besides the public, the conversation at the table starts and ends with football, too. I'm glad I know enough to keep up with what's being said, but I need to brush up on some of the terms being thrown around.

"They're always like this," Kenna says. "If you're wondering."

I smile into my glass of water. She must have caught the look on my face while I was trying to puzzle out some acronym the wide receiver named Cade used. "Single-minded, you mean?"

"You have no idea." Leaning toward me, she lowers her voice. "If you tell West this, I'll deny it with everything in me, but I'm looking forward to it not being football season. Just for, like, a week," she adds quickly. "Then I'll probably miss how excited he gets about it."

I follow her gaze to her boyfriend. He's massive, but the way he smiles down at her and holds her to his side gives me all the good vibes for her. It's obvious he adores her. To have that one day would be amazing. Something real. Something separate from the little glass box I've been put in.

Next to me, Aidan laughs, his chest moving against my body, and I can't help but smile. He has the best laugh. He's always been easy-going and happy. People are drawn to him like bees to honey. The way his teammates hang on every word he says makes it apparent that he's well-liked. It was the same when he used to come visit us. I was stuck in his orbit, floating, waiting for him to acknowledge me, but it never came. Not in the way I wanted anyway.

"I hope you like football," Kenna states, bringing me back to our conversation.

"I like watching it," I offer. I can't say that I've ever played. Not even as kids. While Darrin played in the yard, Mom and I were having tea parties and hosting luncheons where I had to wear frilly, itchy dresses. "I can't wait to go to the next game."

My gaze keeps getting drawn to Aidan. To be his girlfriend, even if it is just for show, and watch him from the stands? My stomach flips just thinking about it.

Kenna's stare moves to Aidan, too. A troubled frown crosses her face, but when she catches me looking, she smiles again. "I'm sure Aidan will love having you there."

I pat his leg. "I'm sure."

He moves his arm from around me and then grabs my hand under the table, squeezing it. I have to hold my breath for a second, reminding myself that he's just really good at this pretending stuff. I'm the one getting drawn in closer and closer. I even tell myself that Aidan doesn't want a girlfriend right now. Not a real one. He explicitly stated he needs to focus back on football and his team.

In order to keep my mind off him, I ask Kenna about herself. I learn she's a collegiate diver, and that she's been diving since she was little. When she asks me what I'm interested in, I nearly fake an answer. How embarrassing to have to tell her that I don't play sports, and that I don't really have any hobbies. My hobbies were my mom's, and the only real thing I enjoyed that she did was reading. Pruning the flowers was hot and annoying. Hosting parties felt more forced than anything else. There was always something so fake about dressing to the nines and sitting around a fancy table.

I can't even think of one lady who would attend that was a good friend to my mom. A real confidant. The conversation always steered to boasting about their children or husbands or what their prized horses did at shows.

That's not my thing. I just have to figure out what is, though.

I should make a list of all the things I've been wanting to do.

My heart stammers in anticipation, and I hide my excitement by sipping the glass of water in front of me. "To be determined," I finally answer. If I find something I'm interested in, I can actually participate in conversations like this and not sound so damn dull.

I give Kenna a small smile as an apology for being so boring, but at the same time tingles run up and down my arms. Coming to Warner was the best decision I've ever made. I'm going to enjoy the hell out of all this freedom. I can tick things off a list one by one, and no one will be there to tell me I shouldn't do it.

Aidan's friend Cade starts telling a story that draws everyone in. Aidan shifts beside me, and I peer down to find him massaging his hand. Without thinking, I reach over, shoo his hand out of the way, and take its place, kneading his palm and fingers.

He stiffens briefly, but then he moves his hand over to give me better access. I start with his palm, massaging it with the pad of my thumb, then I work my way down each of his fingers. It's his passing arm, so that's probably why he has some aches and pains.

"You're good at that," he nearly grinds out, staring underneath the table at what I'm doing.

"What are girlfriends for?" I peer up, giving him a teasing smile, and he returns it.

Leaning closer, he whispers, "If this is what you do for fake boyfriends, I'm wondering what you do for real ones."

The innuendo, whether intended or not, makes my thighs ache. The truth is, I don't know. I've had boyfriends, but they were all my mother's "friends'" sons. The kisses I've shared with Aidan are nothing like anything else I'd ever felt, and considering it was supposed to be fake, how sad is that?

Maybe I'm broken. I've often wondered that. Why

am I the type to go along with whatever my mom says? I date guys I don't want. I don't even find them attractive. Yet, when my mom smiles approvingly at me, it makes it all worth it. At least for a little while.

My hold on Aidan stumbles, and he closes his fingers around mine. "I'm sorry. Don't stop. I like it."

His admission makes my heart race, heat pouring out of me like I'm on fire and he's doing nothing but stoking it. Our gazes connect, and the attraction between us tightens. At least on my side it does.

He gives me a grin. "My hand sometimes aches after practice, so this feels amazing."

Instead of fueling my desire, his words yank me out of the moment. Of course this would feel good to him. It would feel good no matter who was doing it. It's not just because I'm doing it.

Cade must end his story because the whole table erupts in laughter. Aidan and I are still staring at each other until someone calls his name.

We both glance up at the same time, and he waves at a couple of girls that come in as a group. They frown at the lack of room at our table and sit across the restaurant from us.

Kenna sighs. "They'll stop eventually."

"Yeah?" I stare the girls down like I have a right to be jealous that they're calling out Aidan's name. For all I know, they could be real friends of his.

"Most of them are actually good people. They're

friendly. For some reason, they just happen to lose their damn minds when it comes to football players. Honestly, I don't understand it at all."

"It's because we're so hot," Cade says, flexing like a fuckboy.

The guy next to him hits him upside the head. "And modest."

Cade shrugs. "We're athletes in our prime. Of course everyone loves us."

"Not everyone," Kenna pipes up.

He gives her a charming smile. "You learned to."

"It took me a while."

"Hey," West says defensively.

"Not with you, babe. The rest of them."

I poke Aidan with my elbow while the table laughs. "See?" I point out to him. "She called him babe."

He whispers back, "I definitely don't want his nickname then."

I roll my eyes.

"What about you, Bailey?" one of the players on the other side of the table asks. "Were you hanging all over Aidan before you started dating?"

Aidan speaks before I can come up with a response. "Naw, man. She's my friend's sister."

A few of the guys laugh uncomfortably. One of them even says, "I bet you guys aren't friends anymore."

Unlike me, Aidan takes the teasing in good stride. "Please. My boy knows he has nothing to worry about. I'm a true gentleman."

Now the table really laughs, and I make myself chuckle, too. Cade, however, peers over at us, as if he's examining a science experiment. "It could work out, or it could go really, really bad."

"What? Do you have experience, Farmer?"

Another player shakes his head. "He's talking about Reid." The player turns to me, and I wish I could get their names straight. "And by the way, they were perfect for each other."

Cade looks away, smiling.

I glance at Aidan, whose lips have turned into a thin line. "Who's Reid?"

Aidan widens his eyes at me. "I can't believe you just asked me that question."

"What?"

He places his lips near my ear, and I feel him smirking as he says, "You're going to have to study up on football, Angel. Reid Parker was QB1 before me. He got drafted and won Rookie of the Year."

"Is that what you want?" I ask, turning my face toward his. My stare drops to his lips inadvertently, but it's not my fault. We're as close as we were the times we kissed, and I've barely been able to think about anything else. I can't be held accountable for the wild thoughts floating to the surface when he's this close.

71

I'm still ogling them when he says, "More than anything."

I smile. "You'll do it. I have faith in you."

His gaze traces my face, making my heart slam in my chest. If I didn't know any better, it looks like Aidan wants to kiss me, too. It's a terrible idea, of course. For me. I keep smudging the line between faking it and the very real feelings budding again.

He moves forward, and I freeze in place.

He's going to—

Aidan's—

He dodges my lips and places a chaste kiss on my cheek. "Thank you for saying that. It means more than you know."

My stomach churns as he turns away. *Stupid*, I chastise myself. I don't know why I thought he was going to actually kiss me. This is all a ruse. Fake.

If he did kiss me, it would be to keep up pretenses in front of his friends.

Suddenly, I feel silly for enjoying all this camaraderie when it isn't even really mine to enjoy. I'm nothing. I'm no one.

The same player who brought up Reid says, "Don't forget to sign up for the couples fundraiser now that you're with Bailey, QB1."

"Couples fundraiser?" I ask, peering over at Aidan.

Kenna laughs, hard. "Oh, you thought you were getting away with it. This is hilarious."

"Shit," Aidan grumbles.

I turn, looking for someone to clarify. "What am I missing?"

Aidan sighs, knocking a napkin out of his way with his pinkie. "Coach's wife. She's big into fundraising."

I chuckle at his unenthusiastic reaction. "That actually sounds like a good thing."

"It is," he grinds out, his voice in complete contradiction to his words. "It's just that Coach is making every couple on the team compete in her newest fundraising scheme."

Kenna doesn't sound thrilled at the prospect either. "The couple who wins gets to be king and queen of the Halloween Ball."

"It's for a good cause," West adds.

Cade grins, beaming at us. "I've never been so happy to be single."

It would be funny if I didn't notice the reaction Aidan was having. He rubs his hands down his thighs, his leg jumping up and down.

It can't be *that* bad. "What do we have to do?" I ask.

"Participate in short competitions and community projects. There will be a skills game."

West pipes in. "My girl's been working on her arm."

Kenna smirks but continues. "A relationship game. A few other things I can't quite remember, and then it all culminates in a ball that people buy a plate for. All proceeds go to the Step-Up Foundation," Kenna answers. "Oh, and the winning couple both get scholarship money."

"That sounds—"

"Horrible," Aidan interrupts. "Just what I need, another time commitment."

"I'm sure we don't have to join," I tell him, squeezing his thigh.

He pins me with a stare. "Oh, there's no getting around it. Coach asks, we do."

"Well, lucky for you, I'm great at competitions." My whole life has set me up to succeed at these types of things. Plus, earning scholarship money could help. Like, really help. What if I want to stay here but Mom and Dad won't pay for it? I need to be able to fund it on my own.

Cade grins. I can tell he's getting a kick out of all this. "Are you saying you predict you two standing as king and queen at the end of this?"

I lift my chin. "Yep. We've totally got this."

Cade laughs, then glances at Aidan. "I like her, dude. She's a keeper."

Preening under his words, I smile at Aidan. He's got a slight grin on his face now as he watches me. "You're into this, aren't you?"

I shrug. "If we have to do it, we might as well try to win it." Plus, it's different and new. Things I am absolutely here for. A skills competition. A ball. Sounds…exciting.

"Come on, Aidan," West implores, "a bunch of us are doing it. It'll be fun." He waits a beat. "Especially when Kenna and I kick your asses."

I burst out laughing, and Aidan is right there with me. "Oh, it's on, Big Man. You know I can never back down from a challenge." He wraps his arm around me again and nearly hauls me onto his lap. "Bailey and I are in. We'll thank you during our acceptance speeches."

"You keep thinking that."

Kenna rolls her eyes with me, but she looks at West so affectionately. She's secretly loving this, too.

"We'll give you the proper king and queen wave from atop the podium." Aidan waves his hand with a stately flourish.

"Uh-huh, sure."

"You may have opened a can of worms," Kenna tells West.

"I'm not worried." He grins at Aidan. "As couples go, we've been together much longer."

He draws the words out, and my stomach squeezes thinking he knows something. But he couldn't possibly… Right?

Cade calls West out. "Please, you guys are still in the gross touchy-feely phase, too."

Aidan shakes his head at his friend. "New or not, it's on."

"You know it."

Over my head, they touch knuckles, but I can't get West's words out of my mind. They feel like a lead balloon in my stomach. He and Kenna have been together much longer. Actually, they're together period. Aidan and I can't even say that, and I hate the way the lie bothers me right now.

Regardless, we're not backing down from the competition, so we'll just have to be the best couple we can be.

7

AIDAN

I TUCK my notes into my notebook after Professor Huron's brain-melting lesson. I don't mind History, I actually enjoy it, but not the way he teaches it. He makes it as one-dimensional as his monotone voice.

I nod at a defensive player who mopes up to the professor's desk at the end of class. It's no wonder he's having trouble passing this one. He can probably barely stay awake. I pat his shoulder as I make my way around him, sending him condolences that he has to deal with this.

Exiting through the doors, I pull out my phone to see if Bailey's reached out. I don't know what I expected, but she seems to be doing well in her first week of classes. I had visions of her blowing up my messages with all these questions about campus or college or coursework. But it's the exact opposite. She's fitting in great, and when we see one another, it's all smiles and chaste kisses for show, keeping the jersey chasers at bay and her brother in the dark.

It's going so smoothly, I'm wondering why I never thought about a permanent cockblocker before. Genius idea.

The sidewalk leads me out onto the quad where old trees cast enough shade that there are only a few places to get sun. Students are out enjoying the warm weather, and I stop when I spot Bailey's golden halo of hair. She's sitting cross-legged, her blonde tresses falling over her face while writing intently.

Changing course, I walk that way. She doesn't notice me coming until the sun at my back makes a shadow across her. Her face changes from annoyed to smiling when she sees it's me. "Hey, stud."

We both chuckle. She has such a nice laugh. Dainty, almost. But I've heard her roar one out that would rival Farmer's. Either way, it's nice to hear it.

The sun catches on her fingers, and I notice she's taken off her nail polish. She's deglamorized her look from when she first got here. Today, she's wearing a pair of capris and a simple shirt. Honestly, the transformation is sexy as hell. A girl in a beautiful dress with lipstick and the whole nine is gorgeous, but that gives off these unattainable vibes. Right now, Bailey is the epitome of the girl next door. An innocence that is somehow sexy.

Not that my mind should be going there.

"I've been thinking," I tell her. "We might have to rule *stud* out."

"Not feeling very studly?"

I mock gasp while I take a seat next to her in the grass. "Do I look less studly?"

She takes her time looking me over, holding back a laugh when she sees my eyebrow pop up. "Hmm."

"Oh, you're gonna get it."

She beams at me, and I have to look away to stop from contemplating how pretty she is. Instead, I stare down at her notebook. She immediately tries to close it, but I'm too quick for her. I scoop it up. "What's this?"

"Nothing," she says, grabbing hold of it to take it back.

I give her a look. "No secrets between couples."

She matches my look with one of her own and then drops her voice. "Good thing our relationship isn't real."

She gives it a good pull, but I'm not letting it go until I know what it is. "Come on, what is it, Bails?"

I give it another tug, and she sighs, releasing it to me.

Opening it up to the page she was on, I see a bulleted list.

Skip class.
Go to the movies.
Skinny dip.

Cliff dive like at graduation.

I read the list off in my head, each line piquing my curiosity more and more. "What is this?"

"My list," she explains, breathing in deep and staring down at it with determination. "It's everything I want to make sure I do here."

"Cliff dive?" I challenge. "I don't see you as the adventurous type."

She frowns, yanking the notebook away from me for real this time and trying to jam it back into her bag. "Everyone at my high school graduation went cliff diving afterward. It was like a rite of passage. I didn't go."

"Sounds like fun," I tell her, lying on my side and propping myself up with my elbow. "How come you didn't go?"

"Two reasons," she says, lifting her face so that the sun shines on it. "One, because no one invited me. I skipped a grade, so I didn't fit in there. Or anywhere, actually. And two, Mom and Dad wouldn't let me. It's not proper to jump off a cliff and all that."

"But that's why it's so fun."

That statement gets her attention. "You've done it?"

"There's a spot close by." Her eyes nearly sparkle.

"I'll take you some time," I offer before I can tell myself not to.

"I'd really like that."

I stare at her, asking myself why I'm interested in her now. For years I'd see her every summer, and I never even looked at her twice. Now, however, I've been thinking about her a little too much. In fact, when she hadn't blown up my phone this week, I was disappointed. It's better off this way, but still.

"I don't know about the skinny dipping, though," I tease.

"I'm sure seeing me would scar you forever," she deadpans.

My throat suddenly goes dry. I couldn't not picture her, and now I'm suffering because of it. I push the images away. "Nah, your brother wouldn't approve."

"That's what makes it so much fun," she mimics, throwing my words back in my face. "Plus, I remember you guys skinny dipping before."

I tilt my head at her. I tend to remember who I get naked in front of, and I'm one hundred percent sure I've never been naked in front of Bailey.

"You guys went to some party one time when Mom and Dad were out of town and invited girls home afterward." She plays her hand over the grass and looks away. "I watched from my window."

"Why didn't you come down?"

She glares at me. "Yeah, because I really want to

see Darrin in the nude. I'd have to bleach my eyes or something."

She's got a point there. The idea of her watching from her room like an outsider, though, doesn't sit well. When she talks about her life with her parents, she makes it sound terrible. "Why were your parents so different with you than Darrin? It doesn't make sense."

"Because boys sow their wild oats. I have a reputation to uphold, you know."

I laugh. "Yeah, a boring one."

"I'm not boring," she insists. "I just have the appearance of it."

Twenty feet away, a group gathers around a Bluetooth speaker. The first few beats of a song blast out, and they all laugh, covering their ears.

Bails nearly jumps and then glances back, a smile forming on her face. I peer from her to the group that has started dancing, and I can't help but notice the jealousy there. She looks like she wants to do that. Like she's coming out of her skin she wants to join in so bad.

I push her thigh. "I dare you to go over there and dance," I tell her, raising my voice so she can hear me above the music.

Her head snaps back to me. "What? No."

"How come? Doesn't it look fun?"

"I don't know them," she says, her gaze moving back to study them.

I stand. Hell, I don't know them either, but it's

never stopped me before. "How will you ever meet new people if you don't join in?"

I reach a hand down to her. She studies it and then meets my gaze. "I don't think I can." She puts her hand in mine anyway, so that's a good step.

Once she's on her feet, we both face the group. "You're a dancer, aren't you? I bet you could put them all to shame."

She worries her lip. "Ballet. It's totally different. This is a terrible idea." A few seconds go by, and she blurts out, "Will you come with me?"

Well, I can't say no to that. I take her hand, and we walk. The beat starts to pick up, and I double pump her fingers as we approach. She squeezes back, her grip firm and sweaty. As soon as we get there, they notice us and open up their circle. I'm not much of a dancer, but I'm also not shy either. Maybe it's all these years I've had playing in front of a crowd.

My hand swings, and I peer over. Bailey is...dancing. And not just swaying her hips, but jumping up and down, bobbing her head. I join in with her because I really don't have a choice unless I want to lose my money-maker appendage.

Soon, that song ends, and the next one starts up immediately. One of the girls from the group begins to sing, and before I know it, Bailey is all in, too. Everyone's singing. Like total crazies, we dance and sing for everyone to see.

More students join in after that, and soon, this part of the quad turns into an impromptu rave.

The best part about it is the smile on Bails's face. Like pure joy, she's radiant. I'm so distracted that I almost miss a guy backing up. I pull her away at the last moment, and we dance front-to-front, my fingers migrating over her capris until her ass fits perfectly in my hands.

I mean, I am her boyfriend. I'm supposed to be doing this.

The smile on her face turns serious. Her hips take over, her palms tracing up my chest. When I glance down, her stare is filled with something so familiar— like want.

Desire.

Slowly, she maneuvers her hands lower, her fingers gripping the waistband of my jeans, tugging me closer.

"Someone's seen *Dirty Dancing*," I tease, following her lead, letting our hips slide and grind against one another.

"Only my favorite movie."

"Well, I carried a watermelon."

She throws her head back and laughs. "You, QB1, carry a football. And you're damn good at it, too."

She takes my hand to spin out and then back in. I watch the way she moves with admiration as she edges closer. "Where's the scared girl from five minutes ago?" I ask, almost unable to believe it myself.

"She realized she only has one chance."

I hope she's not serious. It would be a shame for the world to never see this side of Bailey Covington again.

Turning, she plants her ass in my crotch, continuing her sultry hip movements. My dick responds in kind. No matter how much I tell it to go back down, it's soon unavoidable.

Bailey doesn't stop, though, until I'm pressing against my jeans and, in turn, pressing against her shapely ass. She turns around again, and I pull her close. The whole quad doesn't need to see how turned on I am right now.

"Is that a watermelon in your pants? Or are you just happy to see me?" she breathes, staring up at me through full lashes.

"Wrong shape," I tell her, my voice suddenly deeper as we stare one another down. "I hope there was something on your list about making a guy hard in a public place."

"Well, I'm definitely going to add it now and check it off."

"Evil," I whisper into her ear.

She shakes with laughter. My dick throbs. We keep grinding against one another until I run my hands through her hair, bringing her face up to look at me.

Just as quickly, I look away. I don't know what I'm doing. This wasn't my intention when I asked her to put herself out there.

Instead of taking it where I want to, I tell her, "We need to stop."

"Oh." Disappointment rings through her tone. "Yeah, of course," she says, stepping away.

I hold on to her hand. "Not too far away. I need you to hide me."

She glances down, and I see the rounding of her eyes in real time.

The Aidan who didn't decide to give up girls a few days ago wants to keep going, but this is also Darrin's little sister. Not to mention a complication. The very thing I swore off of in front of all of my teammates. No more hookups. No more distractions. They're counting on me.

I grab her hands and hold them between us. All around us, bodies still dance. It's like we're the calm inside the chaos, but my mind doesn't have the same peace.

It goes back to Bailey saying she watched me go skinny dipping from her bedroom window, and I wonder if I would've noticed her if she was more like the girl in front of me. Free. Spirited. A down-to-earth girl who likes to have fun.

Before I can travel further down that road, I say, "We need to check more things off your list," only because it's something to distract me from my thoughts.

She grins. "Thank you for pushing me out of my comfort zone. That was so much fun."

I shrug, making it like it was no big deal. I don't answer because it's getting harder to hear her now that we're not caught up in the party. The music seems loud and obnoxious. Reaching down, I rearrange my jeans to make things more comfortable. "I think I'm okay now."

The cutest red dots appear on both her cheeks. "Does that mean you owe me two debts of gratitude?"

"How's that?"

"One for giving you a hard-on, and the other for helping you hide it while it went away."

"I'm pretty sure they negate each other," I tell her, leading her out of the horde of dancers. "Plus, I prefer my erections to go away for different reasons."

Bailey makes a noise and then starts to choke. I pull her to my side and pat her back. She coughs into her hand, and when she's finally calmed down enough, she studies me with tears in her eyes. "Sorry, something got caught in my throat."

There are just too many comments to make to that statement, so I shut my mouth.

We're almost to our stuff when Darrin appears, waving at us. "Bails! Aidan!" He runs up, then peers at the group. "Man, I love college. I swear the hottest girls are dancing over there."

I hadn't even noticed, which is a good thing. My team should be at the top of my priority list, but I can't say it was football that distracted me this time. It was

Bailey. "Wasn't paying attention," I tell him. "Your sister has some moves."

Darrin turns toward me and gives me the most disgusted look. "I just ate lunch, man."

"Oh please," Bailey says. "Like the fact that I'm a woman should turn your stomach."

"You're not a woman. You're my baby sister."

"And you're a dumbass," she argues before leaning to pick up her stuff. I try to take one last peek at her notebook, like I might be able to commit her list to memory, but she jams it the rest of the way into her bag.

Maybe I could make a list for her, too. I could give her some pointers on things she should try while she's not tethered down by her parents.

"Like you should talk," Darrin throws back at her. "You should've seen her trying to do laundry last night."

"At least I tried."

"Aww, you can't do laundry?" I ask, my gaze jumping from Darrin to Bailey. "I can show you."

"I managed just fine."

Darrin snickers. "She Googled it."

"That's what Google is for. I had a question. The question got answered."

"Well, you know, if you need anything, you can always ask me."

Bailey meets my stare and gives me a small smile as

she holds her stuff to her chest. "I have to go. I'll see you guys later?"

"Later," I tell her.

She starts to walk away, but we can't have that, can we? I reach out to pull her back, then kiss her on the cheek. "Later," I whisper, lingering there, taking her in.

"Do I get a kiss too?"

I move away from her and give Darrin the finger. "Fuck off."

"I think I will," he says, clutching his bag higher up his shoulder before jogging toward the group that's still dancing. I watch him go, and when I turn, Bailey is already gone.

8

BAILEY

GOOGLE IS ALSO good for asking things like "What should I wear to my first college party?"

The thing is, I don't trust myself to know if the answers it gives me are good. I don't want to be overdressed, but I don't want to be underdressed either. The horror of both makes for analysis paralysis as I stare at my closet. I now have two categories of clothing: my upscale, throwing-it-in-everyone's-face-that-I-have-money clothes, and the I-don't-give-a-fuck clothes that I've been ordering off of Amazon.

My closet literally looks as if a lazy, topknot-wearing freshman who rolls out of bed five minutes before class lives here. Which is all cool until I'm faced with the reality of my first college party.

My nerves are on high alert. To say I didn't go to many parties in my private school is an understatement. I didn't go to *any* parties. Sure, there were students who rebelled like everyone else, but I wasn't one of them. I was the kind of puke-inducing Goody Two-Shoes that script-writing authors make fun of.

The doorbell rings, and I let out a little yelp of protest. That has to be Aidan, and I'm standing here in my pink giraffe robe over bra and panties with only my hair up and makeup on.

A knock sounds on my door. "Ready for the party?"

Aidan doesn't wait to get asked inside before pushing the door open. I spin and cover myself up even though I'm fully covered as it is. He laughs, then lowers his voice. "Boyfriend, remember? Pretty sure if you were my real girlfriend, you'd be waiting in here naked for me."

I pick up the closest thing I can find to throw at him and blanch when I realize it's my black lace panties sailing across the room. "*Shit*," I protest as I scramble, trying to get to them before he does.

Unfortunately, he snatches them out of the air first and holds them up between us, staring at the lace and then bringing them down so he can look into my eyes. "Well, Bails. I guess I shouldn't be surprised you wear underwear like this."

I attempt to snatch them out of his fist, but he pulls them away, taunting me.

Groaning in frustration, I say, "I suppose I should buy cotton pairs."

He shrugs. "Cotton, satin, lace. None of that matters when they're lying crumpled on the floor."

Heat swamps my face. I grab for my panties again and successfully get a grip. "I think you're forgetting this isn't real."

He lets the panties go, and I sigh in relief. At least they were clean. Yes, I did have to look up how to use the washing machine, but I did it. I successfully washed my first load of laundry. Darrin's dirty clothes are probably still in a pile in his room.

"I haven't, but what if someone asks me a question about the type of underwear you like? I should know these things. Mine is boxer briefs, by the way."

"Who's going to ask us that?"

He shrugs. "Cosmo. Sports Illustrated."

I turn away, throwing the lace panties into my closet. "Yeah, I'm sure we're at the top of their list of couples to interview."

"Not yet."

How long does he think this charade is going to last? My parents will probably only give me until the end of the semester, tops. If I'm lucky, it'll be the end of the year.

Aidan flops down on my bed. "So, are we nervous about our first big party?"

I groan internally. He couldn't have said anything worse to me at this exact moment. I blow out a breath. "I... I don't know what to wear."

He doesn't answer, so I peer over at him to find his gaze scanning my body. "That looks nice."

I resist the urge to find something else to throw at him because with my luck, it would probably be a bra next. I might as well throw him my birth control just to get every embarrassing thing out of the way while we're at it. "Please be serious. You're the quarterback. The big man on campus. I should wear something that, you know, people would expect. You know, since I'm your girlfriend."

I examine his outfit: a pair of jeans and a T-shirt that hugs his biceps. The shirt has a simple collar and is a plain dark-blue color that brings out the blue in his eyes. He looks gorgeous without even trying.

"Wear what you want."

I give him a look. "Completely unhelpful. I guess we really are dating."

He chuckles and gets to his feet. Soon, he's behind me as I stare into the closet again. He looms over me, and my entire backside tingles with his electric current. "I'll have you know, I'm a very helpful boyfriend."

"Should I ask for references?"

His breath hits my ear, making me shiver. "No, because I'm going to show you." He sidesteps me and starts looking at my closet. Going through my clothes, he hums to himself, his agile fingers reaching for and dismissing hangers with precision until he's brought out two pieces and laid them on the bed.

Well... That was easy. These are probably...

I peer at the outfit he put together and immediately think I should turn in my girl card.

"How did you do that?" I snap, tracing my fingers over the soft material of the shirt he's chosen. It's a royal-blue A-line top that I usually wear with a shrug, but it goes perfectly with the black leggings he's brought out with it.

"I look at girls a lot." He smirks, casting an embarrassed glance my way. "If you pair that with a dressy shoe, you'll fit right in. Nothing that'll hurt your feet. I plan on dancing with you again to show you the epitome of first college party experiences. By the way, every girl should dance with the quarterback of their school's football team. But also, don't wear sneakers. You'll ruin the vibe."

"College quarterback waylaying as a fashionista. Or is that fashionisto?"

"I have The Style Network like everyone else, and please, don't use those fancy prep school terms with me. I'm in touch with my feminine side. Fashionista is fine."

I can't help but shake my head. I used to sit back and listen to his conversations with my brother. The way they would tease and play off each other always made me laugh, and here I am doing it with him. I understand what they mean by verbal sparring now.

It's fun.

"Sure, fashionista, now get lost so I can dress."

"Ha," he cackles. He sits back on my bed and gets comfortable. "Don't you think it'll look weird if I leave your room for you to get dressed? Your brother will think something is up."

"Now you're making shit up so you can tease me."

"Changing in front of a dude is just another experience you need to add to your list."

"You're ridiculous."

"Still not leaving," he sing-songs as I grab the outfit off my bed and turn my back. I take a quick peek down my robe and almost die in horror when I realize how much cleavage I was showing. Luckily, the bra and panties I'm wearing will go with the outfit he chose.

"Fine," I grumble. He has a point after all. From under my robe, I start pulling on the leggings.

"Boring," Aidan deadpans from the bed.

"Horndog," I throw back.

He laughs. "Who knew what a prude my fake girl-friend could be?"

I look over my shoulder, shushing him. "My brother could be listening."

"Should we make the bed creak, then?" He shifts his hips, and the full-sized bed hits the wall with a *thunk*.

I spin, nearly tripping over my feet. "Aidan!"

He gets a big smile on his face. "Fine, I'll stop."

I blow out a breath and turn again. Picking the blue

top off the floor, I try to figure out a way to keep myself covered while putting it on, but as soon as I pull my arms out of the robe's sleeves, the material is so slippery it just wants to fall right off me.

The worst part is, I know I'm the one being ridiculous. This should be no big deal. Aidan has made a point to say he's not interested in me, and I'm trying not to be interested in him either. We have a good thing going here for the both of us, and I shouldn't ruin it.

With a huff, I free my arms, and the robe immediately slides down my body and hits the floor. My back is exposed, and I picture what he's looking at: my pale skin against the stark black bra. He's probably picking out imperfections.

Quickly, I place the shirt over my head and tug it on.

The fabric hugs my chest like a glove, flaring out a little at the hips. I move to stand in front of the floor-length mirror, avoiding Aidan's gaze to make sure the halter-style shirt lies perfectly.

His form comes up behind me until he nearly engulfs me. I stare at his eyes through the mirror while he peruses my body, tracing the line of my bra strap. "I think you need a different bra."

I shake my head. "The straps come off." Pulling my shirt away, I unclip the right bra strap and go to reach awkwardly to get the back, but Aidan stays my hands.

"I can do it."

He rolls the top of my shirt down just enough to expose the plastic clip that holds the strap to the main band. He unclasps it and then reaches for the other side as I catch up with him. Then he rolls my top back up, his fingertips lingering on my bare skin.

Goose bumps sprout all over.

"You cold?" I shake my head. The tension in the room has upped by a hundred fifty percent, and it feels like the slightest movement could prompt us off-kilter. Suddenly, he peers up, meeting my gaze. "You look beautiful."

"Promise?"

"I'm your fake boyfriend. I wouldn't lie."

We hold one another's gaze for a beat longer before we both laugh. "That's kind of an oxymoron."

Grinning, he takes a step back, breaking the spell even more. "I think you look perfect for your first college party."

"As long as I look decent enough to keep the other girls off you."

"It's working well enough so far. No girls showing up wearing nothing but robes at my door."

"I guess I don't make a bad fake girlfriend, then."

"Not too shabby," he says, winking.

On instinct, I move to my dresser and spray my perfume, rubbing it in at my wrists and below my ears.

"Mmm, I've missed you wearing that."

I still. "Yeah?"

"It's so *you*," he says quietly as I glance over my shoulder to find him looking slightly uncomfortable. "I just like it, I guess. I don't miss the old clothes you used to wear or anything like that. Only the perfume."

Noted, I think. Keep the perfume. One day, I want someone to look at me like Aidan is right now, but not be faking it at all.

"Why'd you change what you wear, anyway? Not that it's a bad idea. It was a great one, actually."

"Those other clothes weren't me," I explain. "They were my mom. I'm trying to figure out what *my* style is. I like the comfortable chic look."

"Leggings look amazing on you," he says, dropping his gaze to my ass.

I give it a little shake. "Someone is pouring it on thick tonight. Thankfully, I'll be your built-in cock-block because you might be too feisty."

"Nah, just calling it like I see it."

A bang sounds on the door. "If you guys are screwing in there, I'm moving out. I thought we were going to a party?"

I grumble and race to the door. After flinging it open, I glower at my brother with hands on hips, but he has his goofy grin on his face. "Kidding, but are we going to the party? I need the top man on campus to be my wingman."

"You never had any problems getting girls."

"Yeah, but I won't have to work as hard if I can use your notoriety."

"You guys are sick," I state.

"Sick, yet efficient." Darrin shrugs. He moves out of my way as I walk down the hall. "I was going to take a picture of us all to send to Mom and Dad, but you probably don't want them to see what you're wearing."

My stomach churns, and for a moment, I think about changing. I have to really fight against the urge to make her happy. "Don't worry," I call back. "I'll make sure to get a picture of whatever trash you end up with, and then I'll always look like the better option of the two."

"She's got you there, bro," Aidan says in my defense.

I turn, grinning at him. "See?"

Darrin points between the two of us. "I don't like this partnering situation we got going on. It's supposed to be me and Aidan against you."

Aidan claps him on the back. "Sorry, dude, you don't have the pussy."

Darrin pales, and I have to hold back a laugh. "Neither does my sister. I swear to God I will shut your hand in a car door. Let's see you play football with some broken bones."

"You wouldn't do that to me. I'm your best friend."

Aidan walks past Darrin and throws his arm across my shoulders. Leaning close, I notice he breathes in my perfume. The euphoric look on his face spurs my brother on even more.

"I might have to revoke your title."

For a moment, Aidan appears stricken. In the next moment, though, he laughs it off. "I thought you needed my quarterback notoriety to get laid?"

Darrin follows us outside. "You're right. I take it all back."

Aidan grins at me, and all of this seems so real. The banter. The experience. Like in another universe, I could actually be dating my brother's best friend and this is exactly how it would be—my brother weirded out, Aidan using any chance he gets to make sure he's weirded out, and me just laughing along with them.

Finally, in this other universe, I'm a part of something like I always wanted to be.

It's a nice feeling, even though it's not real.

9

AIDAN

SEEING other dudes at this party ogle Bailey as we dance makes my hackles raise. I underestimated how overprotective I would be.

Honestly, I'm having to remind myself that I'm playing a part the whole time. I shouldn't care that other guys are staring at her like they could take her upstairs. Hell, maybe she should. That would certainly be an experience to check off her to-do list.

On the other hand, that would lessen the credibility of our all-important fake relationship.

Despite all these thoughts pinging around my head, Bails is enjoying herself. She agreed to sip a beer out of a plastic cup, but I've noticed she hasn't drunk much of it at all. At this point, it's been unattended for so long, there's no way I would let her drink out of it again.

The party is in what used to be the football house

until they built the athletic dorms and made all the athletes move back onto school property. When I was here just to check out the campus, I attended a wild party in this very house. Reid and his friends Cade and Lex took me under their wing and showed me around. They basically proved there was no other place for me. I needed to be a Bulldog. Of course, it helped that Reid was a no-brainer for the draft. To play backup for him was an honor, and now that I'm at the helm, everything is working out the way I wanted.

Well, except for the recent brief blip of losing sight of my goals, but that's never going to happen again. There's too much at stake.

"Hey," Bails says, placing her palms on my cheeks and making me look at her. "You left for a moment."

There's no use denying it. I'm not even sure I was dancing to the beat. Some first date to a college party I'm being. "Sorry, I was reminiscing."

I tell her the story about how this used to be the football house, and her eyes widen. "That sounds like a disaster."

Chuckling, I answer, "I think it was. Coach was relieved when Warner put the money into building the athletic dorms."

"Keep a better eye on you wild football players," she teases.

Not that it's worked totally. I scan the crowd for Kenna and West as a memory of another time the football team did something very, very stupid. Somehow, she was able to forgive us, though sometimes I'm not even sure how. The rivalry with Hamilton still exists, but if they bring it to our turf again, Coach will blow a gasket.

No one wants that.

Behind Bails, a group of people enter the pseudo dance floor in the middle of the large living room. The house is now owned by one of the new fraternities, but it looks like they haven't done much to the place since they took over. It even smells the same: stale beer, burnt popcorn, with a slight tinge of laundry that needs to be properly washed.

What more can you expect from a bunch of guys living together?

Bails stills, mouth wide, as the group we danced with a couple days ago on the quad encircles us. She joins right in like she's one of them. I grin at her, stomach tightening. This is all she wants. To experience the things she's missed. To no longer feel left out. To feel like she belongs.

I can relate to that.

She turns her back to me, dancing into my crotch, but before we can get into another situation where I need her to block my raging hard-on, I lean down and ask her if she wants some water. She nods in agreement, and I leave her dancing her heart out as I make my way through the crowd. I check the kitchen, but only find the keg on the counter and some liquor bottles lining the peninsula.

Moving to the fridge, I spot even more alcohol, a box of wine, some White Claws, and hard lemonades. When I shut the refrigerator door, the huge body of my roommate moves into view.

"What's up, man?" I give him a bro hug. "Where's Kenna?"

"She went to find Bailey."

Glancing over where I left her, I spot Kenna laughing and dancing right next to her. That's good. Bailey couldn't find a better friend than in Kenna.

"Which, by the way," West's hard voice picks up again, "I haven't told her your shit is a sham."

The accusation in his voice pricks my skin. I peer around like someone else is going to overhear and know exactly what we're talking about. "No one's going to find out," I assure him. "You worry too much, Big Guy."

West shakes his head, a hint of a smile across his face. "I'm not worried. Because I've seen the way you look at her. However, I am worried you're going to scare the shit out of yourself when you realize you might actually like her."

I laugh his words off. I love my friend, I do. But because he has Kenna now, he thinks he's some sort of relationship expert. Like he should have his own column in the Saturday paper where people write in and ask him dating questions. The truth is, he was like me before he found her, except the part where I let it interfere with football. West would never do that.

"I'm good," I promise him. The fact that West thinks that makes me feel better. I don't trust his judgment with relationships at all, so now I know I'm completely safe. "Listen, you know where the water is?"

He nods toward the rear door. "The back porch."

I clap him on the back in thanks. "You seen Farmer?"

"Not here as far as I can tell."

That's good news, I muse to myself. Cade doesn't know his limitations, and I need my guys in tip-top shape while I prove to Coach I won't disappoint him again.

Luckily, I've realized my limits. I'm not drinking at all until the end of the season. No alcohol. No staying out too late. Plus, with Bailey as my cockblocker, I'm practically guaranteed an easy ride for the rest of the season.

Nothing but football, football, football.

I open up the rear screen door and remove two waters from the plastic case. The door shuts behind me while I make my way through the crowd. West has joined Kenna and Bails. He stands there while Kenna sashays next to him. It should look awkward as fuck, but it works for those two.

"Hey, Angel," I whisper in her ear before offering her the water.

She grabs it eagerly. "Thanks..." she hesitates, narrowing her gaze while she stares deep into my eyes —her new thing is trying to figure out a nickname that I'll accept, "you player you."

"You're awful at this," I answer with a laugh.

"You're the one who wants some ridiculous nickname. I just want to call you Aidan. For the love of girlfriends everywhere, do I have to be creative all the time?"

She winks at me, and Kenna and West laugh.

"He's a handful, huh?" Kenna asks. "I figured he would be. You know, my friend Sydney and him had a barely there fling." She peers away. "I told her not to go there."

"Ha-ha," I sneer. There was a little something between Sydney and me, but I eventually chalked it up to mutual attraction. She was fun to hang out with. We had some laughs. But in the end, none of it went anywhere. We're still friends, though.

"She was smart then," Bailey jokes.

"You say that," I tease, yanking her into my side. She jumps, trying to save her water bottle from getting crushed between us before turning toward me, gaze narrowed like she's attempting to stare me down. Unfortunately for her, she just looks like an angry puppy. Nothing threatening whatsoever.

I know what's so attractive about Bailey now. It's this innocent, girl next door vibe she has. Before, she was so put together. It looked like she was a doll that you didn't want to mess up. Now that she's chilled out, though, I can picture her wrapped up in my tousled sheets.

Not that I should picture any of those things.

I squeeze her ass, and this time, she doesn't react when I do it. "You're lucky to have me."

"I know," she says softly. A moment passes between us that's all too real, as if our façade went up in smoke and all that's left is the two of us.

I swallow, my throat suddenly dry. "So, how are you enjoying your first college party?"

Bailey steps away. "Cliché."

"Oh, totally," Kenna agrees. "Drunk people, fights, people hooking up upstairs. We're one huge stereotype here at Warner University."

That being said... "I hope they saved us a room upstairs then."

Bailey looks at me in feigned shock, clutching a string of pearls that aren't there. "Oh God, I would never."

I grin. Her words sound like she's accepting my challenge. I'm pretty sure I've actually seen her in pearls before, and that girl would never end up in a dirty room at a frat house. "I don't know," I say for everyone else's benefit. "I think everyone's first college party experience should end with a moment upstairs."

"Or maybe you're just another horny football player," Kenna tosses at me.

"Touché." I smile at her. "But if I'm a horny football player, then Bailey is a horny football player's girlfriend. Needs must be met. Deeds must be done." I walk toward Bailey with a playful grin.

She edges out of the way slightly, amused. "What?"

"We're going upstairs."

She peers around, watching the other people around us, and if I'm not mistaken, hesitancy has set in. "That's a...terrible idea."

I step toward her again. "I think it'll be an *experience*."

Kenna laughs, and Bailey looks at her and then back at me, a gleam in her eye. "You know what? I should go see what my brother is up to."

I corner her against the group of people we're all dancing with, trapping her against a wall of undulating bodies who are oblivious to anything else going on. "You know you want to..." I sing-song, threading my fingers through hers. I lean in close and whisper, "It'll seem very out of the ordinary if the quarterback doesn't take his girl upstairs at some point." I rock back onto my heels. "Plus, your brother is off dancing with the same girl he left us for when we first got here. He's preoccupied."

Just like we should be, I think before immediately dismissing it. This is all a show. I need to hammer that into my brain.

"Well, he might need me," Bailey says, her futile excuses only making this much more fun.

"Nope."

She presses her lips together to keep from laughing. "Then I have to pee."

Enough with this game. Without warning, I scoop her up in my arms. She squeals when I toss her over my shoulder but throws her hands up in triumph when she manages to not drop her water bottle. Mine, however, goes everywhere, but I don't care. I smack Bails's ass, and laughter erupts around us.

We pass Kenna and West, and Kenna shakes her head. "He's smitten. It's written all over his face."

West only grunts in response, smirking.

Ignoring their commentary, I carry Bailey up the stairs. They have no idea how wrong they are, and it's kind of fun fooling everyone, especially Mr. Know It All.

A guy in a "Stephen King Rules" shirt raises his cup as we pass him. Upstairs, the noise from the party is subdued, tamer.

Bails starts to wiggle. "Put me down."

"Not yet."

"Aidan," she warns. "You had your fun."

Where did my fun, adventurous girl go? It's like she thinks I'm actually going to do something to her. "Stop moving," I tell her, giving her another smack. The leggings leave nothing to the imagination, and damn, her ass is tight.

If I don't stop thinking about it, I'm bound to get hard again.

At the end of the hall, I spot an open door. It just so happens that it used to be Reid Parker's old room—the best room in the whole house. Peeking inside, I find it empty, so I move in and set her down on her feet while locking the door behind us.

Flustered, Bailey moves her hair out of the way and straightens out her shirt. "What was that about?"

"We're at a college party."

"Yeah, and the party is downstairs."

I laugh at her. "If you were an expert college student, you would know that the fun is all up here."

She shakes her head. "I can't tell who you are right now."

I cock my head at her. "Why are you mad?"

"I'm...not," she says, rubbing at her forearms.

Clearly, she is. "What did I do?"

She makes a noise in frustration. "I guess I got self-conscious when you picked me up. It's fine."

I chuckle, and this seems to make her even more mad.

"What?" she fires back at me, her eyes blazing.

I hold my hands up. "Woah, calm down." She peers away, and I can still see that it's bothering her. I never knew she was uneasy about her body. "In a purely platonic way, you're gorgeous, Bails. Do you think I get hard when any girl dances up against me?"

She places a strand of hair around her ear. "Yeah, actually. I thought exactly that."

Technically, I guess it's something that can't be helped, so I throw something else out there. "Why do you think I keep touching your ass then?"

She peers up, and I have to swallow the sudden dryness in my throat. What am I doing? Am I trying to talk us into this?

"Because we're fake dating," she says, brows rising like she's not sure if she should be saying it like a question or a fact.

This isn't going well. I need to steer this back around. "As a friend," I clearly point out. "You shouldn't be self-conscious about anything. I promise."

Awkwardness seems to engulf us as Bailey peers around the room.

"So, what?" she asks. "We stay up here for a little while so people think we did the dirty and then we can go back downstairs?"

I shrug. "Sounds about right."

She smirks. "What's that word you're always using

to describe me? Oh, I know. Boring..." She draws the word out and sends me a look.

From the room next to us, soft moans begin to bleed through the thin walls.

Bailey gasps and throws her hand over her mouth. "There's someone having sex in there," she whisper-yells, pointing that way.

I laugh at her shocked expression. "I have news for you. People are probably having sex in all of these rooms. Cliché, remember?"

She giggles into her hand, and I wonder if the few sips of beer she had are getting to her, or if she's truly that innocent that she thought I was pretending. "You weren't kidding," she muses, then continues to peer around the room. Luckily, I chose one that's decently clean. There's no dirty laundry anywhere, and it doesn't smell like a mold-infested locker room. Whoever lives here even made their bed.

A headboard knocking against the wall comes from the same room as the moans. Bailey laughs again, her cheeks red. "This is crazy." Then, without hesitation she hops onto the bed on all fours. The look of excitement on her face catches me off guard. "I have an idea!" She shifts on the mattress like I did with her bed earlier, and the frame hits the wall, mimicking the sound that's coming from next door. "Perfect."

"What are you doing?" When I'd done the same back in her room, she'd freaked out.

"We're supposed to be having sex. That's what the quarterback of the football team does with his very gorgeous, very new girlfriend." She says the words like she's reading from a spicy novel. "They can't even take one night off from having their hands all over each other. They need each other. Now."

Her tone drops an octave like she took a side job as a sultry sex operator, and I'm all too into it.

"QB1 needs to win at everything. He needs to be louder, sexier than the room next door."

She starts rocking the bed into the wall in time with the couple next door before letting out a passionate groan. I'm instantly hard, my cock pushing against my zipper. But that's not enough for Bailey. She calls out, "Yes, Aidan."

"Jesus Christ," I mutter. It's bad enough that she's saying it, but she throws her head back like she's acting it out.

She stifles a laugh, but she's into it now. "Yes, like that!"

On the sly, I peek down to make sure I'm not showing how much this is affecting me. When I glance back up, she tosses her head back again, her hips making the bed hit the wall. I'm not sure where she learned to do this, but I'm completely turned the fuck on.

She moans again.

Next door, the other girl gives a short cry, and

Bailey covers her mouth to stifle another giggle. "It's working," she whispers, waving me over. "Say something."

I'm at a loss. I'm enthralled at her performance. I'm...completely taken aback. I don't know how to pretend to have sex.

She locks gazes with me. "You're so fucking huge."

Her statement is punctuated with bangs against the wall. It might be my ego come into play, but finally, I lean over, my hands pushing against the mattress to make the springs creak. "You like that?"

Bailey moans in response.

"Take my cock."

Her gaze flies open, and she inhales.

Yeah, it's not so easy, is it? She's about to get a taste of her own medicine.

I let out a moan. "Your greedy pussy."

Bailey's movements on the bed stumble.

"You want more? Tell me."

She moans, her eyelids fluttering closed. At this point, I don't know what's real and what's fake. All I know is that I have a very real stiff dick.

"Aidan." She bites her lip seductively.

The way she locks her gaze onto mine, it's hard to believe that this is anything but reality. Next to us, the girl lets out a scream. The climax. The highlight reel.

I lean over, whispering in Bails's ear. "I think we

can do better than that." Louder, I say, "You feel so good. Fuck me, Angel."

My fake nickname for her slips out, but she doesn't react. She moves against the bed again. This time, more methodical, rhythmic. "I want to—" She shakes her head. "I'm going to—"

"Fuck yes."

"Harder," Bailey cries.

"Yes, Beautiful."

She throws her hips forward, making one final thump against the wall as she calls out my name.

It sounded so real, so...sexy.

My heart is thumping like crazy. She climbs off the bed, not looking at me. "There," she says, still avoiding my gaze. "We beat them."

Her breaths are shallow, voice husky.

Swallowing, her gaze skirts near the vicinity of my chin. "I think I would go to the bathroom at this point, right? To freshen up?"

She sneaks past me, turning sideways. I try to grab her hand, but I miss her, and then the door slams, leaving me alone in the room still so filled with fake tension.

10

BAILEY

OVERHEATED. Anxious. I get just inside the door, lock it behind me, and lean over the counter before I heave out the breath I'd been holding since I left Aidan in that room.

I've never been so fucking turned on.

My core is on fire.

That was most definitely a bad idea. Maybe this whole party was a bad idea.

Who knew Aidan could talk so dirty? It was all my fantasies come to life.

The area between my legs aches. I don't know how I'm going to go back out there and face him being turned on like this. I should take a shower. I should—

I need relief, but I'm in a damn fraternity bath-room. It's not the sexiest place to be turned on in.

Squeezing my thighs together makes it worse. A moan escapes my throat.

Maybe I can...

No, that's ridiculous. I can just go back out there and everything will be fine. I'll ask Aidan if we can leave. Then I can go back to the sanctity of my own room.

My thighs clench on their own accord as I bring up a picture of Aidan. The way he stared at me as he said those sexy things.

Fuck it. I can't take it.

I lower my hand, my fingers tracing across my stomach and down. My muscles jump underneath my touch. They're ready. They want relief. I part my legs just wide enough to sneak my fingers between my thighs over the thin leggings I'm wearing, finally finding my tight bundle of nerves. "Oh God," I whisper. I'm nearly pulsing.

Clamping my mouth shut, I swirl over my clit. My legs threaten to give out, so I lean forward, using the counter to brace me. I don't dare peer into the mirror because I'm sure I look like a sex-crazed maniac. Minutes ago, I was making fun of Aidan about being a horny football player, but what does this make me? I can't even keep up with a ruse without being so turned on I need to take care of it myself.

My legs tremble as I swirl faster. My hips start moving against my palm, then the handle on the door shakes. "Occupied," I call out, my breaths coming quick.

I close my eyes, picturing Aidan over me, jackhammering into me, calling out things like "Take my cock," and a moan flies past my lips.

I've felt his hard dick nestled against my ass. He's girthy, thick.

I moan again.

At the exact same time, hands grab my hips, and my eyes fly open. Behind me, Aidan captures my gaze. "What are you doing, Angel?"

I whimper in response, but to my surprise, I don't get embarrassed. I'm too horny to feel ashamed right now.

"Do you need help?"

"Aidan," I warn. This is a terrible idea. We're pretending. "You should—." Leave. Leave is the correct answer.

He stills my hands, pressing into my clit, and my mouth opens in silent ecstasy. "It's okay," he whispers. "We're both adults."

He rocks into me, and once again, his hard cock presses against my ass cheeks. Moving his fingers over mine, he swirls just like I was, staying there for a few moments while I'm caught between right and wrong. Then, his fingertips slip off. Nudging mine out of the way, he touches me through my leggings.

"Aidan," I gasp out.

He lays his head on my shoulder, his hot breaths hitting the crook of my neck. His skilled, practiced hands bring me right back to where I was within seconds. His lips are so close to my throat that he could kiss me, but he doesn't. One hand pins me in place while the other plays with my clit.

My whole body starts to tremble. I'm so close to the edge, hovering there for what seems like forever, like my body is refusing to give in. It almost hurts, and I hiss, whimpering again while I stay on the precipice.

"Tell me what you need," he urges. "Anything."

Not something I should be answering right now. There are so many things I'd die to see Aidan Michaels do to me. I've only dreamt of this moment. I've laid in bed while he was in the other room and touched myself imagining acts exactly like this. That someday he would see me—actually see me—and he wouldn't be able to keep his hands to himself.

"I need..."

"Tell me."

"Ohhh," I groan. I feel like I could come apart at the seams at any moment, but I'm still there. Still hovering on the edge of a razorblade.

"Aidan."

"You're killing me, Bails. Just tell me. Tell me, Angel."

"Talk dirty to me."

His fingers falter for a fraction of a second, but he's on board in the next. "You want to take my cock?"

I nod eagerly, catching his hard gaze in the mirror.

"Your greedy pussy needs me."

"Yes," I cry out. Already, I can feel the end is in sight. Relief. Sweet, sweet relief.

"You like my dick like this?" He pins me while he rocks into me, harder, faster.

"Yes! Please."

"Tight fucking pussy. So fucking good. I want this. I want you impaled on my dick."

My orgasm hits with the speed and ferocity of a freight train, and I couldn't contain my scream even if I tried. My body convulses, shaking in Aidan's sure hands while he holds me upright, his palm moving over my mouth to temper the volume.

But his fingers...his freaking fingers eke every last bit of aftershocks out of me until I finally open my eyes to find him staring. "That scream? It was meant only for me."

All of this was meant only for him.

My body shudders again, and Aidan holds me in place, slowly removing his hands from all my sensitive places until he's standing behind me, his arms maneuvering around my midsection.

"Only for me," he says again, eyes locked with mine until I nod.

Then, he straightens and leaves. I try to call for him, but he's gone, the door snicking shut behind him.

Heart racing, I peer at my reflection in the mirror

until the thought of repercussions threads into my guilty conscience.

That was a mistake. A terrible mistake.

I breathe in a few calm breaths, then throw some water on my face. I'm flushed, yet completely satisfied. More satisfied than I've been in a long time.

My mind tries to wander to what else Aidan could do to me, but that road is littered with potholes and broken hearts.

I need to find him; to tell him we shouldn't do that again.

Someone knocks on the door, and that finally pries me away from the privacy of the bathroom. When I open the door, it's Kenna. "Oh, hey."

"Hey. Aidan sent me up here to see if you were okay. He said you're a two-sip jersey chaser." She laughs and rolls her eyes. When I don't laugh in turn, she asks, "Seriously, are you feeling okay?"

Her worry pulls me out of my head. "Yeah, I'm fine. Maybe he's right," I tell her, going along with his story. "Maybe the alcohol did get to me."

She loops her arm in mine. "Here, I'll take you back downstairs. You seem a little flushed. It can get hot in here with all these bodies in tight spaces."

Embarrassment claws at me. If she only knew what I was actually flushed from...

Oh my God, in an upstairs bathroom at a fraternity? Could I be any more cliché right now?

"Yeah," I agree absentmindedly. "Tight spaces."

As we descend the stairs, I keep my gaze on the steps. I'm not ready to see Aidan yet. Partly because I have no idea what I'm going to say to him. How I'm going to face him knowing he's touched my most intimate parts. I should crawl under a rock.

"You know," Kenna says, "I used to wonder what kind of girl Aidan would find. You don't disappoint."

"How so?"

"I think you're just as nutty as he is. Please, take that as a compliment. He's so carefree, you know? Fun loving, funny. You took the whole throwing-you-over-his-shoulder-and-taking-you-upstairs in good stride."

I shrug. "Well, that's Aidan."

She smiles. "Exactly. And we can't change the weird parts about our guys. We like them because of those things."

I follow her gaze to find West. The love radiating between those two is so obvious. Almost palpable.

That would be nice to have someday.

A body shifts next to West, and I immediately glance over to find Aidan. He's staring straight at me, and I nearly trip on the last stair. When I regain my footing, he has his hand on my elbow, his commanding gaze threatening to turn my legs to Jell-O again.

"I told you," he says to Kenna. "Two-sip jersey chaser."

I laugh at his playful teasing.

"I'll take it from here." Aidan throws his arm around me, as natural as can be, and just like that, it's as if what happened in the bathroom is forgotten.

Not that I could actually forget. I have a feeling I'll be bringing up that image a lot in the future...when I'm alone in my room.

We may act like everything is fine, but on the inside, the tension between us is like a hundred-pound battle ax poised to fall. He walks me straight through the house and out the front door. The chill night air feels great on my flushed skin. It also knocks some sense into me.

I took that way too far. The whole moving the bed and the moaning... It was too much. What happened was my fault.

Our reaction was normal though, right? We don't need to make a thing out of it. So Aidan had his fingers circling my nub? We're good. Totally good. We don't need to talk about it at all. I, especially, should wipe away all the memories of him saying to "Take his dick."

That's definitely the first thing I should erase.

"I—"

"I'm sorry," I blurt out. "That was... I don't... God, you must think I'm..."

We're steps away from Aidan's Charger when he pulls me to a stop and makes me face him. "I was going to say that I'm sorry I made that part up about you being drunk. It was the quickest excuse that came to mind to get you out of there."

Of course that's what he wanted. He probably wants to take me home and forget anything ever happened.

"But maybe you are a little drunk because you should try finishing a sentence."

He gives me a half grin, and I stare down at the toes of my shoes so I don't think about how handsome he is. "I'm too embarrassed to finish every ridiculous thought that pops into my head."

He grips my chin and makes me look at him. "That was a complete sentence. Good start."

"Ha-ha," I deadpan.

"Well, at least you got *one*," he says, leading me toward his car again with a smirk on his face.

He thinks it's funny that I got all turned on from the joking? The acting out? That has to be it. He was just being helpful in the bathroom, and now he's mocking me. "Just so you know, I could've finished myself," I snap as he leads me to the passenger seat.

I turn away to buckle in, and when I turn back around, he's leaned completely into the car, nearly in my face. "Just so you know, I—" He cuts himself off with a groan and then slams the door before moving to the other side.

When he gets in, the tension is thick for a whole different reason as anger flushes my body. I cross my arms in front of my chest. "So glad I ruined my first college party."

"You're actually supposed to end your first college party pissed," he grumbles. "It's a rite of passage."

"Hallelujah, I can do something right."

He's quiet as he pulls out of his parking spot next to the curb. The engine fills the dead air between us like an angry bystander, the sound doing nothing to help my nerves.

"Just so you know," he starts again, "I wanted to help you. In fact, I wanted to dive my fingers inside your pussy and have you clench around me when you came, but—" He shakes his head. "I was taking it slow."

My whole body heats again. I think I understand now. I'm not the barrier between Aidan and the girls who throw themselves at him, I'm becoming one of those girls. Someone who'll distract him from what he should be doing. "Next time, don't bother."

His head whips toward me, and then he slams on the brakes. The tires squeal relentlessly beneath us, and I shoot my hand out to brace myself on the dash.

"The fuck, Aidan?"

"The fuck, Aidan? The fuck, Bails!" he throws right back at me. "Was that not what you wanted? Was it not me that made you run to the bathroom so you could rub one out? What the hell is wrong with me finishing what I started?"

Nerves skate up the back of my neck. "Because I'm

not one of those girls who fawns all over you. Your distraction. The thing that's going to take you away from football. I had it handled."

I can't believe we're actually arguing about this. This is insane. If this is what I act like in college, I'm out.

He reaches for me, guiding my chin to look at him again. "So we're clear, I had fun with other girls when I was in party mode. I was half-loaded with alcohol and high on being the star on campus. With you, I wasn't drinking at all. I was laughing my ass off. We were enjoying ourselves with being all into that fake sex competition until things just...switched."

I breathe in.

"It was normal," he says. "I wanted you. You wanted me. That's all it has to be. We can call it what it is: a lapse in defenses. We're playing around so much that some lines are bound to be crossed. Don't be embarrassed. It's not a terrible thing."

"Wow, you're really making me feel better." I roll my eyes. "Is this the part where you say it's completely normal to get overstimulated and go relieve myself in the bathroom?"

"Well, yes, it is."

"Then the only abnormal part was you coming in afterward?"

"I was also overstimulated. That's what two people do when they're together like that."

"So, you're fine with it?"

"More than fine."

"O-kay…"

I turn away, and he lets his foot off the brake and starts driving again. I don't know how to take this conversation, but it sounds like everything's normal. What we did was perfectly natural. He doesn't think I'm like the other girls he's trying to get away from.

Aidan points the car away from town, and I try to find the street names to figure out where we are. After a few minutes, it's clear he's not heading to the house.

"It's killing you, isn't it?" he asks. "Why don't you ask me?"

"Is this where you tell me it's also natural to be curious?"

He snickers. "Of course. Everything you do is right and true and perfect," he says with fake enthusiasm.

I fake laugh and sigh afterward. "Okay, for real, where are we going?"

He peers over with a huge grin. "A surprise."

11

AIDAN

I STEER TOWARD THE CHASM, my mind a jumble of thoughts. Trying to convince Bailey that what we did was fine was more me trying to convince myself it was fine.

It didn't take a sex therapist to realize what she was doing in the bathroom by herself. A man with more willpower could've kept walking past the bathroom door. Not me. Instead, I grabbed the doorknob. When it was blissfully unlocked, I took it as a sign.

Seeing her rock into her hand had made me even harder than I already was. A fucking stone statue. I could write a scientific thesis on how blue balls are definitely a thing. Guarantee I'll be rubbing one out tonight thinking about taking her against that bathroom counter.

Considering everything, I think it was a great, if not typical, first college party experience for her. If I had been paying attention to the fake-dating lines we drew, it would've been bleh.

Obviously, what I'm really trying to do is convince myself I didn't just fuck everything up. That devil on my shoulder is hard to ignore.

Over and over again, in the silence of the car, I analyze where the tension shifted. For me, it was those little sounds she was making. The way she loved my dirty talk. Can't say I've ever used it like that before. I went into it trying to be over-the-top intentionally, not knowing it was going to spiral the both of us out of control.

I'm the one who should've apologized to her.

The road in front of us transitions from pavement to rock. Up ahead, weeds grow sporadically out of loose sandstone gravel. Judging by how unkempt everything is, it doesn't look like anyone's been here for a while. We are getting to the end of the season for this, but when I saw that small, scribbled sentence on her list, I knew I had to take her here.

"Where are we?" she asks again.

I peer over to find her squinting, trying to see into the dark night. As soon as I cut the engine, she'll be able to hear the flow of water.

"I hope you were serious about wanting to tick things off your freedom list."

She looks at me cautiously. I can't blame her. I'm

not sure if anything I said to her on the ride over here actually made any sense.

"Are you excited?" I ask.

"I mean, I was, but you took care of that. Remember?"

I shake my head at her. The playful smile on her face makes me heave a huge sigh of relief. "Good one." I shut the engine off and open the car door. She scrambles out after me, peering around like I'm about to lure her into the forest and leave her for dead. Ahead of us, the headlights illuminate the berm that hides the tiny trail to the top of the chasm. However, if you weren't aware that existed, it just looks like we're in the middle of a moonlit thicket of trees. Luckily, with the moon high overhead, there's just enough light to make this only somewhat dangerous.

She meets me at the front of the car. "Aidan, what are we doing?"

Her hand brushes mine, and I grab it, leading her away. "Your list said something about cliff diving?"

Her mouth drops. "You're serious?"

I tug on her hand to get her to walk behind me up the narrow path. The brush scrapes my arms as we follow the twists and turns. "Something about high school graduation?" I prompt.

"Yeah." Excitement bleeds through her words. "After graduation, everyone goes to the Three Mile Cliffs and jumps off."

"And why didn't you go?"

"You know why," she says, voice dropping.

I walk faster. We're almost at the top now, and my stomach squeezes with a mix of thrill and trepidation. As cliff diving goes, the chasm is one of the safest places to do it. Warner residents have been jumping from here for years. Kids, teens from the local high school. All the rookies are made to come up here and dive. Of course, we don't tell them how safe it is before they do it.

I push the last branch away and reveal the nearly twenty feet of flat, vegetation-free ground that leads to a three-story drop into the widest part of the river. Here, the river is loud, more like an echoing roar since the falls are just up the bank. The current, too, is easily manageable, even on a bad day. Basically, it's the perfect spot to jump for a beginner.

Bailey smiles. Moving past me, she reaches out to touch the bench that overlooks the cliff face. "This is beautiful. Even at night. See the way the moon casts a glow?" She points to the other side of the chasm where the rocks hold a golden hue. Ever so tentatively, she steps closer to the cliff edge, leaning over to peer down the sheer drop.

"It's completely safe," I assure her. "I've seen young kids make the jump."

Peering back, she bites her lower lip. "It's really high."

"Higher than the one you missed on graduation?"

She throws her hand out. "Well, I don't know, do I?" Glancing over the edge again, she says, "It looks like it ends in a black hole of nothingness."

I follow her and peer down, too. I see what she's saying. Directly below us, the river is pitch black. The moonlight hits sporadically across the rocks of the chasm. Clear glimpses here and there, but the water itself looks like a shadowy pit. "But you hear the water, don't you?"

She rolls her eyes.

"So, you know it's there."

Timid eyes peer over the edge and then back at me. I move behind her, placing my hands first on her shoulders, then lower, hovering just below her collarbone. Beneath my palms, her heart beats like crazy. "Do you remember why you wanted to do it in the first place?"

Her shoulders lift with a deep breath. "Because I'm sick of always being left out. Because I want to do more things and be free from my cage."

I let her sit in that thought for a bit, but mostly because her words hit home for me too, in a way that's more difficult to explain. I've spent my entire life from five years old until now trying to break free from this thought that I'm not good enough. A kid his birth mom didn't even want. My parents could give me everything in the world, and they have, but some days, I'll still only be that orphan boy in my head.

I take a deep breath of my own. Bails just wants what I want. To be free from the thing that's been holding her back. "What do you think? Are you up for it?"

"Yes," she states confidently. Then her shoulders drop. "No. I don't know."

I laugh, tracing my hands back up to her shoulders where I give her a quick squeeze. There's no way I'm going to let her get away with not doing this now.

"Should we even be doing this?" she asks. "Don't you have practice tomorrow? I don't want to keep you out too late."

"Now you're just making excuses."

"No, for real." She turns toward me. "I'm not supposed to be taking your attention. I'm supposed to be giving you more time to focus."

I blink at her. "You're thinking about me?"

"Well, yeah."

I shake my head. It's stupid that my brain does this. Thousands of people scream my name every Saturday, people seek me out on campus just to say hi, but this kind of attention—the kind that comes from someone who truly cares—still catches me off guard. I've only allowed a few people in my life to get this close to me. Darrin, of course. West. My adopted parents. People I truly trust that I know won't fuck with mine in return. I didn't realize until now that Bailey was getting that role too. I give her my cocky grin. "Well, the longer this takes, the less sleep I'll get."

"Maybe we should do it another night?"

"Bailey..."

She looks into the dark pit again, and I can't help but tease her.

"Gosh, I'm so tired. I wish my fake girlfriend would jump off this cliff with me so I can go home and get some sleep."

"Ugh," she groans in frustration. "You're awful."

I reach behind my back to take my shirt off. Yanking it over my head, I place it on the bench, then step out of my pants. My boxers will do as swim trunks. I wish I'd thought ahead and grabbed a towel, but I didn't. I'm nothing if not a spur-of-the-moment type of guy. Bailey can just use my shirt as one, that's *if* she actually jumps.

When I turn back around, I'm greeted by the vision of Bailey's bare backside: her ass like perfect spheres, the stunning silhouette of her back as it meets her shoulder blades.

Slowly, she spins to face me, and I watch as the color drains from her face. "Oh God..." She wraps her arms around herself, one hand covering her perfect breasts, the other semi-hiding the V between her legs. "Aidan! You only took your shirt off. I thought we were skinny dipping too."

My mouth works, but no sound comes out except

for a laugh. Then another. "I was going to dive in my boxers."

She turns again, snatching her clothes from the ground. Using her shirt to block her tits, she hangs her head, then fishes for her bra and attempts to put it back on.

I walk up behind her, annoyed that she's so flustered. "Don't you dare." My voice comes out low, commanding.

Her back straightens.

"I'm all for the change in dress code," I tell her, my gaze falling on the delicate skin of her shoulder. The same skin I breathed over when my arm was wrapped around her earlier.

"I'm mortified. I can't do anything right."

Reaching past her, I take the shirt out of her hands as she continues to fiddle with her bra straps. They're all tangled, and she growls in frustration. "I swear, if you cover those perfect tits, I'm going to be mad. Turn. Now."

She stills, giving me the opportunity to appreciate her silhouette again. Those sensual curves. That round, supple ass.

Gorgeous.

My dick starts to harden in my boxers.

"If you don't, you're going to miss me taking off my boxers."

"Well, of course no one would want to miss that," she drawls.

Despite her words, she turns, her bra hanging from her right hand.

We keep getting put into positions like this, don't we? Miscommunication. Our fake flirting turning into something more. It's like life is teasing me…

"If I'd known you looked like that, I would've kicked your brother out of our skinny dip party just so you could walk around naked."

"Maybe I have looked like this," she says, sticking out her chest. Her breasts are absolutely spectacular. Her gaze drifts down my front, and she quirks a brow as if challenging me. "Your boxers?"

There's no way I can do this sexily, so I just hook my thumbs and move slow, hoping a big tease pays off. I have to lift the elastic band out and around my stiff cock. It juts there proudly, and I send a thankful prayer that he's making me look good. When I kick the boxers off, she's staring at him, and he preens more under her attention.

This is either a bad idea…or a really good one. Since we're faking everything else, we can get away with naked jumping without serious injuries, right? And I'm not talking about physical damages. I'm talking about making this whole situation more complicated than it already is.

Without thinking, I take my cock in my hand and squeeze, trying to relieve his suffering a little.

Bailey takes in a breath. "So, are we doing this?"

My brain imagines all the things I want to do. Like taking her from behind and then when we come together, we take the jump at the same time— But that's some porno shit. Actually, not a bad porno idea. Innocent college student wants to rebel, so this is how she does it. Sex and adventures.

But I'm not directing a porno, am I? I'm standing in front of my best friend's sister. "Do you want me to go first? Or jump together?"

"Together," she says.

She stretches out her hand, and I take it. Now joined, we step toward the edge.

"It's deep enough, right?" she asks, voice wavering.

"I've done it a hundred times. When you surface, there's a rocky beach to swim to. From there, there's a path that leads back up here."

She nods quickly like she's still trying to talk herself into this.

I watch while she gathers herself. "Okay?" I ask.

"Okay." Before I know it, she steps forward, jumping into the night. I scramble to catch up with her, but I lose her hand.

She screams, her cries echoing around the chasm, and when she hits, that amplifies too.

I plunge in right after her, the cold river washing

over my body in a flurry of goose bumps. For a moment, everything is silent until I kick to the surface. Then the first thing I hear is Bailey's laugh.

The loud belly laugh bounces off the rocks all around us. "Oh my God!" she screams, splashing at the water. She twists, and when she sees me, she pushes her hands forward to splash me right in the face. "You said together!"

"You jumped without warning like a total psycho!" I yell back, wiping the water out of my eyes.

She tilts her head back and giggles into the night. "I have to do that again."

"We can."

"Are you sure? I don't want you to be too tired tomorrow."

"I'm sure," I tell her, running my arm across the water to send a huge wave her way.

She splutters and spurts, then wipes the water out of her face. "You dick."

I shrug. "Yeah, sometimes."

Lunging forward, she splashes me until we're like two preteens at a pool party.

"I got you the best."

"No, I did."

She lunges for me, pushing my shoulders, but I grab her instead, my hands finding her hips. Her legs come around me, and for a few seconds, I'd forgotten we were both naked.

My dick is only semi-hard now, but it finds her inner thighs like a heat-seeking missile.

She gasps, the carefree moment switching in an instant. "Aidan."

I pull away. "Sorry, sorry."

Reaching down, I place my hand over my dick, trying to keep him out of the way.

I chuckle nervously, but she's no longer laughing. She's staring straight at me, her face a mask of desire that I recognize earlier from the bathroom. Shifting her hips forward, she rubs her pussy over my hand. "Bailey," I warn.

"It's natural, right?"

Someone super intelligent said that, and I think it was me on the car ride over here while I was nursing blue balls. Balancing her on my thighs, I cup her tits, needing no other invitation than those three words.

She gasps again, and it sounds so pure to me. Like no one's ever touched her like this.

We struggle to keep afloat, so I lead us closer to the riverbank until my feet touch. We just stand there for a moment, the slight current flowing past us, almost like featherlight caresses.

"Is this a bad idea?" she asks, her worried eyes framed by soaked lashes that are sticking together in points.

I have two minds. One that says yes. The other that

says hell no. "I think maybe we should set some ground rules."

"Like what?"

"Like, friends with benefits?" I breathe out, waiting for her face to change. But it doesn't. "This extracurricular activity could help us keep up appearances, but also, it doesn't last longer than our fake relationship."

She steps closer. "Anything else?"

Her tits are almost pressed against me, making it hard to think. "We don't get attached."

"That sounds reasonable."

"We don't let it interfere with anything," I tell her. "The minute it starts to, we stop."

She nods. "Okay."

I grab her thighs and yank her close. My dick slides against her pussy. "What about you? Any rules you want to add?"

"We go slow," she says, moving with me.

"Your actions say the opposite of slow."

She moans. "It's your fault. It feels too damn good."

I tug her hair until her chest juts out of the water. The fullness of her breasts offered up to me... I can't help but taste and kiss and suck.

She makes another one of her surprised sounds, her feet kicking out as I wrap my lips around her nipple, rolling it between my teeth and tongue. "Aidan, oh my God."

"You like that?"

"I...I didn't know..." she mewls.

I nip her with my teeth, and she places her hand around my neck, tugging me firmly against her breast. The water laps against her there as I taste it and her.

"Aidan..."

Her hips thrash wildly, like she's trying anything to find relief.

Reaching down, I move my fingers up her inner thigh. "Oh God, please. Please."

She's so vocal. I love it.

My thumb finds her nub, and I start to circle it slowly. Her body jerks, and my fingers brush her entrance.

I growl, pressing inside. She cries out, the sound echoing around us. "Aidan, oh shit."

Her unrelenting, jerky movements make it difficult to start a rhythm, so I grip her ribcage with my free hand and then work her with the other. She's so damn tight.

"Take that finger like a good girl," I tell her, sucking her nipple.

Her hold on my neck tightens. "Aidan, I'm going to... Is that okay?"

Is that okay? Jesus Christ, I've barely touched her.

I quicken my movements, flicking my tongue over her nipple until she screams, her walls closing around my finger, squeezing the fuck out of it.

Holy hell.

"Jesus, Bails." I thought she was playing at how loud she could be when we were fake fucking in that room, but she was just mimicking what she does in real life. *Good God.* "I need you," I growl out. I squeeze my dick, angling it toward her pussy. "Please tell me you're on birth control."

"I am," she says.

She clutches my shoulders as I work my cock against her. I'm lined up, ready to push in. "Aidan, I'm a virgin," she rushes out.

"What the..."

12

BAILEY

MY ORGASM still pulsing through me, it's a wonder I even got that much out. I writhe against him. "I needed you to know so you don't hurt me. Just go slow."

It takes me a few seconds to realize he's no longer moving. Actually, he's not doing anything.

I peer at him. "What's wrong?"

He looks white as a ghost. His hands clamp around my waist and then flutter there before creating distance between us. I sink until I find my footing on the rocky river floor.

"I can't believe I almost took your virginity. Bailey." He runs his hands through his hair, looking stricken.

My stomach tumbles over. "It's fine. I want you to. I'm on birth control."

"No, no." He wades out of the river and stands on the rocky beach. Every muscular inch of him is a tease, and it makes what he says next so much worse. "This is fake. I'm not taking your virginity. I would feel terrible."

My mouth unhinges, and the area behind my eyes heats. He would feel...*terrible?* "I'm pretty sure that wasn't a fake finger up my...hoo-ha."

His eyes widen, and if it's possible, he pales even more. "No one had done that to you either?"

Okay, now I'm getting pissed. All of this was going really well until thirty seconds ago. I trudge up the bank, and slip. Aidan reaches out for me, but I slap his hand away. "No. No one had ever touched me down there before either. Do you want to feel bad about that too? Should I hand you a tissue?"

"Bailey. Jesus. This is a big deal."

"It wasn't a big deal until you made it a big deal."

For a moment, I spin in a circle, as if clothes will materialize out of thin air. I'm fucking mortified. I shouldn't have said anything. He would've just done it. I wanted him to.

"Your first experience isn't going to be with someone who's..."

"Who's what?" I challenge. "Fake? I'm pretty sure you weren't faking that hard dick."

"There's a difference."

"I shouldn't have even told you. It's none of your business."

"None of my business?"

"It's not like you wanted my complete sexual history before I said anything." I search around for the path he'd mentioned earlier and walk toward the most obvious spot.

"It's just, your first time shouldn't be with someone like me."

"I know. It's so terrible that you're hot and funny and nice to me. *Wooo.* Guess I better find some moody, disheveled stranger and ride his lap."

I'm midway up the steep path when it levels out and Aidan grabs my hand, turning me to face him. "I mean that the person you do it with should care about you," he growls out.

My mouth clamps shut. I guess there's nothing to say to that. He's made his point. "Wow, okay. We're perfectly clear on that now." I give him a mock salute and wiggle out of his grip.

"That's not what I mean."

"Like I said, perfectly clear, QB1. I forgot that when you're with girls, you don't actually care about them. My bad."

I cringe after I say it but keep moving, only hearing my own thrashes and deep breaths as I make my way up the trail in complete darkness. At the top, I scramble for my clothes and yank them on.

By the time he comes up the trail, I'm yanking my

shirt over my head. I stand there with my arms crossed, avoiding even looking his way. The first tear falls then as I stare out into the dark forest. I wipe it away before he notices and then stomp toward his car.

What an epic fucking disaster.

A few minutes later, Aidan joins me. He starts the engine and backs out without a word.

I'm so lost in my own thoughts that I don't hear my phone until Aidan says, "You're vibrating."

My first reaction is to snap at him, but then I understand what he means. I grab my phone out of his glove compartment where I left it and find a text from Darrin.

> Hey, spend the night at Aidan's, K?

"You're kidding me," I mumble.

"What is it?"

I start to type out a text telling Darrin I can't because Aidan has football in the morning when Aidan asks again. I sigh, putting the finishing touches on the text. "Darrin wants me to spend the night at your place. He must have a girl over or something. I'm going to tell him to fuck off."

Aidan reaches over and places his hand on mine. "Don't. It's fine."

"I don't think you want to be near me right now, and I certainly don't want to be near you."

"Let him have tonight. I promise, it's fine. West will be staying over at Kenna's, so you can sleep in his bed."

My shoulders deflate. I really want to tell Darrin to forget it, but I've been telling him I want space, so if I give it up now, I'll just look like a flake. "Are you sure?"

"Hundred percent."

"Fine."

We drive the rest of the way back to campus in silence. I'm shivering by the time we get there. When he parks, I start to get out, but Aidan reaches over to stop me. "I'm sorry, okay? It isn't that I don't care for you. You know I like you. As a friend, obviously. I just..." He breathes out. "I think your first time should be special and not during a whole relationship that we're faking. We're getting all mixed up," he continues. "You're probably confused. Caught up in the moment."

Every word he utters drives the knife in deeper. I don't say that, though. "Yeah. I'm probably just tired. Confused." *Lonely. Horny.*

"Come on," he prompts.

I get out of the car, and someone yells "Yo, QB1!" from across the parking lot. Aidan waves and comes to my side, placing an arm around me. For a moment there, before tonight, this was starting to feel comforting. Even though I knew we were pretending, I liked it.

Now, his touch is like a hot poker branding me with an undesirable mark.

He holds the door to the dorm open for me, and I walk inside. Aidan lifts his hand to greet the guy at the front desk, then he guides me up to his room. We stop outside the ladies' bathroom. "If you want to start getting ready for bed, I'll grab you some clothes."

"Sure."

It feels like I'm on autopilot as I open the door and step inside to a room filled with stark tile. I curl my lips, wishing I was in my own place. I could be taking a hot bath right now with a bath bomb, some kill-me-now music, and then cuddling in bed with my nice sheets and a favorite movie, trying to forget about tonight.

Instead, I'm in Aidan's dorm.

I shake my head, use the bathroom, and then throw some water on my face. A knock comes, and it must be Aidan because I doubt anyone else knocks on a public restroom door.

Opening it, I reveal Aidan standing there with his shower caddy and some dry clothes. "Hey, bad news. West is sleeping in his bed."

I close my eyes. Of course he is. Because the universe loves fucking with me. "I'll sleep on the floor."

"Like you would be the one sleeping on the floor," Aidan interrupts.

"You have football tomorrow."

He shoves the clothes and shower caddy into my

hands. "We'll both sleep in my bed. For appearances, right?"

My stomach tumbles over, but I guess we really don't have a choice. "If you're okay with that."

He nods down at the shower caddy. "I thought maybe you'd want to get the river water off you. That green toothbrush is new. Feel free to use it."

"Um, thanks. I'll be out in a few."

It would be nice to stay under the water and soak, but the dorm showers are less than desirable and there's some sort of phantom wind billowing out the shower curtain. I end up rushing through my routine, using Aidan's soap to wash up and only rinsing my hair under the hot spray as I wrangle the curtain with my feet.

Afterward, I get dressed into Aidan's Bulldog T-shirt that's way too big for me and brush my teeth. Steeling myself in the mirror, I take a deep breath and peer at my reflection. Did I try to rush into Aidan taking my virginity? I don't think so... I wanted him to. There's a point when a girl just wants it gone already. Like, there's this special group everyone else is a part of, and I'm not even invited.

Although, thinking about it now, it was nice that Aidan wants me to have a good first experience. Though I don't see how that could've been a bad one, but I guess it doesn't matter.

I blow out a breath. He better not snore. I might not get any sleep tonight if he does.

Yanking open the door, I stop when I find Aidan waiting for me.

He sends me a wary smile. "Ready?"

I nod. "You didn't have to wait."

"What kind of boyfriend would I be if I didn't wait for my girl?"

I peer up, assessing him. He's trying to get things back to normal, and if so, I can do that, too. I can forgive him for what he said. And I can forget about what we did. Maybe...

"Thanks," I answer. The truth is, I'm the one who imposed on Aidan. He didn't want any of this. I should stop being weird about it and do my part. "For taking me to do the cliff dive, too. It was fun, regardless of... It was great." My face heats, and I look away.

"I'm glad you had a good time. Now you can tick two things off your list."

Confused, I glance at him again. "Two?"

"Skinny dipping and cliff diving."

"Oh, right."

"How quickly she forgets."

He's wrong about that. I'll never forget the picture of him standing there.

Never.

I hope whoever does end up taking my V-card is as perfect as Aidan.

Right before we get to his room, he brings his finger up to his lips to remind me that West is in there. When I nod, he takes the clothes and the shower caddy from me before opening the door.

Sure enough, West is in his bed, facing the wall, fast asleep. Aidan and I tiptoe inside. I hear him put away the shower caddy, and when I look back, he places my clothes on his desk chair before tugging his own shirt off.

It takes me a moment to figure out that he's already changed for bed. He's wearing a pair of loose athletic shorts, a matching pair to the loaners he gave me.

I wait for him by the bed until he steps up beside me. "What's wrong?" he whispers.

"I don't know what side of the bed you sleep on."

"Scooch toward the wall."

I get in, slipping under the covers. Luckily, he has two pillows, so I take one and place it behind my head. Aidan gets in after me, and my stomach flip-flops. We both stare up at the ceiling, our sides pressed into each other all the way down. The bed definitely isn't big enough for us to have our own space.

Reaching down, Aidan takes my hand. "Good night, Bails. Don't kick me out if I snore."

I chuckle under my breath. "Just get some sleep. Did you set an alarm?"

"Jesus, I almost forgot." He leaps out of bed, grabs his phone, and sets the alarm. The light from his screen illuminates his face. He's so freaking handsome I can't stand it. Any girl would die to be in my position right now.

I shoo away the weirdness from earlier. I don't need to make this any more awkward than it is. He was totally right about the whole taking-my-virginity thing. It was a stupid idea. I was caught up in the moment.

"Thanks," Aidan says as he gets back in bed.

"What are girlfriends for?"

The adorable smile he gives me makes me feel ten times better.

"Well, cuddle up, girlfriend, because these beds are only so big. Don't be shy."

I shake my head at him, trying to be as quiet as possible while we get into a more comfortable position. I end up facing him on my side, my hand under my pillow. He stays on his back, both hands tucked under his own pillow, and if I'm not mistaken, one of his legs dangles off the side of the bed.

I warm at the sight. When he used to visit, I would come down some mornings and there would be Aidan and Darrin, fast asleep after trying to stay up the whole night. Aidan's leg would dangle off the sofa, and I'd wonder how that was even comfortable.

"Go to sleep," Aidan teases.

"I am." I yawn, moving my head into the pillow to mute the soft sound.

My mind is bursting with things to say. I've never slept in a boy's bed before, and my mind races, but when I look over, Aidan's already asleep, so there's no one to talk to but myself.

13

AIDAN

THE IMPRINT of Bailey's ass still tingles along my skin. I woke up spooning her, my right hand cupping her rib cage so I could feel every breath she took. Untangling myself without waking her was a chore.

I breathe in the cool morning air along with the smell of hot muffins from the bakery just off campus. I'd needed to get out of that room before I flipped her over and forgot about the fact that I would be stealing her virginity by taking her the way I wanted, so an impromptu breakfast run was in order. When she told me about her v-card status yesterday, it felt so wrong to continue. Here I was, telling her friends-with-benefits was going to be fun. And there she was, about to let me take her most sacred thing.

Maybe I'm old school, but her first time shouldn't be something she gives up in the heat of the moment without a second thought. It should be with someone who will take it as seriously as the act actually is.

Indecision pricks at me. I'm torn between talking to her about what happened and just letting it go.

"Aidan!"

My head snaps up at the familiar voice.

"I thought that was you," my dad yells.

Surprise ricochets through me as I start jogging toward him. "Dad! What are you doing here?"

He brings me in for a hug and claps me on the back. "I was out this way on a work trip, thought I'd stop by and see how our star is doing."

My face flushes. "Good, Dad. Good." All the bad choices I'd made this last month come flooding back to me all at once, so it's difficult to answer with a straight face. I never told my family I sat some practices out. Or the game. No one has mentioned it either, and I can't tell if it's because they don't know or if it's because they would know I'd be too upset to talk about it.

Coach didn't advertise why he was taking me out of the games, thank fuck. The last thing I need is that getting out to NFL teams. Some of them might strike me off their list right away. I was such a fucking idiot. A month of partying could've cost me my entire career.

Dad peeks at the bag in my hands. "Are those on diet?"

I laugh. "With the way I'm working out, I could eat

a dozen doughnuts a day and you wouldn't be able to tell. But these aren't for me."

"Oh?"

Well, why don't I just step in it? Shit. Upstairs, Bailey is probably still sleeping soundly in my bed, unless West woke her. We only have about fifteen minutes before we need to leave for practice.

A cold sweat sprouts over my forehead. "Yeah, you know, West and whoever else wants them at practice. I'm heading back to my room to get ready now."

"I'll follow. I wanted to talk to you about something."

My stomach churns. There's just something about when a parent says "I want to talk to you about something" that sends a jolt of fear through you.

"Is something up?" I ask as I steer us toward the dorm.

I study his profile, taking in the gray hairs along his temples, and his beard that's almost gray. I saw an episode of some show once where the kid was looking at his father, worried he was going to turn out like him. I won't have that. I have no recollection of my birth father whatsoever, so I guess I won't know if I'm destined to be bald or completely white. Maybe I'll be lucky and get that salt-and-pepper, George Clooney look girls seem to chase after.

I, however, do remember my mom...and sometimes, I wish I could forget I even had one.

Dad opens the main door to the dorm for me, and we walk through. He runs his hand through his beard. "Your mom and I were hoping to come to your next game, but we wanted to check with you first."

"Really? That would be great." My parents don't get to a lot of games. They work a lot. When I was younger, hearing them argue about money always hurt the most because I thought it was my fault. They wouldn't have had to worry about it so much if they didn't have me.

"Yeah, we feel bad we haven't been able to come up before this. We miss you." Our footsteps on the stairs echo, almost sealing those words into me. "You don't call a lot."

I rub the back of my neck. "Busy, I guess."

"We know you're Mr. Hotshot now, but we worry about you."

I lead him to the right, a nagging feeling pricking at me. I don't know why I haven't called. Being at school has brought this weird divide between me and my parents. I can't even put my finger on it. "I'm sorry."

"Hey, what do we always say about that? No need to be sorry. We just want to be involved."

My shoulders droop when we make it to my door. "Yeah, that's on me," I concede. "I'll do better."

My father gives me a small smile. Without thinking, I push the door open. Bailey immediately stands from my bed, dressed in my clothes, and my eyes go wide. My father walks in right behind me, and there's no stopping the moment that's about to occur.

"Mr. Michaels," West says, standing from his own bed. I glance between the two. She runs her hands through her hair and then quickly puts it up in a ponytail while my dad and West make small talk.

She grimaces at me, and I shrug. "Dad, you remember Bailey, right? Darrin's sister?"

My father peers over. Everything happens in slow motion. At first, he smiles, always happy to meet someone, but then he takes in the shirt and shorts she's wearing, which are obviously mine. His stare moves to the bed, then back to her. We all stand there and let him come to the only conclusion there could be. There's nothing I can say to him anyway. Everyone else knows we're dating. I honestly just didn't think I would ever have to mention it to my parents.

"Hi, Mr. Michaels," Bailey says, walking toward him with her hand outstretched. "It's been a long time, but I remember you."

"Yes, how are you?" he asks, sending me a strange look. He doesn't look pissed. He looks amused.

"I'm well, thank you. I was actually just leaving." She glares at the floor, rushing past me.

"Um, Aidan?" my dad says. He stares at the bag of muffins I have in my hand and then at her.

"Oh, right." I spin on my heel. "Bails, I got you these."

158

She pauses with her back to us, sighing. I can tell she really wanted to make a run for it.

"I remembered you like lemon muffins."

Turning, she blinks up at me. "Thank you."

From behind us, my dad asks, "Are you going to school at Warner, Bailey? I had no idea."

"I am," she says, taking the bag from me. "Darrin too. We just transferred."

"Aren't you...younger? You're Darrin's younger sister, right?"

"She skipped a grade, Dad. Can you believe it?"

My dad looks at her, impressed. Bailey looks like she could crawl under a rock to live out the rest of her life and be fine with it.

"Yeah and speaking of, I should probably go study some more. Thanks for the late-night study session yesterday, Aidan. I really needed it. I'll catch you later?"

She practically runs into the hall, and as soon as the door shuts, my dad bursts out laughing. "Late-night study session? For being so smart, she's a terrible liar."

"Sorry, Dad. I didn't know you were coming in or I'd—"

"I'm just glad it was me and not your mom."

Yeah. That would've been a nightmare. I laugh nervously.

"As long as you're being safe."

How does not even having sex sound for being

safe? I don't think my dad would appreciate the play-by-play, though, so I nod and leave it at that.

"Well, I'm gonna get going." West checks his watch. "You got about five minutes."

"I'll see you at the next game," Dad calls out, giving my roommate a quick wave.

"See you then, sir."

The tension in the room builds when it's just the two of us. It feels like a chasm grows with him on one side and me on the other. "Your mom would probably like to know you have a girlfriend, if that's what she is."

The itchy feeling on the back of my neck increases. "It's relatively new. I haven't been holding out for long. When she and Darrin transferred here, things... evolved," I tell him, even though it was more like she was a defensive tackle homing in on me.

The thought makes me smile. She's something else, that's for sure.

"I look forward to getting to know her more when we're up here for the game. We're going to stay for a few days, we think. Send us an itinerary, and we'll hang out."

"Can you come to practice now?" I ask, hiking my thumb over my shoulder in the vicinity of the practice field.

"I actually gotta get back on the road. You know how it is. On company time and all that. But next week, I promise."

I bite my lip. I hate goodbyes. Maybe that's why I haven't been in touch with them a lot. There's nothing to miss if you don't even talk. I walk toward him and throw my arms around him. "Thanks for stopping by, Dad. It was good to see you. I mean it."

He holds me tight, the claps on my back a little stronger than they were when he first got here. "You're making us so proud, Aidan."

His voice chokes a little, and I hold a breath. I can't let us leave on sad terms, though, so I say, "Even with the girl in my bedroom at seven in the morning?"

He chuckles into my shoulder. "I'm impressed. Smart. Terrible liar. Cute. An old friend. No one can fault you for that."

When he puts it like that, Bailey sounds fantastic. And he doesn't even know the half of it.

"I'll have Mom call you with the deets of our trip," Dad says, walking toward the door.

"Deets, Dad?"

"Hey, I'm hip. I know things. Plus, I saw it on MTV. I thought you'd be impressed." He opens the door and gives me a smile. "See ya, Son."

He gives me a two-finger salute before leaving, and I keep a smile on my face until the door closes.

With a sigh, I plop down on the bed. My mind conjures up memories of Mom and Dad, but I have to brush them away in order to focus on my upcoming practice. If they're going to be at the game, I have to make sure my ass is playing.

I breathe in deep. My nostrils flare with a familiar scent. My sheets smell like Bailey's perfume, and I can't help but savor it. The way she high-tailed it out of here, that was hilarious.

Reaching for my phone, I send her a text.

> That was only slightly awkward.
> Sorry, he surprised me. Hope you like
> your muffin. See you at practice?

She doesn't write back right away, and it's probably because she's trekking back to her place on foot. I really didn't plan this morning out well. I should've left enough time to drop her off. Checking my watch, I cringe. If I don't leave right now, I'm going to be late.

> Sorry you had to walk.

> Actually, I'm kind of enjoying my first
> walk-of-shame experience. People
> keep laughing at me.

My hackles rise. If I was with her, they wouldn't be laughing.

Before I can text her back, she says:

> See you at practice.

I release the breath I'd been holding and then grab my bag. Throwing it over my shoulder, I lock the door behind me and make my way toward the field. My mind should be on practice, but instead, I keep thinking about Bailey. About the way she looked peering off the cliff. About the way she buoyed in the water while she glided next to me. The surprise in her voice when I made her orgasm—not just in the bathroom, but in the water, diving my fingers into her.

She was definitely not my friend's little sister then.

My phone pings, and I take it out as I make my way across the quad. It's a picture of Bailey. She's giving me a frightened smile and a peace sign, the message reading:

> I guess everyone knows what you're up to when you still have sheet creases on your face.

I shake my head, zooming in on the picture. Sure enough, she has a bright-pink line streaking down her cheek. I can't help but text back:

> That's how you know you're killing it as a college student.

> Does that mean you give me an A+?

> Don't get too greedy. Maybe just an A.

I'll try harder, then.

Smiling, I take one last look before I put my phone away.

Football time.

14

BAILEY

AIDAN TAKES MY HAND. I can't believe I'm doing this. It was bad enough that his dad walked in on me nearly sleeping in Aidan's bed five days ago, but now we're pretending in front of both of his parents. In front of everyone, actually.

Today is the first couples fundraiser challenge, and we're doing a bunch of athletic skills competitions. *Weee.*

"Oh, I almost forgot," I tell Aidan, pulling back on his hand before we leave my room. I unzip my hoodie, unable to keep the smile off my face. I'd bought us shirts a few days ago and had them ultra-rapid shipped to me. They got in last night just when I was hyperventilating that they wouldn't arrive in time.

He frowns. "Why is there a cinnamon roll on your shirt?"

I run to my bed and pick up his shirt. "Because…"

I reveal his shirt like Vanna White on the final letter of the puzzle.

Power Couple. I throw spirals.

I point to mine that says *Power Couple. I eat spirals.* His has a football where the *o* in power should be. Mine has a cinnamon roll. "Make sense now?"

"You are ridiculous." He grabs the shirt and changes, and I try not to ogle his washboard stomach. It's almost a shame for him to hide that body...if only his shirt wasn't so damn funny.

"Well, come on, Miss I Eat Spirals," he says, smiling. "If we do well today, I'll make sure you get a cinnamon roll as a prize."

"Ooh, talk dirty to me," I tease, then immediately clap my mouth shut. "On second thought, bad idea."

Aidan chuckles some more. "Yeah, we'll get ourselves in trouble again if we start that."

I didn't know how Aidan would react to the shirt, but he wears it loud and proud. He keeps staring down at it and laughing. And when someone comments about them, he sticks his chest out like he couldn't be prouder to be the other half of a cinnamon roll-eating power couple.

Despite the tension between us when I told him I was still a virgin, things have gone on like normal. Tonight, we're going out to dinner with his parents after they watch us mop the floor with the other contestants. I mean, couples. *Football* couples.

As soon as Kenna sees our shirts, she punches West playfully. "Why don't we have matching shirts? That's the cutest thing!"

West glares at Aidan, but Aidan shrugs, tugging me closer like we're an actual team. "My girl bought them."

It's hard not to get caught up in his words. It doesn't matter how many times I tell myself that he's only going along with the idea I had, I can't help the thrill that races through me every time he calls me Angel or his girl. The feeling only got more poignant after the night of the party. At this point, there's no way I'm going to get out of this without some level of heartache, but that's a college experience, too, right? The only thing I want to make sure of is that Aidan never finds out.

A shrill whistle rings out, and Aidan and I turn toward the sound. A beautiful woman with a whistle around her neck waves at everyone. "That's Mrs. Thompson, Coach's wife," Aidan whispers in my ear, sending goose bumps over my body. I nod like he didn't just turn me on with that little move.

"Thank you all for joining us. We're so happy to have you here, and we're really looking forward to raising some money for the Step-Up Foundation!"

Aidan and I clap, and the crowd that's gathered around us cheers. There are a lot of spectators—more than I thought there would be—most of them are wearing Bulldog-blue. I even made sure that the shirts I ordered had blue lettering to match the team's colors.

"There they are," Aidan says while lifting his hand to wave. Following his gaze, I find his parents making their way toward the front of the crowd.

I wave nervously. I've met them on several occasions, but the most awkward has been the morning his father showed up unannounced. I'll never live that down.

Darrin got a good laugh out of it. I see him, too, weaving through the crowd toward them. When he gets there, he yells out, "QB1!" Another round of cheers goes up from the onlookers, drowning out what Coach's wife is saying.

I shake my head, turning back toward her. She's explaining the events we have today. It's stuff that you would see in an elementary gym competition, which is probably the fun of it all. All the players and their girlfriends are about to make asses out of themselves.

There's a three-legged race, racing with eggs on a spoon, a football throwing competition—because *duh*— and a short obstacle course where the couples have to take turns going through it blindfolded while their partner shouts out directions.

My biggest worry is that I'm going to hurt Aidan. Like the shirt says, I like eating spirals. I definitely don't throw them.

Aidan lets go of my hand to start limbering up,

stretching out his legs and arms. I roll my eyes to hide the fear starting to surface. I just know I'm going to screw this up for him. Sure, I'm competitive, but I know my limitations. I'm going to try like hell, but I already foresee myself crashing and burning. There's no way we can beat West and Kenna—who is also a freaking athlete.

"Competition starts in fifteen minutes!" Coach's wife yells, the mic giving her slight feedback that ricochets around us.

"This is going to be terrible," I mutter.

Aidan peeks up at me from his bent-over position of stretching out his legs. "Ye of little faith. This is part of your college experience." He walks up to me, moving the hair that's broken free of my ponytail around my ear. "I really don't care if we win."

"Yeah, that's because you're going down," Kenna states behind him.

I bite my lip as Aidan tries not to laugh. Still, he stares into my eyes like he's trying to convey how sincere he is.

"You're lying," I tell him.

Reaching out, he plays his fingertips along my jaw. "Let's just have a good time. That's what this is all about. Raising money. Having fun." He cups my face. "I won't be disappointed."

I gulp. He touches me like this in public all the time, but it's getting harder to discern what's fake.

169

Which is stupid because it all is. I need to keep reminding myself of that.

"Besides, we're the power couple," Aidan says, getting riled up. "We have the shirts to prove it."

Down the line, one of his teammates boos, and his girlfriend smacks him in the chest. Aidan whirls. "Oh, you just put a target on your back, Rogers! That's a lot of smack talk for a D-lineman."

"Just be thankful I'm not the one protecting your ass out on the field," he shoots back.

The spectators close enough to hear this exchange laugh. My stomach bubbles up with more nerves though. These players are used to competing. Of course they want to beat each other.

"Don't let them get in your head," Aidan whispers in my ear, throwing his arm around me. "First up is the three-legged race. I'll match my pace to yours."

We walk toward the starting line and the blue elastics placed there every few feet. This is going to be an epic disaster. I picture me face-planting for sure. Or worse, causing Aidan to face-plant. What if he uses his arm to block his face and it snaps in half? Everyone will blame me for taking out the most important player on the football team. *Ugh!*

"Hope you've been getting your cardio in," Aidan snarks at one of the stockier players on the team. He's probably a lineman as well. Those guys are supposed to be big and scary, but the girl he's with is super petite.

I don't know how they're even going to compete in this race at all given their stride differences.

"Line up!" a man's voice yells.

There's something about his tone that makes me jump. Aidan too. He places us side-by-side on the starting line as a man comes down the line and moves up the wide, tight elastic piece, linking our legs together. "Thanks, Coach," Aidan says after he's settled us in.

Coach grunts in response, and my nerves fire even more. *This is a bad idea* keeps repeating over and over in my head. Aidan, though, is staring downfield like he can beat the contest into submission. If this is how he looks in a game, I'd be running away from him.

"Promise me you won't get mad." One last-ditch effort to tell him this is really going to go badly couldn't hurt.

He leans over, kissing the top of my head. "Power couples don't talk like that."

Reaching up, he makes me give him a high five by bringing our palms together. "Yeah, but girls who like cinnamon rolls do." I pat my stomach for good measure, and Aidan wraps his arm around me, gripping my hips. "I wouldn't change a thing about you, Angel. Now, let's kick some ass."

I beam at him, butterflies swirling in my stomach. Coach's wife says to get ready, and I maneuver my hand around his waist. I'm as ready as I'll ever be, and

I'm starting to think Aidan won't get mad if I do screw this up for him.

Aidan murmurs. "Outside leg first."

"Huh?"

The whistle blows, and I barely get a step out before I nearly topple over. Aidan barks out a laugh. "Outside first," he says, wrangling me to my feet.

"Oh!"

I tentatively step with my right leg, then the leg that we're bound to one another. Another step and another step.

Just like he said, he matches my pace until we're running like a cracked-out gazelle across the field. We pass the one defensive linemen with the short girl-friend and then another couple who's fallen to a heap on the ground.

We don't win. Not by a long shot. By the way Kenna and West have their hands in the air, they crossed the finish line first, but I'm smiling too much to care. "I'm sorry," I say, chuckling. "I didn't know what you were saying."

Aidan kisses my forehead. "I told you I didn't care." Immediately, he peers above my head, waving to his parents.

Throughout the day, Aidan carries my ass. Of course, he single-handedly wins the football throwing competition, even though my score was actually pretty good. He just didn't need it to pulverize the competition.

He showed off his hand-eye coordination in the egg running contest, while I took my time and didn't drop once.

By the time we get to the obstacle course two hours later, I'm hyped up on blue sports drink and the bananas Aidan brought for us. We're in second place, behind Kenna and West.

"Are you ready to go down?" Kenna asks when we line up at the start of the obstacle course.

"Yes," I answer. "I actually am."

She bursts out laughing. "You guys are the cutest. The crowd is totally rooting for you."

"It's because we're underdogs."

I don't know what she's talking about, though. The crowd loves them, too. Actually, the crowd loves it all. I hope we're helping raise a lot of money for the Step-Up Foundation while I humiliate myself in the process.

Coach's wife stands in front of us, giving out the rules. First, the guys will call out orders to their significant others while we make our way through the obstacle course. Behind me, Aidan wraps a blindfold around my eyes and ties it in the back.

Through my portion of the competition, I have to crawl under a spiderweb of ropes, then cross a short balance beam that's only two inches off the ground.

Then, I have to run up and down a slide before switching the blindfold to Aidan. The tricky part is that if I fall at any time, I have to start from the beginning again.

"We've totally got this," Aidan says. His voice sends a chill through me. I can't see a thing, but I can feel how close he is. He trails his fingers down my arm and then gives my hand a squeeze. "Just listen to my voice."

I nod, waiting. In my head, I'm picturing the layout in front of me. Not going to lie, I already guesstimated how many steps I would need to take before dropping to my knees and climbing under the spider web ropes. The balance beam will be the toughest part.

"Ready?" Coach yells, interrupting my internal run-through.

The crowd starts to cheer, and I panic for a moment thinking I won't be able to hear Aidan.

The whistle blows, and he's so loud. "Five steps and down!"

I nearly come out of my skin. His voice is so commanding, searing like a drill sergeant. He's used to calling out plays in the middle of a packed stadium, so I'm not sure what I was worried about.

I hop off the line, doing what he says. I'd estimated it at five steps, too. Without thinking about it too much, I take the five steps and dive right down.

"Lower!" Aidan yells when my forehead hits the first rope.

I duck under and keep moving. My ass drags along the ropes above me, but I scramble through as fast as I can.

"A few more feet. Two! One! Up!" Aidan instructs as I come out of the web. I shoot to my feet, choking a little on the dust of dirt that must be circling around me. My heart beats a mile a minute.

"Two steps right. Forward three. There." I follow Aidan's instructions to the letter, moving my right foot when he says. Once I'm on the balance beam, I decide to slide along it. I feel when the elbow in the beam comes and veer left on instinct.

"Yes, Angel! Yes!" Aidan screams.

I hope that's good news because the next thing I know, I'm jumping off the balance beam and Aidan is telling me where the slide is. I reach out, fishing for the handrails and then run as fast as I can up the slide.

"Last step!"

My foot hits the top stair just like he said. *Holy shit! We're doing this.*

I fling myself forward butt first and slide down. I don't even get to my feet before Aidan is scrambling at the knot in my blindfold.

"That was amazing!" he says, his voice an excited whisper.

The sun stings my eyes when he whips it off me. I rush to my feet, squinting while I maneuver to his back to tie the knot.

His first obstacle is the monkey bars. I run along with him. "One step to the right! That's right, two more steps," I say, guiding him. "Step up."

He does what I say, but once he's on the monkey bars, he doesn't need any guidance until I tell him he only has one rung left. He swings himself forward, landing on his feet.

The next is a rope swing. If he falls, he has to start over.

"Walk three steps. Step up." Once he's on the platform, I tell him where to reach for the rope that's hanging on a hook. He grabs it, sails forward, and I yell "Jump!" when he's close enough to hit the other platform.

Miraculously, he lands it perfectly. I run to catch up with him. Looking over, I notice we're ahead. There's no one else on the ropes with us. Kenna and West are still back on the monkey bars.

My heart beats overtime. The last obstacle is a net climb. This seems particularly tricky blindfolded. Clips denote a line he has to stay on the other side of so that each player has their own space to climb, or he'll get called to the beginning again.

I guide Aidan to his stretch of netting. "Move right. Right," I yell as Aidan runs forward. He starts up the net, but the judge tells him to get off because he started on top of the clip.

"Two paces *right!*" I scream. He shuffles his feet to the side.

"Good?"

"Now!"

He starts up the netting. There really isn't much to say to guide him. He keeps moving up, finding footing. When he's almost to the top, I tell him he only has a foot to go, and then he's laying over the top beam and trying to find his footing on the other side.

"Let's go, Aidan!" people yell.

He comes down methodically, his foot searching for the net as quickly as possible. "Let me know when I can jump."

"You got about five feet."

I cringe. Good Lord, I'm glad I didn't have to do this one. I don't like heights on a good day, let alone blindfolded.

He jumps off, and I hold my breath.

He lands in a crouch and then spins. I only have to redirect him to run straight ahead and then he's crossing the finishing line, a long yellow ribbon hitting him across the torso.

"Yes!"

I jump up and down and run toward him. He yanks off the blindfold in time to see me launch myself at him. He easily plucks me out of the air and spins me around. "We did it!"

I smile down at him. Without thinking, my lips

find his, and as soon as they touch, it's like a dam breaking. All the tension from the other night hits a boiling point as we find each other once more.

His fingers tangle in my hair, pulling me down to him until we both need to come up for air.

When he sets me on my feet, his parents are there. I stand, stunned, watching while he gives out hugs.

For a moment, it feels so real. So, so real. Like I'm one half of Aidan's power couple team. Like I'm meant to be here. Like I always have been.

And it feels amazing.

15

AIDAN

MY DAD LIFTS his beer bottle. Our nearly empty plates lie in front of us at Cindy's Steakhouse, a Warner treasure. Or so it says on the sign out front. Next to me, Bailey lifts her glass of water as my dad says, "To the winning couple."

A whole-body laugh overtakes me. I'm still wearing the shirt Bailey presented this morning, and when I peer at her, she's taking a sip from her glass, amusement written all over her face.

"I have to admit, it was dope watching you guys," Darrin states. "I didn't think Bailey could move that fast."

"Ha-ha," she snarks, sending him a frosty glare around me, but then it's as if she remembers where we are and smiles sweetly at my mom across the table.

The two seem to have hit it off. They've talked all

through dinner, and whatever awkwardness I imagined there would be isn't there at all. Bailey fits in fine.

Which is awesome...if she was my real girlfriend.

"I'm glad we were able to raise so much for the Step-Up Foundation."

I shrug casually, dampening the thoughts of unease and pushing them way down so I can enjoy this moment for what it is. "It was fun to win, too."

Bailey rolls her eyes. "I was afraid if we didn't win, you'd find someone to replace me."

"Eh," I tease. "They wouldn't have looked as cute in the shirt."

Her cheeks turn red. Next to me, Darrin shifts in his chair, but he doesn't make any comments about wanting to puke in front of my parents. Looks like I'm not the only one on my best behavior.

"You two." My mom sighs, her eyes glittering. "You're the cutest. I can't wait to go to your game tomorrow."

She turns her face and brings a napkin to her eye.

My stomach squeezes, but in true fashion, I say a joke instead. "If I'd known getting a girlfriend would make you cry, I would've done it sooner."

She waves me away. "It's not just that."

My father leans forward, his elbows resting on the table. When he sees me watching him, he smiles, but it's not genuine. Something else is going on. My mind races as I glance between the two of them.

Half of my brain tells me not to pull on that thread. I'm playing in tomorrow's game, and if I don't put on one hell of a show, people will talk. They'll speculate. I need to crush it so no one remembers that I didn't play in the last game.

The other half though...

This is ridiculous. Everything's fine. My insecurities are talking, and I really need to focus on football right now. "I'm glad you guys are here for it. It's going to be epic."

Darrin leans back in his chair. "I can't wait to see you live, man. Bailey and I watch all your games at home, but there's nothing like being in the stadium."

"Sounds like you miss it," my dad muses.

Darrin nods, looking introspective for the first time since he showed up. "Man, I do. A lot."

Bailey hits her knee against mine. "He lives vicariously through you." She gives a terrible impersonation of her brother. "Did you see that play, Bails? QB1. That's my boy, right there."

My mom and dad laugh, but I turn to Darrin. "Why don't you try out next year? As a walk on."

"I won't even be going to Warner next year," he says offhandedly before taking a sip of his root beer.

"You won't?" my mom asks, her gaze flipping to Bailey. "Will you?"

Bailey fidgets in her seat. Her face pales a little, and it throws me for a moment.

I've gotten used to having her around. Both of them. Fun used to be all about going out and meeting girls and talking football, but now, fun has been a whole different adventure. Crossing out items on Bailey's list. Seeing my best friend.

Even after this year, or this semester, she won't be done with her list. It isn't possible. Then what? Her parents are going to make her go to the school with the bunch of uptight, snobby people?

I turn to Darrin. "You planning on going to that school Bailey told me about? The one her parents want her to go to?"

"It's a good school. Dad went there."

"But they don't have football," Bailey interjects.

Darrin's face morphs into a scowl. "Well, I'm not as good as Aidan, so it doesn't matter."

The table falls quiet. "Sorry. Excuse me," he apologizes, throwing his napkin on the table and standing. He pauses a moment, shoulders lifting before moving in the direction of the bathroom.

I watch him go before standing, too, but Bailey wraps her hand around my arm. "I'll go. It's my fault."

Smiling down at her, I pat her hand. "I got it. This is best friend talk."

I weave through the tables, and when I get to the bathroom, Darrin is staring into the mirror above the sink. Our gazes meet, and he sighs as he starts to wash his hands. "You didn't need to follow me in here, dude. Sorry I snapped. It's—" He hesitates, shaking his head.

"What is it, man?"

"Nothing. I don't want to say anything that's going to get Bailey in trouble. I don't know how much she's told you."

My stomach falls out. *Does he know we're faking it? No, that can't be it.* "About what?"

He grabs some paper towels to dry his hands and then throws them away. "It's just, I hope you know there's no way either of us can stay at Warner. This was like a Hail Mary pass for Bails. A last-ditch effort. The way bachelor parties are supposed to be. You know, get your kicks in now and all that."

"Fun before you settle down. I get it. But is this school really that good? Sounds like you both don't really want to go there."

"It's one of the best schools in the US. Tons of past presidents went there. It'll set us both up."

"You didn't answer my question."

He shrugs. "I don't have a choice, and I'm tired of fighting about it. I have to go to school to get a good job, and that's the school they want to pay for. I'd be there if it wasn't for this stunt Bailey pulled."

I lean against the wall. "I don't remember your parents being like this. Making your decisions for you and everything."

"It's gotten worse since we got older. I don't know,

maybe Bailey is right and she's always had it like this. They've planned everything out, and that's what they want."

"Well, what do you want?"

"Shit, I don't know. I've barely had time to think about it when all I keep thinking is that I don't want to do what they want me to do. Then I see guys like you who are thriving, and your parents are so chill. They let you go wherever you wanted."

"I mean, it's where I got the scholarship. It's just a bonus that Warner has a kickass team and was my number one choice."

"But you made that happen." His arms flex, turning his hands to fists as his voice rises. "Even if I was as good as you, my parents wouldn't let me play sports. Doesn't that sound crazy? What parents don't love when their kid is so good at something that people will pay them to do it? It's insane. Your mom is over there crying because she can't wait to see you play tomorrow. My mom would be sobbing for a different reason. 'Throwing my life away' or some shit."

"Just tell them no," I state, getting angry on his behalf. "They can't make you go to school somewhere you don't want to go."

After a moment, Darrin gives me a small smile and walks toward me. "Don't worry about me, man. Make sure you and Bailey live it up before you have to do the whole long-distance thing."

Long distance? No, my brain responds automatically.

Before I can say anything out loud, Darrin's already halfway out the bathroom door. In the distance, Bailey is laughing while my mom talks with her hands. Dad peers between the two of them with a soft, happy smile.

I run my hands through my hair. I don't like the position Darrin and Bails are in. It doesn't seem fair, but I also don't know what to do about it, so I just follow my best friend back to the table.

Once my dad sees us approaching, he calls the waiter over so he can pay the bill. Darrin and I sit once more, and I listen to my mom and Bailey interact. By the end of it, my mom has her and Darrin convinced to sit with them at the game using my family tickets and not student seating, which doesn't take too much persuading considering family tickets are better seats. After my dad signs the receipt, we all stand together, and a pang hits me for not being able to do this a lot. See my family. Have real conversations.

On one hand, I like football because it's constant. The games stay the same. Sure, you play against different players and teams, but the rules, the logistics, they never abruptly change. The way Darrin talks, we might not be able to do this again, and then how am I going to tell my parents that Bailey and I broke up and that she's probably going to marry some dude who runs a software company out in California? That she owns a mansion and dogs and—God forbid—kids, and Darrin is over there every weekend with his wife for parties. And I'm... Well, do I even fit into that picture?

Every once in a while, real life hits me in the face, and it isn't pretty.

My breaths come in short pants, and I close my eyes, searching for Bailey's hand. The panic comes hard and fast like a freight train until my vision starts to blur.

When I was five, I used to have attacks. It was right after I moved in with my new family—this family. Mom and Dad would watch what they said around me because if something ever sounded like they were making a decision about me, I would freak out and hide in my room, lock the door, and cry. It was so bad they had to take the handle off my door.

I try to draw in a steady breath, but it doesn't help. Shallow pants follow one after the other. I feel it in my toes first. A tingling. My body's own version of a warning system that I'm about to boil over like a steaming pot but...

Bailey's fingers finally find mine, and she squeezes me. Her hand grounds me to the present in one swift motion that I immediately feel back in control over my own body.

I force my eyes open and focus on my surroundings. *Nothing is changing right now. Bailey and Darrin are still here.*

I peer down at her, and I can't believe how quickly things become the norm. I didn't even know they were going to show up one day, yet now I'm already worried about their eventual departure.

My episodes are why Darrin hardly ever came to my house when we were kids. My parents loved to have him over, but it was the separation that would get to me. I'd have to gear myself up for it. Mom and Dad would have to pull me aside and remind me that in three days, Darrin had to go back home. Then two days, then the next day. They had to get me used to the idea that Darrin wouldn't be there anymore.

It was different when I was at his house, though. I was the odd one out. It was easier to leave them because I didn't truly belong there. It was more like a vacation with a friend.

The evening air washes over us as we step outside, my hand still firmly clinging to Bailey's.

"Well, I've got a hot date," Darrin informs us, flipping his car keys in his hand.

Bailey balks. "You have to drive me to the house."

"It's okay, I'll drive you," I offer. The truth is, I probably need her more than she needs me right now. When my parents leave, the feeling of losing them will be so much worse because I'll have remembered what it was like to be around them.

...and this is why I like living in my own little world.

We make all the vehicle arrangements, and I hug my parents tight, telling them I'll see them after the game tomorrow. Mom doesn't want to let go. "We'll see you tomorrow," she promises and I feel like that little, scared boy again. "After that, we can come see you more often, Aidan. If it will help."

"I love you."

"I love you, too, my sweet boy. Tomorrow."

My dad has to tug on her hand to get her to let me go, and then Bailey and I are in my Charger, driving to her place.

"Your mom is so nice."

My mind catches on that one moment where she acted funny, but I don't want to think about that right now. "You guys got along well."

"She's funny." For a few beats, Bailey's quiet, then she asks, "What did Darrin talk to you about while you were in the bathroom?"

My fingers tighten on the steering wheel. "He said not to get used to having you two around."

Bailey nods. "Yeah, I think he is finally starting to see what I've known all along."

"What's that?"

"That we really don't have our own lives." She says it so sadly...but then busts out laughing. "It's not funny, but it kind of is. I mean, by almost all metrics, we're adults, but we can't make our own decisions. If I didn't laugh at it, I'd spend every day crying."

My mouth goes dry. "I don't like it."

"Me neither. I can guarantee you I wouldn't have won a couples contest at the other school."

I picture Bailey running an obstacle course with some faceless dude, and I automatically hate him. What would he think about her to-do list? About leggings being her new favorite piece of clothing? Would she even be the same girl she is with me at this other university with some stuck-up rich dude who'll probably want to control her life too?

"Tell them no."

She laughs and starts to change the subject.

"Why are you doing that?" I snap. "Darrin did the same thing. Why don't you just tell them no?"

She peers over at me, gaze discerning. I realize I'm balled up tight and try to relax. I probably look half crazed. "Fear of letting them down. Fear of making a mistake. Fear of not having any money," she states, shrugging. "To name a few."

"If you really want something, you should go for it. You're young. Who cares if you make a mistake? If you end up not liking Warner, go back to the other university. Try it out. Or go to a whole different school altogether. There's more than one way to be successful."

She gives me a small smile. "It's nice that you care."

I straighten up, caught in this weird position. I do

care, but not sure I should as much as I do. "I'm worried about you guys," I concede, but in my heart of hearts, I know that's definitely not all of it. There's more here.

I pull into their driveway, and as soon as I put the car in park, Bailey pushes her door open. "Thanks for the ride. I'll cherish my non-existent power couple trophy forever."

Instead of just dropping her off, I get out with her. "You're not getting rid of me that easily." I search for an excuse. "I have to make sure you get into the house okay."

"Aidan, I'm good. You have a game tomorrow, you should probably go get some sleep."

"Let me make sure there's not an axe murderer waiting for you inside."

"Fine," she sighs, shaking her head. I follow her to the door, and she opens it, switches the lights on, and then walks in. "No axe murderer."

Still not getting rid of me that easily. I close the door behind me, even though I really should be going back to my room and getting some sleep before the big game tomorrow.

"What are you doing?" she asks, backing up.

"Darrin probably wants me to stay with you to make sure you're okay. That's what a boyfriend would do, right?"

"Well, maybe, but my fake boyfriend is a really

famous, really amazing quarterback who needs rest for his game tomorrow."

"I can rest here."

She eyes me. "If you want. I guess."

Turning, she walks down the hallway, and I watch her ass in those leggings. Crazy that I was the one making up rules for her, and now I feel like I want to break every one of them.

The smart thing to do is say goodbye and go back to my dorm, watch some game tape, and fall asleep.

"I'm going to change," Bailey says, slipping into her bedroom. She leaves the door open a crack, and I stay outside, watching her move around in there. She peels off her shirt, and my legs start forward before I can tell them not to.

I nudge the door open, and it creaks. She spins, covering herself up. "Aidan."

I don't care about any of that modesty nonsense. "I've seen you naked," I tell her, smirking.

"Yeah, but—"

I turn away, peering out the windows. "A real boyfriend would make sure no one was spying on you."

"Oh really?" she asks.

"And a real boyfriend would make sure you were settled in for the night."

"Uh-huh."

I spin toward her. "A real boyfriend would make sure his girl didn't go to bed without an orgasm."

191

She sucks in a breath. "Aidan... We did that. It wasn't— It was—"

"It was amazing until it got complicated. It's not going to get complicated this time." I don't know who I'm trying to talk into this. Me or her. "My offer still stands, Angel. While we're faking it, we can be friends with benefits."

"But no sex?" she asks, her brows lifting.

"No sex. Just you and me crossing off items on your to-do list."

She bites her lip. I suspect hesitancy, but before I can come up with another excuse to talk her into it, she says, "I do have something I've been thinking about."

"What's that?"

"Will you teach me how to..." She trails off until her gaze stops on my crotch.

16

BAILEY

I CAN'T GET the actual words out. They sound too dirty in my head, so saying them out loud would surely make me blush and stutter. Like I don't know what I'm doing.

Because I don't.

My experience with guys before Aidan was limited to a few very innocent kisses. My parents have had me locked up tighter than Rapunzel. Honestly, I don't even know why they agreed to let me come here unless they thought I was safe with Aidan.

If only my parents knew I was also getting sex education... They would yank me out so damn quick.

Aidan reaches down. His hand grabs his jeans, and underneath that, I'm hoping his growing cock. "You've never?" The awe in his voice is something to behold. I don't know how to tell him that he's the first person to make me orgasm. That he's the first person besides myself to touch me in any sexual way.

My mouth suddenly goes dry as I watch him. "Never." I didn't know I could feel like this. I've seen movies. I understand the emotion of falling for someone. The intensity. But this is something else. Something *more*.

I lift my gaze to stare into his eyes. "Is that bad?"

He groans, and I don't know how to take it. He was probably hoping for someone more experienced, like the girl who showed up in his room in nothing but a robe. She probably knew exactly what she was doing.

"As your fake boyfriend..." He pauses, and I'm hanging on his every word. Finally, he says, "I have to tell you how hot it is. Also as your fake boyfriend..." he takes a deep breath, and his eyes cloud over, "I should tell you that I'm a bastard for wanting to be your first."

I shake my head. Aidan's definitely not a bastard. He's been nothing but kind to me. He gave in to this silly fake dating scheme. He's actually taken my to-do list seriously.

The sound of Aidan lowering his zipper sends a rip current through me, threatening to take me under. I'm hot all over. My body aches with need in the blink of an eye. The intensity is a bit overwhelming, and I wonder if Aidan feels it too.

He unclasps the button on his jeans and shoves

them down past his ass. His dick presses against his boxer briefs like it's in a cage it wants to be free from. In one swift movement, Aidan maneuvers his boxers out of the way, and the head of his cock pops free.

I squeeze my thighs together. Girls on TV talk like this is something they should do. They don't really want to. But that's not the vibes I'm getting right now.

Aidan sits on my bed. Leaning back on one hand, he uses the other to stroke his hard length. He's still wearing my stupid power couple shirt, and I can't help the thrill that streaks up my spine. It's our worlds colliding. The fake one and whatever this is that's happening between us. Even if it is only sexual.

I hope it's not.

"On your knees."

Holy shit. My toes curl in my shoes.

He grabs my pillow from the bed and places it between his legs on the floor before beckoning me forward. I do what he asks, sinking down until my face is nearly lined up with his cock, a bead of precum forming at its tip.

"Can I see you?" I breathe, my gaze landing on his chest. As much as I love that shirt, it would look better on the floor right now.

"This?" he asks, tugging on the bottom.

I nod eagerly.

His smirk undoes me. Grabbing the hem, he tugs it

over his head and sets it next to him on the bed. "Better?"

"Much," I breathe, studying each dip and ripple of his abs.

He runs his fingers over my head, delving them into my hair. His lips part. The way he stares makes me want to breach the distance to kiss him. It would be so easy. So unbelievably easy.

Instead, he pushes on the top of my head, guiding me down. His firm grip strokes his cock toward my lips. "Take me inside, Angel."

My lids flutter closed. Opening my mouth tentatively, I brace for the feel of him. I lick my lips, and when I do, my tongue brushes against the head of his cock.

He groans low in his throat, the sound stoking a fire in me.

My eyes snap open, and our gazes collide. My stomach rolls like I'm on the precipice of the tallest mountain, and I've found the ends of the earth. It's all here, right in Aidan's topaz eyes.

"Close that gorgeous mouth around me."

I lean forward, his silky skin nudging past my wet lips. His hips jump on contact, sliding even more of his length into me until he hits the back of my throat, and my mouth closes around him.

Oh damn. He's huge. I make an unwanted choking noise, and he grimaces. "Sorry."

He gently pulls himself away, my lips sliding across his smooth, hard shaft.

"We'll take it slow," he whispers eagerly, his hold on my hair tightening. "Wrap your hand around my base so you can control how deep you go."

I bring my hand up, and he helps me close it around him, squeezing me there. In turn, I grip his cock, and he bites his lip. "Yeah, you definitely need to control this before I take it too fast, too soon."

"Is that how you like it?"

"Just seeing your mouth near my dick is exciting, Bails. Now work me into your mouth as you run your lips down me, Angel. Don't be afraid to squeeze me tight. I promise you won't fucking hurt me."

I do as he says, gripping and sucking. He braces himself on the bed with two hands, never taking his eyes off what I'm doing to him. His chest raises and lowers, his fingers sinking into my sheets.

"Fuck, baby. You can run your tongue along me too."

I pull him into my mouth, my tongue playing over his thickness, exploring ridges and veins.

"More pressure with your lips."

So many things to think about, but it isn't a chore. Watching him is like having an out of body experience. I'm doing this to him. Making his breaths come out quicker and quicker.

"Rhythm is important," he moans. Reaching out,

he delves his fingers into my hair again before moving my head forward, down his dick. "Christ, Angel." He guides me nice and slow, just staying near his head until he lowers me further, my lips brushing my fist as he picks up the pace. "Fuck. That's a good girl. Take all of me."

His praise sends shivers through me. I grip his hips with both hands, so I can take him all inside. When he hits the back of my throat, I suppress a gag, and I'm rewarded when he moans my name.

"That's right, Angel. It's like you were made for me. You're sucking me so good."

I flush all over, my hands flexing on his tight muscles before bobbing down his length once more. He keeps eager, fiery blue eyes fixated on me while I experiment a little. More tongue. Less tongue. Licking his tip when I need to come up for air, and then playing with depth and pressure. I listen to his breaths for cues. To the way he moans my name.

He trembles, and I pull back until his dick pops free. He hasn't said anything in a while. "Is this okay?"

He grips my hair more forcefully. "It's fucking perfect. Don't stop."

"Do you think I could make you..." I ask, my brows rising.

"I'm so close, Angel. Wrap those lips back around me and finish me like a good girl."

I take him inside my mouth again with renewed determination. The way his silky skin moves past my lips. The salty taste of his precum. My nipples harden, brushing against the padding of my bra.

"Bailey, fuck," Aidan breathes.

I moan, and his hips pitch forward again, like he has no control.

"These lips. This mouth. This throat." He shifts forward, taking over the pace. "So fucking sexy. Just perfect."

His eyes go wild. Crazy. He holds my gaze, thrusting into me as I work down him. For a moment, it gets so hard and fast, I don't know how I'll be able to keep up. Tears spring to my eyes. If it weren't for the praise flying out of his mouth in a frenzy, I don't know if I could. "So fucking beautiful. Perfect lips. Hot fucking mouth. Innocent...and mine."

With a strangled grunt, he thrusts up one last time, holding me in place with his hand on top of my head. When he tries to pull away, I follow him.

"Bailey, I'm going to—"

I groan. No way is he going to deny me this.

He cries out, his dick pulsing in my mouth, his cum spilling down my throat. I swallow and swallow, closing my eyes while I drink him in. Tears fall down my face as he pins me to the hilt.

When he's spent, he backs up, and I take in a deep

breath, peering up at him through a fractured gaze. His stare zeroes in on my cheeks. "I'm sorry. Did I go too hard?" Fingers come up to wipe my tears. "Are you hurt?"

Am I hurt? Is he kidding? I feel like a goddamn queen. I shake my head. "Gag reflex, I think."

He clasps my cheeks in his hands, watching me.

I start to shift uncomfortably. "I can probably do better next time."

He tilts his head, eyes narrowing. "Are you kidding me? If you can do it better next time, I'm never leaving this room."

"So it was okay?"

"I said you were perfect, and I god damn mean it."

His words linger in the air around us. The stare he gives me says everything. His shoulders raise, and his next sentence comes out slow, practiced. "Has anyone ever licked you here?" he asks, tracing his fingers down to rub between my legs.

I shake my head, my body already tensed up tight. Just his slight touch has me shifting toward him eagerly.

"Can I be the first, Angel?"

I shiver at his words, his nickname sending a thrill to the heart of me. Down to my toes.

I smirk. "I don't know. Are you any good?"

"Oh, honey, I'm the best."

He holds out a hand, and as soon as I take it, he

yanks me up and onto the bed. I giggle until he flips me in one easy movement, parting my legs.

Before I can even gasp, his mouth is on my center. I yelp, his hot breath passing through the layers of my leggings, my panties, until it hits my soaked core. He pins my knees to the bed while he pushes his tongue out to prod and play. What a tease. "Aidan..." I moan.

"It's not my fault you're wearing leggings."

"Take them off," I beg.

He sits back, smirking at me. "If you take your shirt off, I'll take care of these." He wraps his fingers around my waistband.

Lifting up, I maneuver out of my shirt and throw it to the other side of the bed. Slowly, he lowers my leggings, discarding them somewhere on the floor, leaving me in just my bra and panties. Exposed to him.

"You're wet," he purrs, staring between my legs.

My core flexes. "I've wanted this for a long time."

"From me?"

My eyelids flutter closed. It wasn't a coincidence that Aidan's name came out when I told my parents I had a boyfriend. He's the only person I've ever crushed on like that. The forbidden brother's best friend. "Would you be mad if I say yes?"

"Are you kidding? I'd be fucking honored." He waits a beat before saying, "But now I know you might do anything to get it."

I rush in a breath. "Like what?"

"Take off your bra."

I stare at him. This is intimate. This isn't just two people getting off for pleasure. We could do that with clothes on. Or as many clothes as needed on.

He lowers my panties, circling my clit with his thumb. "Please?"

"Aidan," I moan. Everything he does feels amazing.

"Take it off, and I'll give you whatever you want."

I want much more than he's willing to give, but I'll play his game. I unclasp my bra from the front, fanning it open. His gaze zeroes in on my erect nipples.

With his free hand, he reaches out to tweak one. "When I first saw these, I needed them in my mouth."

His thumb hasn't stopped working me, and I can barely concentrate on anything he says. "Aidan, I don't think I'm going to last long. If you're going to do this—"

His hard stare brings me up short. He slips his thumb down, coating the pad of his finger in my juices, and then moves back up again to circle my tight nub. With his other hand, his fingers tease and play with my nipple.

I'm lost in pleasure. "I want your mouth on me, Aidan," I warn again. My orgasm is building. I'm going to miss out. "Please lick me. Please. I'm begging."

"Here?" He leans over, his tongue finding my nipple.

I cry out, my body jumping up to meet his. His

thumb swirls quicker, tightening his movements. My jaw unhinges as my orgasm barrels forward. I give a silent scream as I come, my hips moving against him until I stutter, shivering to a stop.

I smile, in a haze. "You said—"

I'm interrupted by his tongue circling my clit.

"Aidan!"

I'm so sensitive. Too sensitive. He moans into me, and my eyes fly open to watch. I've never seen anything so erotic.

He peers up, flattening his tongue while he pins me with his salacious stare. I take a mental picture. "Oh shit."

He smirks, his lids closing again before returning to his work. I don't have anything to compare it to, but I don't need another experience to know that Aidan is good at this. He takes his time, quickening and slowing his movements when I get too close to the edge.

"You were too turned on," he explains between strokes. "If I'd tasted you then, you'd have come apart in no time. I want this to be an experience." He flicks his tongue over my clit, and for a moment, I forget to listen to him. All I catch is: "Like mine."

I work my fingers through his hair, and he lifts his head before gripping my hips and returning to my clit. He licks the length of me, moaning.

"I taste good?" I ask, breathing heavily.

"Angel, you couldn't taste bad if you tried. I'm going to make you come on my tongue. I'm going to drink your juices like you did mine. And I'm going to savor every fucking second of it."

Aidan gets in a rhythm, a flow that has my hips working into his face of their own accord. Miraculously, I think I'm going to orgasm again. "Oh God."

He watches me, his gaze intent, studying me like a scholar of the game until I think he can fully play me whenever he wants. When I'm hovering over the edge to the point where it's starting to hurt, he works me and works me.

I watch in bewilderment as he works my body like he's fine-tuned it before. Like he made it, honestly. He knows every nuance. Every movement that drives me higher and higher.

"Aidan!"

He hums over my clit, spurring me on. White light blinds me for a split second while I come so hard I scream.

Aidan's relentless. I try to push him away, but he holds me there. Just like he promised, he licks and sucks and drinks me in. My climax keeps coming, my whole body vibrating until he mercifully slows his movements and I fall back onto the bed.

"I think..." I breathe out, not entirely sure I am thinking correctly in my sexual daze, "you did that better than me."

He tweaks my nipple, and I swear my pussy reacts, squeezing again. I moan.

"Did I break you?" he whispers in my ear.

"Is that possible?"

Expecting a snarky response, I wait for it, smiling. Instead, I get, "I think you broke me."

17

AIDAN

"HEY," a soft voice whispers. For a moment, I think it's my mom. My *mom* mom. The one who put me up for adoption at five. I struggle to hold on to the voice, but then my brain does that thing it does, reminding me she gave me up.

It's the push I need to shake out of the feeling.

"Hey."

My eyes open at once, searching out Bails. This wake up is much more welcome. I stretch out in her bed, which has a lot more room than mine. "Hey."

"Sleepy head." She leans over, her lips brushing my ear when she says, "You're so lucky your fake girlfriend wants all the good things for you. She made you breakfast."

I blink, my body locking up. "You made me breakfast?"

"Pretty sure the most important player of a celebrated college team needs a good, healthy breakfast before a game."

She tries to stand, but I close my hand around hers. "Seriously?"

She nods, patting my hand with her free one. Slowly, my grasp releases, and she gets up, picking my clothes up off the floor and draping them over the edge of the bed. She's already dressed in a pair of royal-blue leggings and an oversized shirt falling off her shoulders.

"Figured I'd feed you before you do the walk of shame." She chuckles to herself. "No complaining either. I had to do the same."

Fuck that. There's no walk of shame here. It's the walk of someone who knows what he wants. There was no way I was leaving this room last night. We watched game film on my phone until she fell asleep next to me. She'd listened as I studied the defensive line out loud. She'd even pointed out that the right tackle wiggles his hands when he's going to blitz.

I sit up in bed, looking around her sparsely decorated room. Every time I come in here, there's a little something more, as if she's piecing her life together slowly, making sure it's right. Like she doesn't want to add anything unless she really likes it. Unless it means something to her.

"I think we should talk," I tell her, watching as she tosses some clothes into the hamper in her closet.

Her back straightens. Turning, she looks anywhere

but my face. "After the game, 'kay? Everything can wait until after the game. This is your big moment. Your mom and dad are here. They want to see you at your best."

She forces a smile to her face while looking just past me. "You know, if you don't hurry, Darrin's going to eat everything." She turns to walk away but stops. "And please throw some pants on. I've already been teased relentlessly. If you show up practically naked, he might have a heart attack."

I shake my head as she walks out. Hopping up from the bed, I tug on all of my clothes. Afterward, I make a quick stop in the bathroom and throw some water on my face and through my hair to tame it a little.

Staring at my reflection in the mirror, I realize I've been kidding myself. From the moment Bailey showed up here, I was intrigued. Her fake dating idea. Her to-do list. Everything she wanted called to me. At the same time she was coming out of her shell, she was yanking me out, too. The real me. Not the kid who made all the mistakes before she came.

"Hurry, Aidan!" she yells from the kitchen. "He's got the bacon."

Oh, now that's going too far.

I throw the door open and walk down the hallway to find Bailey slapping her brother's hands away from the good stuff. She urges me with her eyes, and I hustle over to scoop some up. "Whoa, where's the bro code?" I ask.

"Oh, that went away when you started dating my sister."

"Ha-ha." The looks on their faces while they stare at each other—first hard, then smiling—makes me long for that kind of connection. I'd always wanted a sibling when I was younger. "Smells good," I tell her.

"I'm just finishing the eggs. I didn't want to cook them too early."

"Since when do you even cook?" Darrin asks.

At the stove, Bailey shrugs. "I kinda like it. It's like brewing a potion or something."

Darrin and I share a smile, but since he's her brother, he can't let that go. "Well, I hope you didn't screw it up."

"Well, you don't have to eat it."

He mouths to me, *But you do.* I nod, grimacing. Darrin hides a laugh. "Did you Google again?"

"What is your fascination with me Googling? And yes. There are all these food blogs, and they're helpful, but I have to scroll through their whole life story to get to the actual recipe. What does their third-grade teacher have to do with scrambling eggs? It's ridiculous."

Turning from the stove, Bailey holds a frying pan in front of her and walks toward the table. She scoops eggs onto the three plates set there, and I take a seat at the one across from Darrin. On the counter, the toast pops, and Bailey nearly comes out of her skin. "Shit, the toast. I forgot."

She scoops the last of the eggs onto Darrin's plate and then hurries to the counter, mumbling to herself.

"So," Darrin says, "You ready for the game?"

"Hell yeah. I predict," both he and I lick our pointer finger and then act like we're making a tick on a board, "one for the win column."

He laughs. "I'm stoked to watch you play. I went to the store on campus and got a shirt and everything."

Bailey sighs as she butters the toast. "Wish I'd thought of that."

"Oh, I got something for you to wear," I tell her.

"You do?"

"Well, yeah, it's tradition for the girlfriends to wear their boyfriend's jersey."

"Oh," she says softly.

Turning with a plate in her hand, she looks at me and seems surprised that I'm staring back. She pauses for a moment before continuing, placing the plate of toast in the middle of the table.

"What are you guys waiting for?" she asks, sitting in the spot next to me.

I look at her spread. Eggs, toast, bacon, there's even a little dish of jelly next to the toast. Judging by the color, it's strawberry. My favorite.

I reach under the table to squeeze her leg. She

smiles at me, and it nearly takes my breath away. "Thank you."

"Yeah, thanks," Darrin mimics, stuffing eggs into his mouth.

"You're welcome."

Her cheeks turn pink, and a small smile crooks her lips.

"Wow, Bailey," her brother says around a mouthful of food. "These eggs are good. Did you put cheese in them?"

"Yeah," she answers, grabbing a piece of toast. "Several different kinds, actually. The Google told me."

We eat, talking about old times. Well, it's mostly Darrin and I talking about things we did at his house. Bailey is quiet, and it hits me that she never participated in anything we did. Not one thing. The thought is unnerving. She was a bystander in her own house.

I steer the conversation toward the couples games. "Did you see Bailey rip up that obstacle course? I was impressed."

Darrin nods. "I didn't think she had it in her."

"Hey." She shoots her brother a look.

He shrugs. "Just being real. The crowd next to me was yelling 'Baidan, Baidan,' so I guess you guys have a nickname now." He rolls his eyes.

"Baidan, huh?" I ask, stomach flipping. "I like it."

"You know," Darrin offers, glancing between the

two of us. "Don't get me wrong, I've felt a little sick to my stomach here and there about my sister dating my best friend, but all in all, not bad. Three out of five stars."

"Three?" Bailey asks, choking on her orange juice. "That doesn't sound good at all."

"It could be a one."

"Okay, but this breakfast is a five," I state, shoveling more eggs into my mouth.

Bailey reaches over and squeezes my arm. "QB1 needs his energy."

Darrin hisses. "That comment was like a two out of five. I threw up in my mouth a little."

Bails's whole body shakes with laughter, and she has to set the orange juice down before spilling it. "I can't wait for you to get a girlfriend so I can rate everything *you* do."

"No sense in getting a girlfriend." Darrin shrugs. "It wouldn't last long."

He studies the two of us, but I refuse to think about the context. This is their life. They can do what they want with it.

Bailey stares down at her plate, and I squeeze her leg again, my fingers playing absentmindedly over the soft material of her leggings.

My phone pings, and I take it out of my pocket with my free hand to find a text from West.

You good?

Good. Never better.

While my phone is out, I check the time. Three hours before game time. My stomach starts to squeeze with nerves. I hurry and finish my plate, pushing past the pregame nausea. This is a big game. My parents are here. My girl. My best friend. Excitement ramps up as I move to the sink to rinse off my plate.

Bailey comes up behind me. "Anything else I can do?"

"Yeah," I tell her. "Meet me at the fence before the game so I can give you my jersey to wear."

"Yeah?"

I turn to lock eyes with her. "Of course."

She looks like she wants to say something, but she just nods.

I leave a few minutes later, throwing myself into my game time routine. Locker room, warm-ups, Coach's talk. The closer it gets, the more I start to buzz.

There's nothing like the excitement of a game. I live for moments like this. For a game I adore.

Before we head out onto the field, I check my phone one last time and find a text from my mom. It's a picture of her, Dad, Bailey, and Darrin. Their smiling faces settle in my stomach, a sense of completeness ringing through me.

For so long, I thought I was missing something. As an adopted child, I went to therapy. I know all my feelings of being an outsider are valid, but this picture... Something about it just clicks.

It's exhilarating and fucking scary at the same time.

Cade slaps my back a couple times. "My hands are ready, QB."

"So are mine."

He lets out a yell that fills me with fire. That thrill of competition. Nothing beats it. Except... Shit, except maybe the high of seeing Bailey.

I take a step back at that realization. Nothing ever compared to football. Not really. Now, I can see that gap decreasing each day Bailey and I pretend.

Fuck pretending. I'm fooling myself.

I grab my spare jersey out of my locker and follow the rest of my teammates into the tunnel. Nothing compares to a home game. There aren't many in a season, but when they happen, a special snap fills the air. Elation.

We wait in the dark passageway, the crowd screaming for us as the announcer's booming voice introduces "Your Warner Bulldogs!" The eruption of cheers and horns and bells sparks my whole body. On the TV screen in the corner, the cameraman pans over the crowd, and I pick my family out right away. They're on their feet, yelling, jumping up and down.

Bailey too, her face painted with my number.

Her face painted with my number.

I run out with my team, the marching band starting the fight song that couldn't drown out the crowd if it tried. They vie for attention until the crowd yells, "Fight, fight, fight!" with the few short horn blasts at the end.

I tip my helmet up, so my facemask sits on my forehead, then run to the gate in front of where my family's seated. I crook my finger at Bailey. The crimson on her face deepens. *I told you to meet me,* I mouth.

Darrin tries to shove her forward, but her feet stay planted.

Well, we can't have that.

I jump over the gate and run up to the wall, hauling myself up the few feet of concrete until I'm leaning against the metal handrails, staring Bailey down.

"Hi," she squeaks.

I turn her cheek toward me, admiring the number one glittering there. "You look good."

"The cheerleaders insisted."

I'm hyper aware that my mom and dad are staring at me. "I told you to meet me."

She murmurs, "I forgot," but she's clearly lying. I'm not sure she has a deceptive bone in her body.

"I want you to wear this." I offer up my jersey, trying to display my number and my last name as best I can while not falling off the wall. The last time I saw a teammate of mine climb into the stands, it was West going after Kenna.

"Aww," my mom coos, fanning her face.

Bailey looks like she could crawl under a rock and die.

"Aidan? Where's Aidan?" the quarterback coach barks behind me.

"You're going to get me in trouble," I tease.

Bailey takes my jersey, and I grin as she pulls it over her head.

The way my throat dries up seeing my number plastered to her front only solidifies that I'm a goner for this girl. For real. I'm not faking. Or joking. I'm fucking falling for her.

"Now, have you ever wanted to kiss the quarterback who had the best game of his life?"

"You haven't even played yet."

I shrug. "I feel it. In my toes."

Coach must see me because he yells, "For God's sake, Aidan!"

"You better hurry," I tell her, laughing. I'm not getting down until I get what I want.

Thankfully, she doesn't make me wait. She shakes her head, leaning over the wall. Our lips touch, and I swear the crowd's roar defies sound barriers. Just like Darrin said earlier, a chant of *Baidan* rumbles through the spectators.

The kiss is short and perfect, her laughter breaking it up. "I guess we can't deny our fans."

"Hey, I was going to say that."

My coach yells again, and Bailey peers behind me. "He looks mad."

"He'll forgive me when I have the best game of my life."

She tsks. "So full of yourself."

"You know it."

I drop down and turn toward the field, tugging my helmet on.

Game time.

18

BAILEY

I CAN'T STOP SMILING.

Aidan grins at me from the other side of the room, flanked by dozens of people. Everyone wants to talk to him. Everyone wants to congratulate him.

I don't know how he did it, but he really did have the best game he's had all season. He freaking surpassed the record for total passing yards in one game that was previously held by Reid Parker, and Reid Parker went on to play for the NFL.

The reason I know this? Everyone's also coming to talk to me. Maybe it's because I'm still wearing his jersey.

Cade walks up to Kenna and me, shaking his head. "He had a hell of a game."

"You did, too," I point out. "He wouldn't have completed so many passes if you weren't there."

He smiles, his dark hair tousled. "Remind me to tell Aidan how much I like you."

Butterflies erupt in my stomach. For the first time ever it's like I have a built-in friend group. If they're friends with Aidan, they're friends with me. The other day, I dropped my books everywhere, and one of the linemen not only helped me pick them all up but walked me to my next class.

"Seriously," I tell him. "You were great."

He waves at me to keep going. "I could listen to accolades all day. What else you got?"

"That one touchdown?"

"Which one?" he asks, and the rest of us laugh.

Behind him, Aidan meanders toward us, and my tummy does a flip. His stare catches on mine and keeps it, like a magnetic pull. He leans into Cade, still looking at me. "Trying to steal my thunder?"

"Well, as your girlfriend so eloquently pointed out, you wouldn't have completed so many passes if it weren't for me."

Aidan's smile grows wider. "Oh, she said that, did she?"

"I wouldn't lie. I think she also said she wishes she had a guy like me. Better at football. I think those were the exact words she used. Oh, and more handsome. Mature."

Aidan playfully shoves him out of the way. "Now I know you're bullshittin'. My girl only has eyes for me."

The way the butterflies erupt inside is insane. It's like hope and excitement exploding in a glitter bomb. He wraps his arms around me, reminding me of the way he greeted me after the game, then he leans down. "You want to get out of here?"

I hug him back, holding him to me. "You sure? Everyone wants a piece of you right now."

He chuckles, the warmth of it making me sink deeper into his embrace. Aidan gives the best hugs. His long arms surround me like a cocoon. "I'm sure."

I nod into his chest. First, we'd gone out to have a celebratory ice cream with his parents. They barely got to see him because everyone at Scoops had arrived from the game, and it was a madhouse. After that, we came out with the whole team to celebrate at a bar in town. Half the population of college students are in attendance.

Aidan releases me, and then tucks me into his side. "We're out. Check you guys later."

"What?" the group near us cries. "Come on." I distinctly hear Darrin's voice among them, but he's been wrapped up in a girl.

Aidan shrugs. "I've got plans."

I peer up at him, wondering if I'm included in those plans as the crowd parts for him. We meander our way to the front entrance and then out to his Charger. More people call his name, and he waves politely.

"You're a stud tonight," I tease when he gets in on the other side.

"I'm a stud every night, Angel."

"In your own mind."

He grins, backing out of the space. "So, do you want to hear about my plans?"

"If you want to tell me."

"You'll love it."

"Again with the modesty."

He barks out a laugh. "I promise you, you'll love it."

"Are you sure you don't want to celebrate your win some more?" I feel bad that we left his celebratory party. Most of the team was still there.

"I will be celebrating my win. Just with fewer people."

Aidan pulls out onto the main road, and I sit back in the car, watching the moon through the trees. "Your parents were so happy," I tell him. "Your mom especially. She gets so nervous when you're out there. Every time someone tackled you, I thought she was going to have a heart attack."

Aidan chuckles. "She's been like that since peewee."

"How lucky that your parents put you in something that turned out to be the exact right thing. Look at how it's shaped you."

He nods. "I never thought about it like that." The green glow from the dash lights gives him a mysterious look. "But you're right. I guess you could say there are a lot of what-ifs."

"Oh, I think about that a lot," I confess. "Like, what if my parents had let me go to public school my whole life?"

"You wouldn't be who you are right now."

"True," I muse.

I turn my head to peer at him. "What if I had told my brother's best friend that I thought he was cute?"

Aidan reaches over, dropping his hand on my knee and giving it a squeeze. "You mean instead of making him pretend to be your boyfriend?"

I chuckle. "Yeah, that."

When Aidan turns onto campus, I side-eye him. He parks in front of a building I haven't been inside yet. "Where are we?"

"You'll see."

"Is this a good time to tell you I'm not really a surprise person?"

"Nope."

After shutting the car off, he runs around to my side and opens my door. He holds out his hand, and I take it. Walking together, he leads me up the sidewalk before knocking twice on the door. It opens immediately, the smell of chlorine hitting my nose, stinging my eyes a little.

A security guard waves us forward, and we walk into a huge pool area. To the right, there are a bunch of platforms and diving boards. Still, buoy-less water waits below them. The uniformed employee steps into my view and says, "You have three hours."

Aidan shakes his hand. "Thank you. I appreciate it."

The guard nods at him and hands over a football I hadn't realized he'd been carrying. After Aidan signs it, the man smiles and walks away, his footsteps echoing before he leaves out a side door.

Aidan places his arm around my shoulders and walks me toward the side of the pool. When we get closer, the flicker of candlelight dances off the walls and bleachers. There are beach balls of every color bobbing in the water as well as a large, circular floaty half in the water.

"What is this?" I ask.

Aidan holds up a finger and then runs around the other side of the pool. He reaches down, and immediately, a beam of light illuminates a screen on the edge. He grabs something else before jogging back over to me, a shit-eating grin on his face. "You said you wanted to go to the movies."

"We're going to watch a movie? Here?"

"In this," he says, pointing at the large circular raft. Next to that, there are other smaller floats with snacks on them. One has popcorn. Another has candy. Another holds cups.

"This is...adorable," I rasp. I peer up at him, my

heart constricting. "But there's no one here to pretend for, Aidan. If we wanted to keep up appearances, we should've stayed at the bar."

He reaches out to cup my cheeks. "I thought you realized, Angel. I'm not pretending anymore. I'm not sure I ever was."

My lids flutter closed. He strokes my cheek, and I get lost in his touch. I've waited so long to hear those words. "Are you sure?"

"I am. And unless I completely misread the signals, which I don't think I did because I'm excellent at reading defenses, you feel the same."

Popping up on my tiptoes, I press my lips to his. He wraps his arms around me, holding me. There's something special about this kiss, something...understood. It isn't a kiss to show off. It isn't a kiss to pretend. This is a capture of feelings between two people, like a picture that depicts a moment for all eternity.

I pull away, savoring the feel of him. "I can't believe you did this for me."

"I can't believe you caught that lineman's tell. You saved my ass on that one play."

It's hard not to beam under his praise. I don't know if he's only teasing me, but I don't care. "Always happy to help."

He reaches around, squeezing my butt. "Now, get that fine ass in the floaty. We have a movie to watch."

Leaning down, he nudges the raft all the way into

the water and holds it in place. I frown, not sure exactly how I'm going to do this. I keep envisioning me toppling into the water and making a fool out of myself. It seems pretty stable but...

"You're just going to have to trust me."

His gaze fixes on me, and I know he's talking about not falling off the floaty, but there could be so much more context to what he's said, too. Knots form in my stomach. In front of me is the boy I always wanted. What he's offering is a dream come true, but I also have to trust him. Trust this.

I turn, squat down, and then let myself fall backward. Miraculously, I hit the floaty and bounce.

I hope falling into this with Aidan will be just as easy. So far, being with him has been as natural as breathing. Putting a real label on it shouldn't make a difference.

"Keep it near the edge while I put the food in."

The raft starts to drift, so I lean over the side and paddle to stay close to the edge, but I end up going around in circles instead. "Um..."

Aidan peeks over and laughs. "What are you doing?"

"I'm trying," I call out. No matter how hard I try, though, I end up spinning like a dog chasing its tail. "It's more difficult than you think."

He finishes sending the food into the water on their own little floaties and then places his hands on his hips, cocking a brow as I splash and splash, making no real headway. "Aidan!"

He doubles over, laughing.

"I'm glad you think this is funny!" I'm paddling so fast water splashes me and the raft. If I keep going, I'll sink this thing.

"I've never seen someone so bad at floating in a pool."

"Well, if *someone* was thinking ahead, they would've put the snacks in before they shoved the girl onto the floaty and expected her to work miracles."

"Oh, comments from the peanut gallery. Is that how it's going to be?"

"Oh, that's how it's going to be."

"Well then..." He backs up away from the pool and eyes the distance between the edge and the float.

"Don't you dare!" I call out.

He dares.

He runs forward, throwing his hands out like Superman until he lands on the huge float, sliding into the backrest.

I cry out, waiting for him to send both of us into the water, but it doesn't happen. "You're crazy!"

He flips over on his back, spreading his arms out wide. He eyes me shyly. "This was supposed to be romantic."

"It is," I insist, pressing my lips together to stop my giggles.

"Yeah, a romantic comedy, maybe."

He scoots closer, maneuvering so he's seated next to me. He drapes his arm around me like he likes to do, but then he immediately drops his head back.

"What?" I ask.

He points to the side of the pool where blankets and pillows are stacked. I can't help the giggle that spills out. "Watch it, Angel, or I'll have you swimming to go get them."

"We can do this," I tell him, putting on my serious face. "Now that we're both here to paddle."

Since we're all the way on the side of the pool near the screen, it takes us a minute or two, but eventually, we get to the other side. I'm the closest, so I scoop up as much as I can and throw it in the float before we bounce off the edge and start back out to the middle of the pool.

We spread the pillows out behind us, making a comfortable little spot. Aidan reaches out with the remote—at least he remembered that—and presses Play. On the screen, the beginning credits of a movie start.

He holds me to him, and I take a deep breath, wondering how I went from one extreme to the other. From being around people who treated me as a show-piece; from being at a school where people pretended I didn't exist; from always being on the outside... to being perfectly happy nestled next to a guy I used to have a crush on.

I don't think I ever want to leave this place.

Warning bells go off in my head, but I push them away. I can think about the fact that my parents are never letting me stay here another day. Right now, I like being right here. Right where I'm supposed to be.

"Um, Angel?"

"Hmm?"

"I think we're sinking."

"What?" I sit up, and the float starts to depress, sending my feet up in the air.

Aidan laughs. "The float is deflating."

"Probably because you leaped onto it like a ninja."

"You have to admit. That jump was pretty badass."

I turn, scooting onto his lap. "You, sir, have a big head."

"Don't I know it."

He peers down my body and back up, taking me in. "I suppose we should get off this thing."

Shrugging, I cuddle closer. "We can go down together."

"You won't kick me off the door like Rose did to Jack?"

"Never."

"Fake dating you might have been the best thing I ever did."

"You're welcome."

He tickles my sides until I stare up at his rueful smile. His hips lift out of the water briefly, but it's enough for me to feel his hard length, and my body immediately responds.

"I feel like I want to tell people how happy I am."

"Except we were already happy."

The look he gives me tells me everything. He kisses me, taking his time, delving his tongue into my mouth, showing me his true feelings. He brings me so high, it feels like a dream.

Until water starts to fill the float.

"We're going down," he says, lips moving over mine with his words.

"I don't want it to end."

"It won't."

Like the gentleman he is, he rolls off the raft. Taking his weight out of the equation helps buoy me. He stands, towing me to the side. With a grunt, he pulls himself out of the pool and then helps me onto the edge, water shedding off him until there's a puddle at his feet.

"What a mess," he says.

"I guess you're not good at everything. Noted."

"Keep talking, Angel, and I've got something else to occupy that mouth."

I wrap my hands around his waist, not caring about how drenched he is. "Why don't you take me home?"

"I thought you'd never ask."

19

AIDAN

NERVES SETTLE around me like tiny pinpricks nipping at my skin. Bailey walks down the hallway, and I'm right behind her like a lost puppy. Luckily, Darrin is with the girl he's been hanging out with, and he'd already texted Bailey that he wouldn't be coming home tonight.

...Because he definitely needs to not come home tonight.

She enters her room and looks over her shoulder. It's almost like she's making sure I'm still there, and I can't believe I ever turned her down. I can't believe I was kidding myself that what we had was anything other than real. From our first kiss, I felt it. The connection was undeniable.

Those thoughts jumble in my head, making my hands shake. The weight of every game is on my shoulders, and I feel that now, too. The need to perform.

The need to make everything perfect. Bailey's first time. It should be special.

I'd wanted to woo her with the movie and the candles and the floats. It took us a long time to break everything down and put it in my car, and even though we worked quickly, we worked quietly. As if our thoughts were consumed with the same thing. For me, I still feel the lingering tension from when she sat on my lap and kissed me. It's a tightness in my chest that I'm not sure I want to ever go away.

"So, what do you want to do?" she asks, closing the door behind us. "I have some movies. A deck of cards."

I stare at her. She keeps her face a mask of innocence until she bursts out laughing. "The look on your face."

I mimic her, but it's all for show. I'm too consumed with her to tease.

"I was joking," she says, edging nearer. She blinks, her eyes slow to open. When they capture mine, it's as if my own never want to leave. "Aidan?"

"Yes?"

"I want you to be my first. In case it wasn't clear." She studies my lips, then moves up again. "But I want to know if this jersey is a symbol for something real. If what you said back at the pool is true. Is this really what you want?"

"You're my angel."

She sucks in a breath, her lashes fanning over pink-tinted cheeks. It takes several moments for her to respond. "I'm nervous."

"Should we go back to the river? You didn't seem nervous there."

"I was pumped full of hormones then."

A smirk pulls my lips apart. "I'm pretty sure I can pump you up with some more hormones."

"I don't know," she teases, gaze twinkling. "Now that I know you're fallible, maybe this wasn't a good idea."

I shake my head. "Now you really shouldn't have said that."

"I thought you liked a challenge?"

"You're my favorite challenge yet."

She walks her fingers up my chest. "Trying to act like I wasn't affecting you? Like you weren't falling for me every moment of every day?"

I clasp her hands over my heart. "That wasn't a challenge. That was stupid."

She wiggles out of my grip then reaches down to grab the hem of my wet shirt. "At least you're pretty," she says, eyeing my muscles once she drops the shirt on the floor.

"I've got nothing on you," I growl, backing her toward the bed. Her nipples press against her shirt, and I need them in my mouth. I need my body on hers. There's this voice in my head that says to take it slow, but we've been working up to this since she showed up

232

in my room that night. Since that first time she kissed me.

I fall onto her, her legs spreading wide. I maneuver my knee between her thighs and lean over, teasing her breast through her shirt. I nip at her, and she sighs. The memory of her fake fucking me at the party surrounds me. I started to see then. My eyes have opened wider and wider since. She's the person I laugh with. The person I'm the most real with. What we thought we were faking turned into an inevitability.

"Hey," she rasps, grabbing my cheeks. "You okay?"

"Just wondering how I didn't see you for so long."

"You know, I've wondered that myself. I should have left you sinking on that floaty."

"You wouldn't. You like my dick too much."

"I like *you* too much," she whispers, immediately peering away, cheeks turning red.

I kiss her collarbone, my lips traveling up her neck in feather light touches. She shifts against me, just tentative hip movements at first, her core sliding over my thigh.

I move my hand down, pressing the pad of my thumb into her clit. She throws her head back, working up into me. "I'm so glad you like leggings," I growl. I can feel everything: her hard nub, her soft flesh, the way she's soaking through her panties. "But I need to see you."

Reaching to her waistband, I tug her leggings

down, revealing her stomach, then her hips, then her upper thighs, my jersey lifting up to her belly button. I can't help but sit back when I discard her bottoms, pushing her knees to the bed, exposing her. If this isn't the sweetest picture. The perfect girl wearing my number in one of the sexiest positions.

"You're not going to make me wear this the whole time, are you?"

"No, because I want to see these." I trail my hand up under the jersey covering her soft skin and then squeeze her breast right over her flimsy, lace bra. She moans, spurring me on. Pulling the cup down, I tweak her nipple, and she thrusts her chest into my eager fingers.

"Can I see you?" she ekes out.

I stand, unzipping my pants and then pushing them down past my knees. I step out of my shoes and clothes, all while she stares at my cock. A shiver runs through me. "Say it again," I whisper.

"Say what?"

"That you want me to be your first."

She smiles. "Aidan. Stud. QB1. Terrible floaty expert... I want you to be my first."

My breath hitches watching the different emotions play over her face. From humor to sincerity. The playfulness we both share. I've never wanted anyone more.

"You want me here?" I ask, moving my hand up her

thigh until I hit my target. I swirl her nub as she nods. "Sit up."

She does so, and I help take my jersey off her before tossing it onto a chair and then unclasping her bra. My stomach knots in anticipation. She slides up the bed, lying back onto the pillows and then pats the spot next to her.

I take my place, facing her, my heart beating like mad. She reaches for me, her fingers tracing my cheeks before kissing me. Her lips soft and eager, I revel in the way she tastes; in the way she takes her time, savoring every last moment of our connection. I work my hand between her thighs, dipping in her juices before finding her entrance, pushing inside her with a gentle thrust.

She moans, her eyes widening until the noise ceases, dying on her lips with an intake of breath. Her hips move against me, taking more and more of my finger deeper inside. "You're going to be on top," I tell her.

"What?" she asks, panicked. "Is that the best idea?"

"I can't think of anything better than you dictating everything."

She licks her lips. "But I want you to enjoy it."

"I don't know what else you think I could be doing."

"Aidan, don't tease me right now," she groans, my

finger still moving inside her. "I want to be good for you."

"You will be, Angel. You're going to be the best."

She reaches out, fisting the base of my cock, running her grip along my length, trying to match my pace. I kiss her neck, tracing up her jaw. Short sighs fall from her lips.

I'm so hard I could bust right now.

The next time I retreat my fingers, I switch to two and then push inside. She's so damn tight. Fuck. I scissor, and she squeezes my cock in response. I play with her until she's writhing, each sound from her lips like a prayer.

Without hesitation, I pick her up, settling her over my hips until she's straddling me. She stares down with wide eyes. "I don't know if I can."

"You can," I promise her, reaching into her nightstand for a condom.

Her mouth drops. "What? Where did that come from?"

"I have ways," I say, shrugging.

She bites her lip. "Oh, you're a lying liar. How long have you had condoms in there, Mr. Fake Boyfriend?"

"I'm not telling."

I tear the condom open and show her how to roll it down my length. She guides it to my base and then waits, her perfect breasts calling me. I reach behind her thighs, yanking her forward until I'm lined up. "Sit on me."

She shifts up, but at the last second, I have another idea.

"Wait one second, Angel." I scoot down while holding her in place, then I grab the back of her thighs until she's straddling my face and not my cock. She falls forward, her hands hitting the wall when she cries out. "Aidan!"

"I need to taste you first." I lick up her length. I could make an excuse about needing her wet, but she already is. She's soaked. This is purely selfish. I just want to make her come on my tongue.

Grabbing a handful of her ass, I yank her down, her knees spreading wide while I flick and taste her. "Oh my God," she moans. Once I hear her, I can't stop. I drive my tongue into her pussy, then circle her clit. She keeps lifting off me, telling me it's too much, but I yank her back down every time, sucking.

"Aidan!"

"Mmm, give it to me," I murmur against her nub. I want her juices to spill over my lips. I want her pleasure. All of it.

Her hips start to move, riding my face. My dick is so fucking hard, it's straining against the rubber.

"I'm going to— Aidan!"

I keep going until a tremor rocks her body, her orgasm hitting hard and fast, and then I move her down, holding my cock near her entrance. I don't even have to tell her what to do. She lowers herself, taking just my tip as she rides out her orgasm. She rocks again and again, squeezing me.

"You sneak," she says breathlessly when she comes down, and I swear to fucking god, watching this woman ride me is the most erotic thing I've ever seen.

My mouth goes dry. "We're going to go slow now. You haven't taken all of me yet."

She nods, bracing her hands on my abs as I urge her hips forward. Little by little, she takes more of me. Watching her explore, her fingers sinking into my chest, gives me chills. "That's a good girl. Does it hurt?"

"It's a mix. Pleasure and pain and..." She finally presses down, sinking over me to the hilt, and I groan, holding her hips in place so she can get used to me. "There you are."

"Fuck, baby."

Her brows rise. "Does it hurt?"

"Only because I want you so damn bad."

She lifts up again and lowers. I tip my hips, and her mouth unhinges. "I like that."

She drops forward, her hands hitting the bed. We move against each other, finding our rhythm in a mix of pants and frantic heartbeats.

My cock swells, loving it inside her. I lift up quickly, coaxing her into a faster rhythm. She moans. "Oh...oh my—" She dissolves into a groan.

"Uh-huh," I tell her.

Leaning up, I lock my lips around her nipple, flicking her with my tongue. She moves faster, calling out my name. I touch her everywhere, sliding my hands over her ass and then squeezing her breast, tweaking her nipple.

"This feels amazing," she mewls.

"It doesn't hurt still?"

She shakes her head, using her hips to slide down me.

"That's good because you're killing me."

She stops. "I am?"

I smile. "It's the perfect torture, Angel. Don't you worry."

Leaning forward, she kisses a trail up my chest, over my neck to my jaw. Eventually, she presses her lips to mine, kissing me lazily at first, then with more passion. Her movements get jerkier. I thrust up, grabbing her ass to bring her down.

Feeling her body work over me and knowing this is her first experience, I can't get past it. I want more. I want it all. I want this first thing in the morning and before I go to bed every night. I want this as my prize for winning a game.

The more I think about our future, the more I lift up into her. "Aidan, yes."

I hold her in place and thrust up into her. She

writhes against me, both of us frantically trying to finish.

I know the moment Bailey realizes she's going to come. I watch as her movements even out, taking me in long and deep. When it hits, she cries out my name, and I jerk inside her, following after her with a long groan. Her eyes round. We keep moving together, moaning in tune with the other.

Breathless, she stares down at me. Beads of perspiration gather between her breasts, and I lift up to lick them off.

"You came, too, didn't you?"

"Why would you think I wouldn't?"

"Because I don't know what I'm doing."

I cup her cheek. "Angel, you definitely know what you're doing because it's me. We're in sync and so are our bodies."

She drops her head to my chest, and I hold her until our breaths even out. Until the moment is over, but not gone. It'll never be gone.

It sounds so damn cheesy, but I'm going to treasure this. That someone trusted me enough to take care of them in such a vulnerable moment, I have to be doing something right.

"Next time we do this, I want you on top."

I chuckle. "That's what you're thinking about?" Here I am waxing poetic, and she just wants more of my dick.

Nodding, she says, "I want to see your moves."

I roll her over, and she squeals while I kiss her collarbone. Shifting up, I hold the top of the condom while I pull out.

Traces of blood redden the rubber. "Are you sure you're not hurt?"

"Nope. Not at all."

I frown. "We might have to take it easy. You bled a little."

"Really?" She peers down her body, shrugging.

I walk to the bathroom to throw away the condom, but I also grab a washcloth and wet it down.

She's sitting on the edge of the bed, but I ease her back down. "Hold on. Spread those legs, Angel."

She smiles, leaning onto her elbows. I wipe her up, making sure the traces of blood are all gone. "Let me know if you need pain reliever or anything."

It hits me then that I've never taken care of my partner like this before. This is a first.

"You really are a gentleman, aren't you?"

Only for her. "I try."

"Well, you're doing a damn good job."

Bailey reaches for her clothes, but I refuse to let her get dressed. Instead, I pull her onto the bed with me, and we spend the rest of the night watching a movie.

It's the best end to a great game day.

20

BAILEY

I WAKE to soft kisses across my shoulders, the featherlight touches giving me goose bumps. A moan of content escapes my lips that surprises me.

Turning, I find Aidan kneeling on the bed next to me. His eyes roam over my body in a slow perusal.

"What time is it?" I ask.

"Not too late."

I stretch, feeling the ache in my limbs and between my legs. It's a good kind of sore. "You turn into a furnace in the middle of the night," I chastise.

"Me? You're one to talk."

"Sounds like we're just fire together."

He smiles, working his hands through my hair before cupping my cheek. "Are you sore?"

I don't know how to answer because I don't want him to blame himself. "Maybe. Not too bad."

"Maybe?"

"Okay, a little." He starts to frown, so I say, "It must be that monster dick of yours."

My joke does exactly what I want it to. He laughs. "You're good for my ego." He leans over, placing a soft kiss on my lips. "I drew you a bath."

"A bath? Why?"

"I thought it might help."

"Aidan..." I can't help but laugh. "Girls everywhere lose their virginity every day. It's not a big deal."

"I don't care about girls everywhere. I care about you."

My heart nearly melts. I could get used to him saying these kinds of things to me. I reach out my hands, wiggling my fingers. "Then take me to my bath."

He helps me to my feet, and I start for the door, but he holds back on my hand. "Darrin's here, so you should probably throw some clothes on."

A sliver of embarrassment races through me. That wouldn't have been good. Darrin's been cool about us so far, but I'm sure me walking out into the main house naked would send him over the edge. "Good call." I throw on a Warner Bulldog shirt I find on the bed that's Aidan's. The crumpled leggings on the floor will also do as I make my way to the bathroom.

Really, the pain isn't all that bad. I have a sneaking suspicion he went easy on me.

To my surprise, he follows me into the bathroom

243

and sits on the counter to watch me undress. Warmth flares all over. "You want to join me?" I ask, stepping into the tub. The bubbles tease my skin in a nice caress.

He groans. "Evil woman. I would love to, but Darrin's literally out in the kitchen."

The warm water coats my body as I sit, sloshing up over my breasts to my neck.

"Does it feel better?" he asks, hopeful.

I nod. This is the sweetest thing ever. "So," I start, wiping my arms down with the vanilla-scented bubbles. "When can we do that again?"

Aidan smirks, looking away. "You really are trying to kill me."

"Guilty," I tease.

In the other room, my phone starts to ring. Aidan hops off the counter. "I'll get it."

"Don't bother," I try to tell him, but he's already out the door, leaving it open a crack.

The ringer cuts out right before I hear him say, "Bailey's phone. She can't talk right now." I chuckle, shaking my head. This guy... "Sure. Of course, Mrs. Covington."

Oh shit. I suck in a breath, scrambling out of the tub.

Heavy footsteps run down the hall, and I'm just stepping out when Aidan comes in, his face white. *I'm so sorry*, he mouths.

I try to act nonchalant, but I reach for the phone with shaking hands before holding it up to my ear. "Hey, Mom."

She doesn't say anything for a few seconds. "Was that Aidan?"

"Yes, Mom."

She doesn't have to voice her disapproval. It's written in the long pause and all over her tone when she says, "Isn't it a bit early to have visitors?"

I try to slow my beating heart, racking my brain for an excuse. I can't tell her I lost my virginity to my fake boyfriend—Actually, scratch that. Aidan and I are much more than that, but regardless, I'm not going to tell her I lost my virginity at all. She'd probably run to pick me up at this very moment. "He and Darrin went for a run this morning. I'm about to make them breakfast. That's why I couldn't come to the phone."

"You're going to make breakfast?" she asks coldly.

"Yeah, I enjoy it. Who knew?"

"Hmm."

"What's up, Mom?" I ask. She hasn't called me the whole time I've been at Warner's and suddenly, here she is.

"What's up?" She dissects the words like she doesn't understand them. "I'm checking in. Your dad and I saw you and Darrin on TV last night. What an interesting choice of attire."

I peer up at Aidan and roll my eyes. Inside, however, my stomach is churning. My mom has a way of making me feel small in as few words as possible. "It was a football game. We were dressed for the occasion."

Aidan tilts his head like he really wants to know what we're saying, but I turn away. I can't talk to my mom while he's staring at me like that.

"I see," she says. "Was that marker on your face?"

"Paint."

"Hmm."

I want to lash out. I want to ask her what the big freaking deal is. Most everyone at the game looked just like me—but of course, she saw that. She saw that and she didn't like it.

"Did you watch the whole thing? Aidan had a great game."

"No, your father and I had better things to do."

My fingers on the phone squeeze harder as I sit silently. I need to ask Darrin if he got the third degree about the game, too. Probably not. "Well, if that's all," I finally prompt.

"Actually, no. I was calling because there's a soirée you're requested to attend later today."

I put my finger over the speaker and turn toward Aidan. "What time is the Step-Up thing today?"

"One."

While he's answering, my mother says, "What's that, Bailey? You were muffled."

"Mom, I've got plans at one today."

"That's when the luncheon is."

I take a deep breath. "You'll have to make my apologies."

"Bailey Covington. We did not raise you to cancel plans at the last minute."

"Exactly, and the only plan I made is the one for the Step-Up Foundation. It's for a good cause. A charity. Aidan and I are helping raise money for this organization that his coach's wife is involved in." I don't tell her anything about the competition. She wouldn't understand. She would especially hate something like Aidan and me wearing matching T-shirts.

"That sounds nice, but I RSVP'd us for this luncheon months ago, Bailey."

"I don't know what to tell you."

A firm hand settles on my shoulder. I peek up, and Aidan is mouthing to me that I can go to the luncheon, but I shake my head. There's no way.

"Maybe Darrin can go with you. Or Dad."

There's silence on the other end of the line for quite some time. It takes everything I have not to fill it with an apology or inform her to forget everything I just said and that I'll go, but Aidan is counting on me.

"I'm not happy about this," Mom finally states. "About any of this."

The phone clicks off.

My mother just hung up on me.

Aidan's still staring cautiously, so I say, "Yes, okay. Talk to you later," before pretending to hang up the phone.

"Is she mad?" he asks.

I place my phone down on the counter, and he weaves his arms around me. Lifting up on my toes, I give him a short kiss on the lips. "A little."

From outside the bathroom, Darrin calls out, "Hey, why's Mom texting me to ask if Aidan and I went running this morning?"

Aidan's eyes widen, then he disentangles himself from me and runs out the door.

He explains to Darrin what happened, and my brother gasps. "Dude, you answered the call when it was my mom?"

"I didn't even look to see who it was."

Darrin tsks. "Rookie move."

I get back in the water, letting the warmth take me away again. Eventually, Darrin's and Aidan's voices disappear, and then it's just me with my own thoughts.

It's been a blissful couple of weeks without my mother. It's a horrible thought, but I can really be myself here. Who cares that I wore face paint with my boyfriend's number on my cheek? Who cares that I was wearing leggings out in public?

I imagine she had a heart attack about that one.

Being with Aidan is amazing. At Warner, in our own little bubble where I'm in his world, and he's not in mine.

In mine, it certainly isn't proper to answer your girlfriend's phone at an hour when she should probably still be in bed. Mom didn't believe the lie at all, which is why she asked Darrin.

Good thing Darrin will lie for us.

But I can't lie to her our whole lives.

I sink into the water until it covers my face. I wipe my hands down my cheeks, scrubbing before pushing myself out of the water again.

Dammit. I was on such a high this morning, but now I'm in this funk, knowing my mom not only won't approve of Aidan, but she's certainly not going to let me stay at Warner much longer if he keeps answering my phone like that.

A knock comes on the door. "It's me."

"Come in."

Aidan enters, shutting the door behind him. He grimaces. "Sorry, I wasn't thinking."

I shrug.

"Darrin told her we were out running this morning. She also asked him what you're making for breakfast, and he said pancakes. I'm pretty sure he's going to cash in on those pancakes since he's lying for us."

I roll my eyes. That sounds like him. "Tell him to get the ingredients ordered."

"He already did. And he paid extra for immediate delivery."

Aidan's quiet for a little while, and I'm too in my own head to make conversation. "So, does your mom not like me? I always thought she did."

Well, that's a loaded question. I don't even know the real answer myself. "She's just being overprotective."

The truth is, I'm not sure. I always thought she did too, but when his name came out as the person I was dating, I saw the hesitation there. The tiny bit of disapproval.

Any other family would be ecstatic to have their daughter dating a quarterback from a championship team, but I saw the look my parents shared.

I haven't quite figured it out myself. At the time, I didn't really need to. Aidan was only a fake boyfriend. An excuse for me to have a few months of freedom.

But now, I'm going to have to pull on that thread.

I peer up at him with a smile. "Can I ask a question?"

"Shoot."

"Are we real? Boyfriend and girlfriend? We can stop saying fake, right?"

A grin teases Aidan's lips. He jumps off the counter and slips his socks and shoes off. His sweats are next until he gets into the tub with me. "I'm going to pretend that wasn't a real question, Angel. Do you think I almost drown on a floatie with just anyone?"

Then he kisses me, making me forget about everything that happened...

Almost.

21

AIDAN

THE LITTLE TERRORIST they dared to call Sweetie Pie shakes in my hands, spraying me with water. The dark-haired terrier glares up at me with a snaggletooth.

To my right, Bailey laughs. "You and that dog."

"It hates me," I whisper. At the same time, I smile at the family who brought him in as they take my picture with their pet.

Operation Dog Day for the Step-Up Foundation is in full effect. Families from around the county are bringing in their pets to get shots, vet checkups, groomed, and bathed. Since the only thing that the football players and their significant others are able to do is give the dogs a bath, that's where Bails and I are.

The little fiend growls low in his throat, and I stare down at it. "You're a cute little thing, aren't you?" I say with a forced smile.

This dog and I are enemies. I don't know why. I don't know how. But it is what it is.

And I love dogs. Just not this hairy thing with eyes like the devil.

"I'd offer to switch, but Peanut and I are in love," Bailey coos. She hugs the golden retriever she's bathing, and the dog eats it up, its tongue lolling out of its mouth like it wouldn't want to be anywhere else.

I know the feeling.

When she pulls away, the front of her light-blue shirt is wet. It reads: *At Step-Up, We Paws For Puppies*.

Seeing Bailey's smile again is heartwarming. She was quiet all morning after that phone call. I half expected her mother to show up to take her to the lunch date, anyway. Luckily, she didn't. But Bailey didn't really get excited again until she saw what we would be doing today.

She lifts Peanut's paw, shaking it at me. "Say bye, Aidan. This sweetheart is all fluffed." Her voice takes on that cute dog-talking tone.

The dog in my hands barks, and it's so piercing I think it scared away a few of my brain cells.

On the other side of me, West laughs. "Hurry up and get it over with, man."

At the same time, Cade walks by with his phone, videoing all of us, and I plaster another smile on my face. I'm not fooling him, though. "Bigger, QB1." Then his voice drops to a whisper. "You look like a dog beater."

I will fucking kill you, I mouth.

He shuts off the recording. "Well, that's going on my Snapchat."

I glare at him until he slowly walks away. Bailey moves up beside me after giving Peanut back to her owners, bumping me out of the way with her hip. "Can I rinse this little sweetie?"

I'm about to shield her from his ire when the dog literally runs its head all up in her palm, sighing and rolling over for her.

"Look at you," she exclaims, taking my spot.

"How did you do that?" The dog literally glares at me, sending me a warning growl again before Bailey turns on the special handheld sprayer. Sweetie Pie elongates his neck, letting Bailey rinse the shampoo off him.

"He seems sweet," she says, rubbing him under the chin. I honestly have no idea how she does it.

"You just sweep your way into every man's life, don't you?"

"Only the cute ones."

I pinch her butt, and she presses her lips together.

The family waiting on Sweetie Pie asks if they can get a picture with all three of us. Bailey lifts the dog out of the bin, and I stand behind her shoulder while they take the picture.

"That is the cutest thing," the wife says, staring at the picture on her phone.

The little kid with them lifts up a notebook and pen. *Well, this I can handle.* I wipe my wet hands on my shirt and walk toward them. "What's your name?"

"Ronnie."

"Hi, Ronnie. Do you want me to sign that for you?"

"Yes, please."

I take the notebook and pen from him, and he jumps up and down. I scribble my name, smiling. There was a time when I literally practiced signing my name. It was Reid who told me I better come up with something short and sweet. Something that still looked like my name but wouldn't take me forever to write down when there was a line of people waiting.

The guy knew what he was talking about.

"Do you play?" I ask when I hand him back his stuff.

He stares down at my signature. "Mm-hmm. I want to be quarterback for Warner, just like you."

Kneeling on the hard pavement, I reach out my hand, and he puts his palm in mine, wide-eyed. "Well, Future Quarterback for Warner, we have to stick together."

"We do," he says in awe.

"Future quarterback?" Bailey questions excitedly from beside me. She has Sweetie Pie wrapped up in a Warner University towel they're giving out for free with every donation to the Step-Up Foundation. "That's impressive."

The family thanks us for bathing their dog. They put his collar and leash on him, and he walks away, his little legs moving at rapid speed.

"So, no terriers?" Bailey muses.

"Huh?"

"When you graduate and have your own dog and your own house, I'm guessing you're not going to get a terrier?"

"Hell no. Did you see the way that thing looked at me?"

She laughs. "He liked me."

"Well, that's not fair. Everyone likes you."

"It's a curse," she says with a shrug, then walks toward the intake lady to grab the next dog in line.

I make my way back to the basins they set out for everyone and start washing them out when a deep voice states, "You better watch out."

I peer up at West. "What do you mean?"

He glances around and lowers his voice. "I told you fake dating her was a bad idea. You like her."

A dopey smile fills my face. I really do like her. Turning over my shoulder, I spot her talking to the head of the ASPCA for Warner County. Her hair is out of place, flyaways framing her pink cheeks. Her shirt is soaked through in some places, but she's so beautiful.

Turning back to West, I shrug. "We're not faking it anymore. We're the real thing."

He nods, staring at me. His silence irks me. "What?"

"I thought you said you were going to lie low for a bit?"

I return my attention back to the basin, spraying it down with the shower-like head while I figure out what I'm going to say. I never expected a reaction like this. Not from West. He's my friend. Can't he see that I'm better with her?

"Were you there for the game I had yesterday?"

He holds up his hands. The boxer he's sudsing up turns his head to look at him and then licks his hands. "Hey, it's not like that. I like Bailey. I think she's good for you. I'm only repeating what you said to me. But if you think this is best, then that's great, Aidan. Really. I'm happy for you."

My stomach churns. I can't think of one thing that Bailey hasn't made better since she showed up outside my dorm. If anything, she's made sure I stick to my rules about getting to practice on time and being the best I can be for the games.

Of course, there's only been one game.

But it was the best game I've ever had.

"You think this is a bad idea?"

"No," West says, but it sounds too forced.

He does. He must, or else he wouldn't have said it.

I stare at Bailey, who's moving toward me with the prettiest copper goldendoodle. "This is Luna," she says.

Luna must know what she's doing because she walks up the steps and sits right in the basin. Leaning over, she licks my face. "Pretty girl," I tell her, petting her behind the ears. "Do you want to get a bath?"

Her ears quirk up.

Bailey pats her on the head. "There's another terrier over there, so I bit the bullet for you, QB1. Didn't want you to be intimidated. Or lose an arm to the ferocious beast." She grins at me and walks off.

"Ha-ha," I call out after her.

I start rinsing Luna down while I think about what West said. It's early for Bailey and me, but I'm different around her. I'm not the guy I was when I was partying it up and forgetting about all of my dreams.

Girls are a distraction, though.

"How do you do it with Kenna?" I ask West. I peer around him to see her giving a huge Great Dane kisses.

West shrugging makes me look back at him. "It's just easy. I guess that's how you know. She doesn't take away from football, she adds to it." He takes a deep breath, grabbing the sprayer to start hosing his dog down. "I'm not saying it's always easy. Football takes up a lot of time. So does school. So does life. I guess just make sure you find someone to do all those things with."

"Bailey likes football," I tell him. Kenna goes to

West's games, but she never liked football until him. In fact, she hated it.

"Well, is she staying at Warner? Didn't you say this was temporary?"

"Yeah, she's staying," I state immediately, but my hands freeze. Luna takes the opportunity to lick them.

"You sure?" West asks.

Shit. I glance over at Bailey, who's snuggling up to a black and white terrier. She has to stay... I'm sure she wants to. She's so much freer here. Plus, I'm here. There's no mistaking the chemistry between us. It's something we both want to pursue.

My chest constricts, that feeling of being separated stretching its dark, shadowy tendrils toward me. I close my eyes, breathing in deep.

I wish there was a way I didn't have to feel like this again. Like an outsider.

Bailey could easily not stay at Warner. Then what? A long-distance relationship? What happens when that doesn't work? A month from now. Three years from now. I have a lot of years left here. At least two and a half. Possibly a third season if my draft chances don't look good.

Luna places her head on my shoulder, and I instantly relax. She leans her weight into me, and I reach up to stroke down her spine. My parents had talked about getting me an emotional support dog when I was a kid, but then it turned out that Mom was allergic, so we couldn't.

This is ridiculous, I chastise myself. I'm not going to go down this line of thinking anymore. When Bailey and I are alone, I'll ask her.

I'm sure she'll say she's staying, and I'm freaking out over nothing. It's what I do. It's called abandonment issues. Had them since I was five.

That doesn't make them any easier to deal with, though.

"You good?" Bailey asks.

I hug Luna in front of me. "Just hanging out with my new girlfriend."

"Oh, I see how it is."

I pull away, and I swear the dog smiles at me. Mouth open, panting, this dog and I are on the same wavelength. "She's not going anywhere, is she, pretty girl?"

As if she can understand what I'm saying, she licks my cheek.

That's what I thought. I'm right. West is wrong.

Bailey isn't going anywhere, and I'm certainly a better person while she's here. She won't impact football negatively like I let myself slide into in the past.

I have my head on straight now, and it's staying that way.

"Hey," I say to Bailey, nodding at her.

"Yeah?"

"Is that a wet dog in front of you or are you just happy to see me?"

She shakes her head, chuckling. "I'm not sure that makes any sense. Good thing you're handsome."

"Here, here," Cade says, videoing us again. This time, Luna and I pose for his camera, and he walks on by, giving us all a thumbs up.

22

BAILEY

"THAT WAS A SUCCESS!" Coach's wife exclaims, beaming. The head of the ASPCA is with her, peering down at a clipboard, but she also wears a smile.

All the players and their significant others stand around them. The sun is going down, and the chill in the air makes all the wet spots on my shirt feel even colder.

"That was fun," one of Aidan's teammates comments. "We should do that again."

"We had such a great turnout." Mrs. Thompson is beside herself with happiness. "We raised over $5,000 for Step-Up today!"

My eyes nearly bug out of my head. I was not expecting that. I bathed a lot of dogs, but I can't imagine helping that many people. Wow.

"The donations we received were incredible," the

ASPCA lady announces, eyes brimming with tears. "Simply incredible. I want to thank you all."

Aidan leans over, bumping his shoulders with mine. "It's because we had an incredible game yesterday."

I want to laugh at him for how full of himself he is, but in this case, I think he's right. Everyone came to congratulate the team on how well they did. One family even paid for their dog to see every single player. It was all on a pay-what-you-can basis, and I'd be willing to bet, there were some families who paid a lot more than what a bath is actually worth. That's not to mention the shots and vet services.

We did a good thing today. Plus, I finally felt like I fit in. People didn't look at me just because I'm Aidan's girlfriend or for who my parents are or how much money I have. They genuinely like *me*.

"As you know, we asked everyone dropping by who they were here to see," Coach's wife states.

With the amount of fun I had today, I forgot that this was part of the competition. The families weren't assigned a dog bather randomly. They chose the player and girlfriend team to wash their pets. Whoever bathed the most dogs came out on top in this competition.

Next to his wife, Aidan's coach perks up. His stare skims down the line of us. He seems like a no-nonsense type of guy, but he's also super nice. He even talked to me earlier, asking me how I'm liking Warner and what my major is. Under his scrutiny, I give him a smile, and he returns it before continuing down the line.

The lady from the ASPCA hands a piece of paper to Coach's wife. It shouldn't matter what's on it, but like Aidan, I like to win. Plus, there's also the added benefit of a scholarship. A part of me has started to believe that maybe I could stay here even if my parents want me to leave.

And trust me, they want me to leave. A scholarship could help sway them.

Who am I kidding? There is no swaying them, but a scholarship could help sway myself and all the doubts I have about making my own life.

Coach's wife smiles down at the paper. "West Brooks and Kenna Knowles!"

Next to me, Aidan turns to his friend and shakes his hand, whispering something into West's ear that makes him laugh. Afterward, Aidan turns to me and places his arm around my shoulders. "We'll get them next time."

One of the linemen yells out, "I want a recount."

Cade laughs. "No one cared about seeing you. Pipe down."

The whole team jeers.

Aidan squeezes me. "Let's get out of here."

Warmth fills my stomach. We've had a bumpy twenty-four hours. The highest of highs, and a *low* low, but I can't think of anything better to top it all off than one thing.

"I was thinking," I start as he takes out his car keys.

"Yeah?"

"Well," I draw out the word, smiling at him. "Since our ruined date yesterday turned to sexy times, I was wondering what you would think a great date would turn into?"

"As in?"

I shrug. "Skinny dipping?"

The truth is, I want a redo of our cliff-jumping moment. I want to bleed that other image out of my mind with a new, sexier one now that we're on the same page.

He holds the door open for me. "You found a kink, didn't you?"

I mock gasp. "Me? It's only my first day of not being an innocent. Ravaged by the quarterback. Stolen my—"

He kisses me to shut me up. "Ravaged by the quarterback. Sounds like a romance novel."

"Sounds like a new T-shirt," I respond, smiling. "I'll wear it under your jersey to every game."

"Oh, your parents would love that."

I grimace. I've tried not to think about my mother all day, grasping on tightly to the moments with Aidan. It's been in the back of my mind, though, like a burrowing animal. My mom doesn't let things go. I fully expect to get more and more phone calls from her.

Let's hope I can hold her off.

Aidan helps me into the car and then does some sort of fancy footwork around the front, something I've seen the team do during practice. "Limbering up," he informs me as he opens up his door.

He starts the car, places his hand on my knee, and then exits the parking lot. In five minutes, we're parked at a different spot near the river. This one is farther out into the woods. Off my side of the car is a trail through some brush and trees where I can see the bank of the river beyond.

"It's a little chilly," Aidan notes.

"You'll keep me warm," I tell him as I unbuckle my seatbelt and make a break for it.

"Hey!" he calls out. I turn down the trail. My heart is racing, this complete and utter feeling of freedom passing over me.

My mom called and I told her no.

I'm dating a guy I swooned over since I was younger.

He looks at me like he's in awe.

I don't think I could have it any better right now. Really.

When I get to the edge of the water, I slip my shirt over my head and turn toward the trail exit. Aidan is marching my way, his hand already at his pants and tugging the zipper down. "We definitely should've started skinny-dipping together sooner."

"I don't know," I tease, kicking off my leggings. "I think everything happens for a reason." Standing there in my bra and panties is liberating. Courses of electricity jolt through me, and when Aidan tugs his shirt over his head, that electricity turns to warmth.

I back up until my heels hit the water. It is chilly, but nothing unbearable. I keep going, goading him farther and farther in. He steps out of his jeans, his cock pressing against his boxer briefs. He saunters toward me, and I take him in. His physique is something to behold.

"Don't you have to be naked for this to count as skinny dipping?" he asks, lifting a brow.

"Hmm. Maybe we'll call this 'fooling around in the water,' and then I'll cross it off my list."

"You need to cross off getting a real boyfriend."

My heart pounds at his words. Real. I finally feel like I'm actually living my own life. I have something *real*.

He slides his hand up my spine, then back down to my thighs, gripping me and hauling me up. I cross my ankles behind his ass, and he walks us into the river.

"Are you sore?" he asks, the tension mounting.

"I wouldn't tell you if I was." He frowns, but I shrug in response. "Just being real, stud."

"Hmm," Aidan says, nipping at my lips. "Since

we're being real, I think we need to go back to a party so I can actually take you upstairs and compete against the couple in the next room."

"Well, aren't you dirty? I think I'm too innocent to be associating with someone like you."

He grins. "Of course. Because you've never touched yourself in a public bathroom."

"Never."

"Never let the best player in the league finish you off."

"I have morals," I tell him with fake shock.

He stops for a moment, staring at me. "How are you so perfect?"

I wrap my arms around him, holding him tight to me.

"It's so weird," he muses, his voice softer, more introspective.

"What?" I stroke my fingers down the nape of his neck.

He shakes his head. "I've always felt like I could lose everything at any moment, you know? Nothing seemed fixed or settled. Even at home, I think a part of me always created distance between me and my parents because I was scared of losing them. Scared of being given up again. A product of being adopted and all that."

I pull away, watching him. I hate that for him. No one should feel like that, especially not with their family, and I'm ashamed I've ever complained about my situation. Aidan has had it harder than me. Harder than most.

"You feel good, though, Bails. Really good. You let me say all of my ridiculous things. You cook me breakfast on game day. You do all these crazy things with me —and even think up most of them. It just…"

I smile, smoothing my palm down his neck. "Feels right."

He nods, and I couldn't have said it better myself. What should've been a ridiculous offer that day when Darrin and I showed up at his dorm, Aidan went with it. He sees the humor—the possibilities—in everything. It's a breath of fresh air.

"You can always feel at home with me," I tell him. "I mean it."

In that moment, I know there's no way I'm going to let my mom come between us. Or anything, for that matter.

People. Distance. Nothing.

Aidan tugs me toward him, pressing his cock between my legs.

Our redo. This is it.

"I want to taste you," he says, eyes hooded. "Then I'm going to hold you like this, guide you down on my cock, and make love to you like I should have before. Okay?"

I nod before kissing him, swiping my lips over his urgently.

He turns us, walking me backward until my backside hits a hard surface. He sits me on top of it, pushing me away while he glides his hands across my hips and tugs my panties past my knees.

I'm on a rock jutting out into the river. Aidan notices me staring at it and says, "This is Oral Rock."

I gasp. "It is?"

He smiles. "Nah. I made that up, but I do think we could christen it that way." He tosses my panties onto the bank and slides my heels onto the hard stone, my legs automatically opening.

Goose bumps sprout over my wet skin as the cold rock mixes with the heat of my body. He reaches up, moving the cups of my bra down to reveal my breasts. The wind hitting my hard nipples sends a chill through me.

The sky overhead is turning dusky pink, the last vestiges of the sun sliding away. It's still light enough to see anything that goes on between us, and because of that, butterflies erupt in my stomach. "Do you think someone will see us?"

Aidan shakes his head.

"How do you know?" *On second thought...* "Never mind, don't answer that."

Aidan takes that opportunity to lick up my center. "If you're wondering if I've ever brought anyone here, the answer is no." He teases my clit with the tip of his tongue. "This is our place."

He runs his hands up my rib cage, grabbing my breasts while he goes down on me, moaning and purring into my pussy until I'm moving against his face.

If I was sore, I'm not feeling any of that now. All I feel is the heightened sense of pleasure when he tweaks my nipples, rubbing them between his fingers as he sucks on my clit. "Aidan..."

I run my hands through his hair, holding him to me. "So fucking good," he responds, stroking me. "Sweet, pure ecstasy. Remember when you came on my face?"

A strangled cry rips from my throat. He teases and licks, and my hips move involuntarily against his mouth. He's so good at this. Too fucking good at this.

My body shakes. The river carries away my moans when he slips a finger inside my pussy, circling me and then pistoning in and out in rhythm with his tongue.

"I want to feel you," I rasp.

"Soon."

"Aidan..."

"I like it when you beg."

"Aidan, please." I sit up, nudging him away by the shoulders. I scoot toward the edge of the rock and slip off, forcing him to catch me. Pushing his boxers down, I wrap my legs around his body until he's at my entrance.

I lift my eyebrows, waiting, biting my lower lip. He caves, slamming his mouth to mine while he works his cock inside me, feeding it into me inch by inch. It's a fullness I crave. A fullness I savor when he starts fucking me. He pins me against the rock, sliding in and out of me. The water ripples away from us, muted by our joint sighs and the sound of the falls in the distance.

He tugs on my hair, holding me while we stare at each other until my body starts to quiver. "Aidan…"

"I know. Come on my cock, Angel."

He quickens his pace until I'm nearly Jell-O in his arms, and finally, I erupt in pleasure. Aidan follows soon after, clutching me to him when he empties inside me.

"Oh my God," he pants. "Bails!"

I smile, working my fingers into the hair at his nape when a flashlight beam nearly blinds Aidan. "Hey down there!"

Aidan and I both freeze, clutching one another.

"This is the Warner Police Department. Please make yourselves decent and meet me at your car. Don't bother running. I know it's you, QB1."

Shit.

23

AIDAN

"WELL, THIS IS AWKWARD."

My idea to make light of the situation isn't working on Bails. Her fingers shake while she frantically yanks her clothes on, her face stricken.

"It's okay."

My attempt to comfort her fails. The look she gives me tells me I should just shut up. She slips her feet into her shoes. "How do you figure?" she finally snaps, whisper-yelling at me. "Aidan, we were having sex in public. Only our second time, by the way. Oh my God." She runs her hands through her hair. Going to her, I wrap my arms around her. She's shaking from head to toe.

"I'm sorry," I state, pulling back enough to tug my shirt on over my head. "It was reckless."

"It was my idea. I'm mortified. What's he going to do?"

The truth is, I have no clue. I've never been in a situation like this. I could see it going badly but, honestly, I could also see us getting away with a slap on the wrist. He knows who I am. Leniency might be in the cards.

"Do you think he saw anything?" Tears gather in her eyes.

"No," I growl, taking her chin to make her look at me. "I promise you, he didn't." I'm not going to lie, the image of ripping this cop's eyeballs from his head crosses my mind at the thought of him seeing Bailey like that. "He didn't see anything, and even if he did, your back was to him."

"This is so bad."

Her eyes are wide with fear. Shock. I don't know how to calm her down other than keep trying to soothe her. "I'll take care of it. You stay here, okay? He won't even see it's you. I promise."

"Like there's some other girl you've been dating that you can pretend it's her. We're Baidan, Aidan."

"Maybe he's not a football fan at all?" I offer, shrugging. "Just stay here, okay? I'll take care of it."

I squeeze her hand and take a deep breath. What a fucking reality check. One second, pure passion. The next, the deepest horror.

Holy shit.

I swallow, trying to force down the nerves that are bubbling to the surface. Tree branches claw at me as I take the path back to the road. As soon as I exit the path, he shines his flashlight on me. It doesn't hit me in the eyes but directly at my chest, as if he's got me ensnared and there's no way to get out.

"Fancy meeting you here," he says. There might be a hint of a smile, but it's shadowy, and now that I'm staring at a man in unform who has the power to take me away in handcuffs, my stomach twists, and it's taking everything in me to focus.

"Sir, I'm extremely sorry. My girlfriend and I—"

He points his flashlight down the path. "Where is she?"

"Waiting back there. She's upset. We both are. I told her I would talk to you."

The police officer turns off his flashlight and leans against my car, crossing his arms in front of his chest. "Local kids come here all the time. We have to break up parties regularly, but I was surprised to find you here."

"It wasn't my best decision," I tell him, giving him an attempt at a rueful smile and scratching the back of my head. My skin feels like it's on fire. I've never been in trouble like this before. Judging by Bailey's reaction, neither has she.

"Do you know there're such laws as public indecency? Lewdness? Disorderly conduct? They're all misdemeanors, QB1. I'm a friend of Coach's, and I really don't think he'd like hearing about me catching you here."

My stomach falls out from under me.

"Your girlfriend got folks?"

"Yes, sir." Fear crashes down on me. They would yank her out of Warner so quick if they found out. Hell, they never even wanted her here in the first place. "Please, I'll take the charges. If you could leave her out of it."

He tilts his head, as if my answer has caught him off guard. "I take it this isn't some random hook up, then?"

"No, sir. Not at all. Her parents are strict, and if they found out..." I swallow. I'd rather deal with Coach's wrath, and even that would be terrible. Possibly devastating.

What a fucking shitshow I've put myself in. Stupid. Fucking stupid. And here I was hours earlier telling West that I was different with Bailey.

Am I really?

The cop is silent for what seems like forever. Time enough to make my palms go sweaty and for the chill of the air to send a shiver through me.

Finally, he kicks away from my car. "I don't want to get you in trouble, Aidan. I don't want to get your girlfriend in trouble either. But think of it from my point of view. If people could have sex wherever they wanted, whenever they wanted, that wouldn't be a good thing. What if a family had decided to take their kids to the river to go for an evening swim, and there you two were? Think about how this town looks up to you."

My stomach knots as if someone has fisted my insides and gave them a sharp tug. "I understand. It was stupid. It won't happen again."

"I've worked on the force for a lot of years, and do you know how many times I hear that and catch people doing the same thing again and again?"

Shit. This isn't going well. "It won't be me, sir. I've learned my lesson. My girlfriend is mortified. I'll be lucky if she even agrees to have sex with me again at this point."

I press my lips together, wishing I could take the words back. Sometimes my humor comes out at inappropriate times. The cop smiles at me, though. "That sounds like punishment enough."

My heart leaps, but I'm too scared to ask what that means.

He walks forward, placing his hand on my shoulder. "Listen, you're a good kid. You've got a great career in front of you. I don't want to be the one to put a wrench in those plans. I'm not going to charge you with anything, and I won't say anything to Coach either, unless I find you back here doing the same thing."

"You won't. I—"

He gives me a hard stare, silencing me.

"Let me give you a little advice: Just because things sound like a good idea doesn't mean they are. If you ever think about doing this again, remember how you feel right now."

"Yes, sir."

He squeezes my shoulder. "Tell your girlfriend that everything is okay and to have a good night."

Relief floods through me, and I nearly collapse.

"You're a good guy for worrying about her."

I don't feel like a good guy right now. I feel like a dumbass. "Thank you, Sir."

He nods at me, then walks to his car and gets in. He doesn't look at me again as he backs up, stops, and continues down the road.

"God, that was stupid," I chastise myself.

Behind me, a twig snaps, and I turn to find Bailey coming out of the mouth of the trail. She peers up and down the road. "He left? Are we in trouble?"

I shake my head, and the relief on her face makes me feel a little better. "He warned me not to do it again." I wait a beat before saying, "He said he was friends with Coach."

Her eyes widen in horror again as she walks up to me. "Is he going to say anything?"

"He says no, but..."

"Shit."

I nod, taking everything in. If he'd charged us for any of those acts he listed, Bailey's parents would've found out. That would have been the exact opposite of everything she wanted to accomplish here at Warner. My parents wouldn't have been happy either, but Coach... Shit. Bad PR for the team. He would be forced to take a stance on it, and that stance would've been worse than me showing up late to practice, I'm sure.

My mind goes on a downward spiral while I walk Bailey to the car and get in. We drive in silence back to her place.

"Hey," she says, reaching out to stroke my knee. "I'm sorry. It was my idea."

I pull into the driveway, park the car, and turn toward her. "If you think I'm upset about doing that with you, you're wrong. There was nothing wrong with the act, Bails. We probably should've been smarter about where we did it. Man, I've got so much going on." I take a deep breath. "And if your parents had been called, they probably wouldn't let you date me, let alone stay here at Warner."

She swallows, not denying anything.

Little by little, I feel myself withdrawing, my brain hyperfixating on shit. I pull out my phone and send a text to Darrin.

Dude, you home?

Yep.

> Cool. Bailey is coming in.

I pause, staring at my phone. She shouldn't be alone right now, but I can't... I just can't do this right now. I need to think shit over.

I lick my lips, glancing up at her. "I'm really tired. I think I'm just going to go home."

"Oh. Yeah," she says. I see the disappointment in her gaze, and it kills me. I'd be worse off for her if I went in though. I know that.

"I'll see you tomorrow, though."

"Right. Yep." She pushes the car door open, and I reach for her hand, holding it until she peers back around toward me. Her eyes glisten, and I look away. "What?" she asks.

I pull her hand up, kissing her knuckles. "See you tomorrow. Text me, 'kay?"

My heart squeezes as she agrees. The car door shuts, and I watch her stride up the sidewalk to her house. She turns at the door, and I give her a short wave. She returns it before slipping inside.

Immediately, I take out my phone again and text West.

> Where are you?

> Kenna's.

> Can I come over? I need to talk.

Of course.

I take the short drive to Kenna's place, the whole time chastising myself. Despite it being Saturday night, the city is rather quiet. Few people are walking the streets and even fewer cars. The car horn echoes when I lock it after getting out.

I knock on the door, and Sydney opens it. "Aidan, hey."

"Syd." I give her a big hug. "It's been a long time."

"I know." She retreats, smiling at me. "I saw your girlfriend at the game. She's the cutest thing. I'm so happy for you."

For some reason, her words feel like an anvil to the chest. "She's...great."

"Oh, Sydney," Kenna calls from the living room, "Aidan wants to talk to West. Come watch TV with me."

"Oh. Oh." Sydney's eyes widen. "Sorry. You guys talk. I'll get out of your way."

"It's no big deal," I find myself saying, but everything feels like a big deal right now.

She passes West in the hallway, and I hold up my keys. "Want to take a drive?"

"Sure, but we'll take my truck."

"Ooh, the Hulkmobile."

He glares daggers at me, but behind all that, I recognize the concern in his gaze. If I'm upset, can he still tell me to shut the fuck up about his car's nickname?

He snaps his mouth shut, turning away, and I decide right there that I must not be hiding my freak-out well.

I walk back outside and head toward West's ginormous truck the local dealership gave him as part of an NIL deal. My own are slowly coming in, but I try not to think about them because if I do, it messes with my head. I saw the circus West had to go through when shit hit the fan with his dad and how he had to play into keeping his sponsors happy. That's not something I want to deal with.

Another reason why I shouldn't have been so reckless.

The truck growls to life, this beast even louder than my sports car's engine. It's totally West, though. The insignia on the side, West "Hulk" Brooks, is the icing on the cake.

He backs out of the driveway and asks, "So, what's up? If this is about me giving you a hard time earlier, I'm sorry. You know I really like Bailey. It wasn't my place."

I shake my head. "Dude." I blow out a breath. I'm usually not so embarrassed to talk about sex, but this is different. This is about Bailey and me, which makes it mean more, and worse, it's about us being walked in on. "So... Ugh," I growl in frustration, my fingers curling into my thighs. "I don't know how to say it, but after the ASPCA thing, I took Bailey down by the river and we...*were together*, and a cop found us."

West peers over at me, eyes bugging out of his head. "Shit. Are you okay? Is Bailey okay?"

"Everything's fine." I rub up and down my arms like I'm cold, but I'm not. "We're both embarrassed. The cop scared the shit out of me. He was talking about misdemeanors and telling Coach."

"Fuck."

"He said he wasn't going to do it, but, West, what the fuck? Am I just bad at this?" I ask, the words tumbling out. "I feel like I'm fucking everything up. First, I fucked up with the team. That got better, partly because of Bailey, but now I feel like a failure because I almost screwed it up again, with her *and* them. If Bailey's parents found out..." I shake my head. "West, you don't even know. They're so strict."

"That's heavy shit," he says. Silence fills the car for a bit. "Let's go from the outcome back. You're fine. Bailey's fine. No one got in trouble."

"But only because I'm me!"

"Wait, wait, wait. He could've just as easily turned you in because you're you."

I bite the inside of my cheek. Of course West would have this perspective because of what his dad did to him. "That's true," I agree.

"So, what are you most upset about?" he asks. "Is

283

this about football? Or is this about letting Bailey down?"

"Both. They seem intertwined somehow." I glance over at him. A lot of the guys on the team have girlfriends, but I had an up close and personal take on West's relationship with Kenna. If you'd asked me before if college kids could fall in love, I'm not sure what I would've told you, but I do know that what West and Kenna have is the real thing. They'll be together for the rest of their lives.

A sick feeling squeezes my stomach. I blink, suddenly understanding where all my apprehension is coming from.

It's fear. One hundred percent. People don't stay with me, they leave me. It's been engrained within me since my real mom left at five. I've been guarded from my own parents because I don't want them to ever leave me.

My eyes prick with heat. "I think the problem is that I'm falling for her."

West reaches over to put a comforting hand on my shoulder. "I know you told me not to, but I happened to tell Kenna that you guys were faking it, and she laughed at me. She said there was no way either one of you were faking anything. You were lying to yourselves."

"You told Kenna? Dick."

He smiles, replacing his hand back on the steering

wheel. "Just assume that when you tell me to keep a secret, it means from everyone but Kenna. You probably understand that now."

I take a deep, rattling breath. "It's scary."

He looks over. "It can be. You know I've had my own shit with my dad and mom being...them. It's not comfortable putting your heart in someone else's hands when you've been through something like that. Something like you have, too. Does she know about you being adopted?"

I nod. "I told her, but I haven't told her everything. I probably screwed that up, too." Sighing, I wipe the fog from the window. "I left her with her brother tonight. My brain wouldn't let me act normal, and I think I hurt her feelings. I'm sure I hurt her feelings."

"You should tell her. I know it's scary. I get it. But that's where trust comes in. Let's not forget that I fucked it up with Kenna before. We all know I did. Thankfully, she saw what I was doing, and she's the one who made me see."

Jesus. If people could hear us now. We sound like two saps. "I wish I knew that she was staying at Warner, but even that is up in the air. Her brother told me the other day that he wouldn't start something with a girl because his parents won't let him stay. I can't do long distance, West. I need her here."

I blow out a breath. It feels so fucking good to talk this out. I'm understanding myself more and more.

Bailey never promised she would stay. In fact, she said at most she would get one semester in, but now that we're in so deep, we have to make this work. I can't go through someone I love leaving me again.

"What's their issue with Warner?"

I shrug. "It's not really with Warner, I guess. They want her to go to this other school, and before you say she should be able to go to where she wants, in theory, that makes sense, but she has this thing about letting her parents down." Plus, her parents holding the purse strings. That can't be easy. "It's different from our parents. We got scholarships, and we're football players, but not everyone is like us. Her situation is different."

"I get that," West says. "Did you see that video about the player who committed to Florida and his mom walked out of the press conference because she wanted him to go to Bama?"

"Copeland? Yeah. It's fucked up."

"Parents should be supportive." His own history marks his face, and out of all things, I know West gets it more than others.

I run my hands down my face. "I don't know how I can have everything. And what will happen to football if she decides to take off?"

"Football is a crutch for guys like us. We use it as an excuse for everything. It's serious, especially when you're talking about our long-term goals. It's fucking scary. But around all that, life is still happening. We could get hurt tomorrow—"

"Jesus, don't fucking say that."

"It's true. That's what I'm saying. We have this mentality of all of our eggs in one basket. The fucking pressure," West grinds out.

I'm glad I'm not the only one who feels it. When I first started for Warner, I had all this anxiety to be as good as Reid. Being the quarterback, it's like putting the whole team on your back and carrying them. "Are you trying to talk me into Bailey? Or out of Bailey? I can't tell."

"I'm saying you should treat football and your relationship separately. As much as it's amazing that Kenna is there for me with football, if football went away tomorrow, I'd still have Kenna, and that's..." He takes a deep breath. "That means a lot to me. With her, it might feel like shit would be bearable. She'd tell me to get over myself, and I would. Eventually. I mean, I'd be a crybaby at first, but eventually I could function."

"I don't know why it feels like I can't have both. Like somehow, if things are going well with Bailey, football will suffer—like with the stupid stunt tonight."

"It's because it's raw."

"Okay, Dr. Phil."

"What I mean is, everything worked out. No one got hurt. You didn't get arrested. Coach won't find out. Bailey's parents aren't aware. Literally, nothing happened. You're scared of a what-if. It's your job to now make sure that what-if never happens."

Shit. That was profound. I sit up straight. "You're like a relationship guru, man."

"I am pretty good at it. I mean, I did bag the prettiest girl on campus."

I smirk. I'm going to let him have this one because he just helped me. A lot.

"Tell Bailey about your fears. It's better that way. Don't make the mistake I did and pull away. Especially if you think she's the one."

I blow out a breath, exhaling all my nerves. Aside from my parents, I've never truly talked with anyone who wasn't a therapist about my adoption-related struggles.

When I started football, it seemed unnecessary.

But they're there still. Obviously.

"Want to drop me at Bailey's?"

West grunts in response, turning the truck around.

I might as well lay it all out for her.

24

BAILEY

I STARE DOWN at the texts that just came through from my mother. My stomach plunges. She wants to talk. She wants to come to Warner tomorrow.

This is bullshit.

I march out of my room and up the stairs. Darrin is playing a video game with headphones on, and when he sees me standing at the entrance to his room, he slips them off.

I hold the phone out to him and march forward. "Did you get texts from Mom?"

He checks his phone. "Nope." He reaches for mine and scans my screen, shaking his head. "I don't know what you expected."

My stomach falls. "Darrin, are you kidding me?"

"No!" His voice is like an explosion, and I take a few steps back. He takes his headphones from around his neck and throws them onto the table next to him. "You've been living in la-la land, Bailey. We're not staying here, and this morning, your boyfriend answered your phone. What did you think would happen?"

"Oh, I don't know. To be treated like an adult. You didn't get texts, Darrin. You didn't get an early morning phone call saying you had to go to some important luncheon that you were just then hearing about."

His face twists in confusion. "That's why she called you?"

It's my turn to explode. "Yes! For fuck's sake, it's always something. I'm expected to follow along with whatever she does. I thought I would be safe for a while. We live a couple of hours away now!"

"And you didn't know about the lunch?"

"Are you new here?"

"Bails..."

"Don't *Bails* me." I turn in a circle, nearly pulling my hair out. "Did you know she gave me shit because she saw us on TV at Aidan's game? My clothes weren't right. I had paint on my face. I shouldn't have been acting like that.

"Mom wants the daughter who sits quietly next to her at those stupid luncheons with all of her fake-ass friends. Someone who only smiles and nods, and who'll eventually push out a couple of well-polished kids.

Possibly daughters like me. Except mine will most likely disappoint her because they won't just stand there with their mouths shut and look pretty."

Darrin reaches for me, but I pull away.

"Don't be like that," he says. "I know Mom is tough on you."

Tears threaten to spill over. "I can't be who she wants me to be anymore."

"Because of Aidan?"

I groan in frustration, my hands turning to fists. "Because it never should've been that way in the first place. I'm my own person. What if I don't want to wear pantsuits in the middle of summer and use a gallon of hairspray just so I can wear my hair curly?"

"Are you even talking in English anymore?"

"You had it so much better than I did," I growl out.

"Me?" He stands from his chair, scowling. "Bullshit. I couldn't do anything or be anything without it having to mean something. I couldn't just enjoy football because if I was good at it, I had to be the best. I couldn't just be a good student in class, I had to be the best."

"At least you had friends."

"I had to fucking plead with them every year to let Aidan spend a couple weeks with us! Every fucking year. And you know what? For weeks after, Dad would sit me down and we would go over why Aidan was such a better player than me. Yeah, it was a great fucking time."

I suck in a breath. "But they like Aidan."

He laughs and shakes his head. "Are you kidding me? Do you know how I got them to let me invite Aidan over? I told them we would practice. They never agreed until I pushed them to see what a benefit it was. If Aidan wasn't good at football, Mom and Dad never would've let him stay. He didn't go to a fancy-ass private school like all my other friends."

"Well, that's fucked up!" I snap, furious. I'd been wondering what the look was between Mom and Dad, and now I know.

Darrin lets out a breath. We stand there, breathing heavily. They put us both in a box, held down by restraints, and neither one of us saw it in the other. "It always looked like you were having so much fun," I tell him. "Everyone at school liked you."

Tears well up in his eyes. "Bails, do you remember the weeks I spent in the hospital when I was a freshman?"

"Yeah, you hurt yourself at football."

"No." A single tear tracks down his face. "I tried to — Fuck, I took too many pills. On purpose."

The world pauses for a moment, and when it starts up again, it's tilted. Like nothing is right. "What?" I rasp. "Why didn't— You didn't—"

"Mom and Dad didn't want you to know."

I run forward, throwing my arms around my brother, squeezing him. He wraps his long, lanky arms around me, and I just hang on tight.

How could I not have known? All this time, I resented him because it seemed like he had it so much better than me.

I bite my lip, but it's no use. I cling to my brother, tears coming and coming. Tears for him. For me. "I'm so sorry I didn't know."

"It's not your fault. I was going to tell you so many times, but I didn't want you to worry."

"This is some kind of fucked up," I say, pulling away. I've left wet marks on his shirt. "Was it the pressure? Did you tell Mom and Dad?"

He shakes his head. "They just thought... I swear to you, they just thought I was weak. They gave me a lot of leeway after that. I think that's when Mom went crazy on you. She didn't want you to do the same thing."

I move around him and then pull him down so we can sit next to each other on the sofa. Placing my elbows on my thighs, I hang my head in my hands. "They're going to make us leave here."

"There was never a chance we were going to stay. You knew that going in. But it'll be okay. You and Aidan were doing the long-distance thing before, you can do it again."

I cringe. I can't lie to him anymore. Not after what he's just revealed to me. "Don't be mad."

He drops his head. "What?"

"I lied about Aidan. We weren't secretly dating."

He tilts his head. "So, you're not dating?"

"Well, we are now. I mean before." I stand again, walk toward the TV, then turn around to face him. "When I told Mom and Dad I wanted to go to a different college, I used Aidan as an excuse. He was the only person I could think of that Mom and Dad liked, the only person I could use as a reason why I would want to go to Warner. I put two and two together, and then it popped out that he and I were dating."

"Let me get this straight. When you and I showed up at Warner, you were not dating my best friend?"

I shake my head.

"Then you somehow talked him into it? Within minutes?"

I shrug. "It was kind of easy. He needed a jersey-chaser blocker so he could focus on football."

"You're making my head hurt." He sighs, running his hands through his hair. "But now you are dating? For real?"

"For real, for real," I tell him. "Though we just got into trouble, and he's upset at himself and won't talk to me about it."

"In trouble?"

"Don't get mad."

"If you say that one more time, I'm going to get pissed."

I grimace. "Um, so, we were in the river...naked. A..." I clear my throat. "A cop kinda sorta found us out there."

Darrin jumps to his feet. "Jesus Christ, Bailey."

"It's not like we meant to."

"Are you in trouble? Did he give you a ticket?"

"No, he let us go. He knew who Aidan was, but we were scared shitless."

"Oh my God, if Mom found out..."

"I know! I'd be leaving right now."

"Oh, he's going to hear it from me." I give him a look, but he waves it away. "No, Bails, not this time. I gave him a pass about dating you, then come to find out you weren't dating, so he used his Get Out of Jail Free card on a fake relationship. Now it's on."

"Can we not go there right now? Darrin..." I sit back on the couch next to him and turn to face him. "What are we going to do? Do you like it here? Do you want to stay?"

"It's not an option."

"Well, that's bullshit."

"Mom and Dad aren't going to pay for you to go to Warner, so forget about it."

"Okay, but should that matter? Darrin, kids all over

the world go to school and I'm sure their parents don't have money. They must do something."

"Yeah, loans."

"Okay, we'll get those."

"I don't know. Don't you think we kind of owe it to them to toe the line on this one? They're terrible people. They want the best for us, and if you put Warner and Carnegie side-by-side, Carnegie wins."

"But at the expense of our identity? Our happiness?"

"They're just going to say you're making a decision for a boy. And hell, maybe you are. What's so terrible about going to Carnegie? They have a great reputation. Great professors. Good class size."

"What are you? The brochure?"

"I'm only saying, a lot of people would kill for that education."

I rub my palm up and down my arm, thinking. "So we wait it out a couple more years?"

"I don't know, you're Miss Smarty-Pants. You'll probably have a degree after a year and a half. It's not that long."

I roll my eyes. "It's not fair."

"They're not being malicious about it, Bailey. They want us to get the best education."

"What if they don't offer what I want to study?"

"And what's that?"

"I don't know."

"Then you can *I don't know* at Carnegie. This is about Aidan."

"It's about freedom, Darrin. It's not about Aidan at all." *Well, maybe a little.* Aidan's a part of that feeling. He makes me feel like I'm soaring through the clouds. Reckless. Happy.

"Bails..." He stares down at his hands.

"Yeah?"

"They already matriculated us. We start in January."

My stomach falls. Darrin starts going on and on about how the tuition is paid, about how they told us this was just going to be a little break. Almost like a tiny gap year, except it's nothing like that because we're still going to school, just not *their* school. "This can't be happening."

"If I were you, I'd tell Aidan sooner rather than later." He blows out a breath. "Faking it or not, I'm pretty sure if you guys are the real thing, he'll understand."

I stand as if in a daze. Like thick fog has rolled in and I can't seem to get my bearings.

Before, I had hope. Now, I have nothing.

It's done. They went behind my back and did it. They knew this was never going to be anything. They gave me a couple months. If that.

Mom is coming tomorrow... Is she going to tell me that I have to leave right away? Did Aidan answering my phone in the morning really spook her that much?

I turn to my brother, trying to dissect the look on his face. "Are you okay with this?"

He shrugs. "I don't have an Aidan, Bails. I knew coming here we weren't going to stay. I've been treating it like a nice retreat. But Carnegie's not going to be all that bad either. It'll be like here."

"Except we have to wear uniforms."

"I know, you're so attached to your leggings now."

I shoot him a look, and he lifts his hands. "I'm sorry. I knew you were going to be upset."

"Aren't you?"

"Like I said, we'll still be out on our own, we'll just be out on our own on a different campus. It really doesn't matter to me. I'm..." He lifts his hands. "Glad to not have daily probing, if you know what I mean."

My throat thickens, tears threatening again. I don't understand why I'm so angry about this. I never thought I'd be able to get away with going here anyway. Maybe Darrin is right. Maybe this is all about Aidan... But if it is, is that so bad? I want to be with him.

I get up and march out the door.

"Bails... Come on, Bails..."

"I need to be alone," I eke out before running down the steps, racing through the hallway, and throwing myself onto my bed.

I can't tell if I should be more sad or more angry.

Both emotions flicker through me at the rate of rapid Morse code.

In the end, I think I'm more mad at myself. I got the taste of freedom, and now I don't want to give it up. It might have been better to remain blissfully unaware.

25

AIDAN

I KNOCK on the front door, harder this time. I'm about ready to haul it off the hinges. A minute has passed, and no one is answering, even though the lights are on.

Finally, Darrin yanks the door open, scowling. "I should punch you in the face."

I step back. Bailey must've told him what happened at the river. Or maybe I really did hurt her feelings. "I'm sure I deserve it, but can it wait? I need to talk to your sister."

Darrin wraps his arms around himself, glaring at me. He and I have always been about the same size, but for some reason, I feel like he's towering over me, his look of disappointment shortening me by the second.

I try to push past him, but he pushes me back. "We're not done."

"What is it? Is Bails here? Will she talk to me?"

"She said she wanted to be alone, but, dude, this isn't going anyplace good."

My stomach clenches. "What the fuck are you talking about?"

"I'm talking about you and Bailey," he hisses. "Both of you. You're going to get hurt. You should break it off now. It'll be better."

My heart beats like crazy. "What are you talking about?"

There's a seriousness in his eyes. His clenched jaw is like a brick wall. "I can't see her hurt."

"I'm not going to hurt her. That's the last thing I would do. Dude, we're best friends."

"Which is why I'm asking you to walk away now before it gets more serious than it already is. I just watched my sister have a complete meltdown. I know how bad it can get, bro. The pressure she's under is fucking real. You're a complication that will only make it worse."

A complication? A fucking *complication*? "Let me fucking talk to her." He blocks the doorway when I attempt to barge through. "You're my friend, but I will knock you on your ass."

The need to fight for Bailey bangs against me, unrelenting.

"I don't want to see you hurt either," Darrin grinds out through gritted teeth.

"If I don't get to talk to her..." I force out, confusion

and anger sweeping through me like a Molotov cocktail mix.

"Talk to your fake girlfriend," Darrin spits out.

Shit. "She's not fake anymore."

"Maybe you're lying to yourself. Maybe you're just caught up in the moment."

"Maybe I'm not good enough for her? Is that what you mean?" I scream, pushing him.

"I didn't say that."

Old insecurities bark like snapping dogs into my ear. All I have is football to remind me that I'm actually okay. That I actually deserve to be here. I thought Bailey could be that for me, too.

I run my hands through my hair, tugging at the ends. "I'm sorry we lied to you, I really am, but you don't know what you're talking about when it comes to Bailey and me."

"I do, and that's why I'm telling you to get lost. Forget about her. Focus on football, man. In a couple of years—"

"In a couple of *years?*" I roar.

"Aidan?"

That small, sweet voice.

I peer over Darrin's shoulder to find Bailey staring at us from the hallway. The confused look on her face makes me glare at Darrin. "I want to see her. Now."

"Darrin, it's okay," Bailey says, coming up behind him and placing a hand on his shoulder.

He turns his back on me. "You're going to get hurt."

"I'd rather feel pain than be empty."

He stands up straighter. "You know what, you both can count me out when this explodes in your faces."

He pushes his sister's hand off him and stalks toward the stairs.

I watch him go, my anger dissipating to sympathy. When I finally lock gazes with Bails, something primal takes over. I clutch her cheeks with my palms and walk her backward. Her eyes widen with each step until I kick her bedroom door closed behind us. My brain keeps snagging on things to say to her. I want to ask her what that was about. I want to know why her brother is so mad at me, why does he think we're better apart, but all I can do is kiss her.

I want to consume her. What I can't say with words, I can say with the way my tongue holds her mouth hostage. If she breathes, she breathes in me. If she tastes, she tastes me. If she feels, I'm the one enveloping her.

She moans low in her throat. "Aidan, hell. Are you okay?"

Her lids flutter open as if she's been drugged. The feeling is mutual. "Bails, I didn't handle the cop and the river well. I fucked up. I'm sorry."

"What do you mean? You saved me from embarrassment."

"I mean afterward." I take a deep breath. "I started

303

to spiral, and when I start to go down, it's like a freefall. The cop said he was friends with Coach, and if Coach found out, it would be bad for me. Warner doesn't want troublemakers on their team. They've made that abundantly clear. They have a zero-tolerance policy."

"So, he scared you?" she asks, reaching out to grip my elbows.

"Scared the shit out of me. I was thinking about losing football and losing you. It kept getting darker and darker and—"

"I can be that person you talk to when shit gets dark, Aidan," she says, brows lifting.

But as soon as she says it, her face gets guarded. Strained.

The tension in the air shifts and tears gather in her eyes.

"What is it?"

She shakes her head, pressing her lips together. "After. We can talk about you."

"Bullshit," I tell her. "My girl's in pain, and I want to know why. Is it Darrin? Did he say something to you?"

Her lower lip trembles, and Darrin's words come rushing back to me. *I just watched my sister have a complete meltdown.*

"You better tell me before I burn the world down trying to figure it out myself."

"It's...everything," she says, more tears tracking

down her face, and she gives me a wobbly smile. "I got a text from my mom. She's coming here tomorrow. Darrin tried to kill himself in high school. I found out Mom and Dad already signed us up for Carnegie. But I'm...I'm in love with you, Aidan, and I'm worried."

Her words are an onslaught. Blow after blow. Until I hear those five words.

I'm in love with you.

Then nothing else matters.

I dip down, claiming her mouth again. Her lips are salty. I kiss and wipe the tears away as they fall down her cheeks. Very few people have told me they love me. I can't even remember my birth mother saying that. I've tried and tried, but the few things I can remember aren't words of love or devotion. They're words of goodbye.

A few words, a simple hand squeeze before a car pulled up to the curb. She straightened my shirt, and then off I went. I didn't even realize it was forever until I was introduced to my new parents in a sterile office.

I kiss Bailey until my lips ache. Until I'm tired, but I'll never be tired of hearing what she just said. "You love me?" I ask when I finally let her come up for air.

She nods.

I can probably count on one hand how many times I've said those words in my life. What a strange, odd feeling that it's bursting out of me. That I feel like I will come apart if I don't say it. The words are missiles, counting down to ignition.

"I love you, Bailey Covington." The raw honesty escaping me makes tears form in my eyes. "I fucking love you. Everything you just said, we'll figure it out together." I grab her hands and hold them in front of me before dropping my forehead to hers. "I promise."

She gives me a wobbly smile. "You do?"

I nod, and she throws herself at me. Catching her in my arms is a moment of pure bliss. Second to none. It's Bailey's heart in my hands and then the feeling I get when I run out onto the field. Both of them are like soaring through the clouds but having roots at the same time.

Chills run up and down my arms. West was right. I can have both. Actually, the more I think about it, the more complete my life will be when I have both.

I kiss her again, my hands roaming freely. She arches into me and any resolve I came in here with melts off me.

I choose love.

I choose to live in the moment.

I could let the other things threaten to take me down, but not when I have this.

"I want to feel you," I tell her, kissing up her neck.

"We should talk," she whispers, but her hips move against mine.

"Mmm," I moan into her ear. "We should."

My words belie my actions. I squeeze her ass, then work her shirt over her head so I can bury my face in her cleavage, nipping and sucking.

She throws her head back, gasping. "There are things to discuss," she tells me, her voice wavering as I work her core over my lengthening cock.

"Important things," I agree.

"Aidan, we have decisions to make."

I nod, moving the cup of her bra out of the way with my teeth so I can take her nipple into my mouth, lashing at it with my tongue.

Pulling back, I say, "I agree. Like do you want my mouth here first?" I reach between us to press on her clit.

She moves into my hand.

"I'll take that as a yes."

"Aidan, this is important," she says while I lay her down on the bed, spreading her legs, but she pulls me on top of her in the next moment.

I give her the smallest of smiles. "The only important thing right now is this. That I get to show you how much I love you." Working her leggings down, I reveal her creamy skin before discarding her clothing on the floor.

She's right. We do need to talk, but I need her to know what's the most important.

This. Us.

Not everyone knows that growing up. That love

really is the only thing that matters. What they should fight for.

"I love you," I tell her.

She reaches up, working her fingers through the hair at the nape of my neck. "I know."

I say it again, and she laughs. "I know."

I work my pants down, discarding my boxer briefs with them. Then I reach behind me to take my shirt off, and pretty soon, I'm naked in front of her, staring at my mostly naked girlfriend.

Eyes fixed to mine, she reaches behind her and unclasps her bra, throwing it off the side of the bed.

She's so beautiful. I trace the inside of her thighs until she shudders. My thumb circles her clit, and I can't think of a better way to take her than like this.

I reach for the pillows at the head of her bed and place them under her hips, propping her up for me. Her stare moves from my cock to my face.

I grab my dick at the base, then reach over to grab a condom from her nightstand, working it down my length. I'm still playing with her nub when I enter her, and she cries out, "Aidan!"

"I want you like this, Angel. So I can see every perfect part of you."

I start with slow, measured strokes—movements that drive me crazy as much as her. Her pussy takes me in so good, so fucking good, like she was made for me, molded for my cock.

"Mine," I grind out, working faster.

Her hands flit around the bed, grabbing the sheets in her fists, then letting them go. Her breasts jiggle with every stroke.

"Touch your nipples," I instruct.

"Aidan," she groans.

"Please, I'm desperate for it."

She licks her lips, her fingers finding her hard nipples. Her jaw drops in pleasure, and I'm overcome with an intense need to fill her. To claim her.

"Mine."

"Yours," she breathes out.

My hips piston forward faster. She cries out, her chin tilting up to the ceiling when I drive inside her.

My brain repeats *"Mine, mine, mine"* until I come, emptying everything I have. Her walls close around me at the same time, clenching and unclenching.

"Aidan!"

I thrust inside her one last time as I stare down at her from above. Our gazes connect, and I know, this is it for me. This is the only woman I'll ever have for the rest of my life.

And I can't wait.

Nothing will ever tear us apart. Ever.

26

BAILEY

MY STOMACH CHURNS as we wait for my mother. Darrin and me...and Aidan.

He insisted.

He pulls me onto his lap, and I melt into him. He opened up to me last night, telling me how he's always felt like an outsider. How he has abandonment issues from his birth mother giving him up for adoption. I held him while he told me everything. It was like an exorcism of his past trauma, and while I was still reeling and raw, he asked me mine.

We've been up nearly all night. My eyes are dry and tired. I've shed every tear I've had in me.

When Darrin woke, we both hugged him. I understand now that he doesn't want me to suffer the same fate as him, but there's one difference between what Darrin went through and what I am: I have someone else to confide in.

Aidan's still here, even with the threat of my mother.

"She's not going to make you go to Carnegie," he keeps telling me, but worry settles deep in my bones. It was obvious yesterday that Aidan wouldn't be able to handle a long-distance relationship. Not with his abandonment issues. I feel for him in a way I never thought I'd have to.

The doorbell rings, and I clam up. Truthfully, I don't know exactly why she's coming here. To tell me about Carnegie? To take me away now? We don't know what we're dealing with, and that makes the worry that much worse.

"I'll get it," Darrin says.

Aidan nudges me, and he's right. I have to show her that I'm not scared. "No, I will."

I stand up, squeezing Darrin's hand. "Remember, this isn't your fight. You can go upstairs."

He shrugs noncommittally, and I honestly don't know if he will be my friend or foe when my mom walks in and starts talking.

The doorbell rings again, and I make myself walk forward. After tugging the door open, my mother turns, her gaze sliding from my head to my feet until she frowns. "What interesting attire."

I smile, trying not to let her jab get to me. "Thanks. I wore it yesterday, too."

Her stare darkens to a glower. "I see this campus is having such a great impact on you. Like I thought."

Before she can get another word out, I reach up and hug her, squeezing her shoulders. Memories come flooding back, and they're not all bad. They truly aren't. I love my mother. "I've missed you."

"Oh."

"I'm glad you came by." I move out of the way and gesture down the hallway. "Aidan's here to say hi, and Darrin, obviously."

She clears her throat. "I was hoping to speak to just my children," she says, voice haughty as she steps into the hallway.

"Well, he's here." I move her forward. I'm practically on her heels the whole way. It feels like a walk of doom, but I have to stand up to my mother at some point in my life. It might as well be now when I'm surrounded by people who care.

When she enters the kitchen, Aidan jumps up from a seated position and holds his hand out. "Mrs. Covington, great to see you again."

"Aidan, hello."

Her fake smile is plastered on her face, and it glitters with inauthenticity. After she shakes his hand firmly, Darrin wraps her in a hug. She studies the small kitchen with a frown until Darrin backs away and Aidan offers her the chair he was sitting in.

She sits, her gaze still darting everywhere. "I thought this would've been bigger."

Well, it's definitely small compared to our house back home if that's what she's comparing it to, but it's also massively bigger than Aidan's dorm room. "It's the perfect size," I tell her. "Darrin and I don't need much space. It's only the two of us. Can I get you something to drink? Water?" I quickly offer because I realize we don't actually have anything else. Plus, that's a trick I picked up from her: know how to work your guests.

"Water is fine."

The contents of my stomach slosh around as I fill a glass from the cupboard with water and offer it to her. She peers at the cup, looking inside like she's going to find something gross floating in the contents. Without drinking, she sets the glass on the table.

Internally, I bet myself five dollars she won't even take a sip. A cold sweat starts to form on my forehead. She's being even more snooty than I imagined.

"How long are you staying?" I ask, standing in front of her. "Should I make lunch reservations? There are a couple really great places downtown to eat."

She sneers, and all the pretense she walked in here with vanishes. "Bailey, I don't understand what game this is, but I'm done playing it. I came here for one reason: to take you home."

"Mom," Darrin sighs. "You said you'd give her the semester."

I put my hand up. Even though a hollow hole has opened up in my stomach, I trudge forward because she needs to know I don't want that. Maybe if I explain it to her... "No, I expected this."

"Of course you did." She smiles, peering at me hopefully. "Because you know what's best for you. I agreed to this so—"

"Being here is best for me," I interrupt. Nerves skate over my skin until I'm buzzing. "I'm staying at Warner. Darrin told me you matriculated us at Carnegie, well, you can rescind my application. I choose to stay here."

My mother laughs abruptly, but she still has that air of sweetness about her like all she has to do is make me see her way and I'll be agreeable again. "I know you *think* you want to stay. I feel for you, I do. Your father and I have made the decision, though. You're coming home to prepare for Carnegie."

"Mom, you can't make decisions for me anymore. I'm an adult."

She glances down at the water, twisting the glass in circles on the table. "An adult screaming at football games? Whose boyfriend answers her phone calls at an ungodly hour? That's not you, Bailey Covington. I certainly didn't bring you up that way."

"I apologize for answering her phone," Aidan states. My heart clenches when he talks. His voice cracks, and I look over to see real worry on his face.

I try to send him a reminder with my eyes that I'm handling this, but he glances away. I wish I could go to him, but that might make things worse right now.

My mother straightens her shoulders. "I'm worried about the lasting impact this...place will have on you. The both of you," Mom says as she focuses on Darrin and me.

"What's so bad about me cheering my boyfriend on at a football game? Come on. It was a little paint on my face. It was fun."

"It was tasteless."

"Mom."

She folds her arms across her chest. "I just want more for you."

"So, you want me to play in the football games instead of watching?"

"Oh, don't be ridiculous. You're losing sight of what's really important, sweetheart. It's not boyfriends and football games. Your future is on the line, and you're getting entangled in things that don't serve that."

She means Aidan. My heart thumps. She really does have a problem with him, of what he represents. Anger builds in me. The arrogance wafting off her turns my stomach. How can she place such high importance on our life back home? Darrin and I are happy here. "You're worried about my future..." Wave after wave of indignation crash into me. She's being willfully blind to the facts. "What about the lasting impact

Darrin had from taking too many pills? That happened on *your* watch. Not here."

Mom gasps. My words cut like a battle ax, and for a moment, it feels amazing, but within seconds, my mother's eyes turn glassy. Her fingers flex in her lap, and that's the only tell that shows I've shocked her. Not only by my knowledge of what happened to my brother, but that I would actually say it. "You're throwing Darrin's suicide attempt in my face? How peculiar."

"What's peculiar is that you never told me, and I beg you to see that he's actually happy here. We both are."

She swallows, shaking her head a little like she's trying to rid herself of my words. "I've always wanted the best for you both."

"She knows that, Mom." Darrin shoots me a threatening look and moves to rub her back.

Emotional blackmail. She's going to act like the victim now, and dammit, I should've kept my anger in check.

My mom isn't a terrible person, she just knows how to work angles. This is an angle to her now. Once she gets her way, she'll be all smiles again. But her smiles are only façades—perfect but laced with barbed wire.

"I'm only pointing out that Mom might not have a good grasp on what's actually best for us."

"And Aidan is what's best for you?" my mother

argues, grabbing a tissue out of her purse. "You're going to ruin your future for a boy?"

Aidan grimaces, and I move next to him to reach for his hand. "No, I'm making decisions for myself. If I fail, it's on me. If I thrive, it's on me."

Determination makes me lift my chin, but my mother isn't having it. She's so stubborn when she wants something. It's her personality trait. She waves her tissue dismissively. "We're not paying for you to attend Warner. We agreed so you could get this flirtation out of your head. I thought you would've worked it out of your system by now, but when I saw you on the TV, I knew I had to step in. We're paying for you to go to Carnegie. A real school. And that's that."

"Well, the *flirtation* isn't out of my head," I tell her, glancing at Aidan. "In fact, it only got stronger. We're—"

"Don't tell me you're pregnant." She sucks in a breath and somehow, simultaneously, stares at my leggings in distaste.

"Jesus, Mom," I snap. "We're in love. We're young, but we're not stupid. I like these leggings. And not because I'm getting fat from carrying a baby. They're comfortable, and they go with so many things."

Aidan chuckles next to me, and I hit him with my elbow. He shrugs it off. "I was just thinking that you look great in leggings, but maybe that's not the point to make right now."

"Leggings aren't the point!" I turn to my mother, frustration raising my voice to a shout. "I want to live my own life!"

My mother peers between all of us, exasperated. She latches onto my brother. "Darrin, please tell her. Make her see."

He presses his lips together, his gaze falling to the floor. "I don't want to be in the middle of this," he starts, but his voice strengthens the more he talks. "But, Mom, I've seen Bailey thrive here. She has friends. She's doing well in her classes. What she and Aidan have is real. I think it would be a mistake to take her away from here."

I knew I loved my brother. I give him a thankful smile.

"This is preposterous," my mother states, standing so fast that Darrin has to take a large step back. "The movers will be here in five minutes. They're packing this place up today. I already ended the lease with the landlord. Talking with you was only a courtesy."

I gasp. "Mom—"

"No, I won't hear it," she snaps. "I knew this was a terrible idea, but your father insisted. He thought it would be good to give you a bit of freedom before you went to school—a real school—but I knew this would end terribly. Look at you."

"What's so terrible about it?" I exclaim. "I'm a straight-A student. I have a boyfriend. I have friends."

"We want better for you." Her husky voice breaks along with her façade. Real tears form now, and they come faster and faster. She wipes at her cheeks furiously. "Bailey, Carnegie is where your dad and I went. It's such a great school. It's going to set you up for life. Everything you've ever wanted will be in the palm of your hands. There for you to take."

"Set me up for *your* life, you mean." I shake my head. "Mom, I love you, but I don't want to *be* you. I want to be my own person."

Her mouth drops, opening and closing like a wayward fish. After a few moments, her face crumples, and my heart sinks with it. She brings shaking hands to her face, and I walk over to her, wrapping my arms around her.

"I'm sorry."

"This is...unacceptable." She tries to keep her strong voice, but it catches with a sob.

I hold her tighter. "If that's how you feel, that's how you feel." What Aidan told me yesterday flits through my head. All that stuff about how much it hurts to have been abandoned, and for the fraction of a moment that I saw my mom's face when I told her I didn't want to be her, a piece of me wondered if I did that to her. If it felt like I was letting her go. "I don't want this to change anything between us, Mom. If you want to cancel the lease, if you want to move everything I own out of this house, it doesn't matter. I'll still love you. I just want to make my own life. You'll still be in it, I just don't want you to run it."

"But...for a boy?"

"Aidan's...the chocolate drizzle on a sundae," I tell her, smiling to myself. *Jeez, she's really going to think I'm pregnant...* I try to find a different analogy and fail. Instead, I speak from the heart. "I know you're worried about me. I am too. But I've been lost. I tried to be the best daughter you could want, but in doing so, I gave up on being myself."

My voice cracks, and I try to knit myself together. "I wish I'd known what Darrin was going through because we would have had a lot to say to each other. And I didn't know how to tell you that living with you felt so stifling. But I am old enough now and ready to make decisions for myself, and if I screw up, that's on me. It's not on you. If I fail, it's not because you did something wrong. Failing every once in a while just happens. It makes you stronger."

I chuckle to myself when I realize where that thoughtful statement came from. I was at one of Aidan's practices, and Coach got in Aidan's face. He'd grabbed his facemask, and I stood up like I was going to shield him, but then I heard his words. He told Aidan not to get down about the incomplete pass he'd thrown.

Failing makes you better. Failing means you figured out one way that doesn't work, so you can discard that and look for a different way. Now, get out there and find a way that works.

Aidan must recognize them too because he starts to rub my back. In turn, I squeeze my mom even tighter, and she actually hugs back. "That sounds so grown up of you."

"I think you'd like grown-up me if you gave her a chance."

She pulls away, her smudged mascara giving her a moody, crazed look. Not something I'm used to seeing on her. "You're my little girl."

"Yeah, and you don't have to let her go. You just have to give her space."

She lets out a ragged breath. "I still don't like this idea."

"You don't have to."

She steps back to sit in the chair she'd vacated, but this time, the raw parts of her are showing. The woman who doesn't have it all together. The woman who's scared. I like her. I like her a lot. She doesn't make me feel less than for not being perfect.

I take her hand. "Please, will you stay for lunch? I want you to see Warner the way I see it."

"But the movers."

I'm about to tell her they can work while we're at lunch because I honestly don't care what happens as long as I stay here, but Darrin speaks up. "Cancel them, Mom. You know it's the right thing."

She swallows. "But you might never come home."

Her words send an ache through my heart. Beside me, Aidan wipes at his eyes. "Mom, you're being crazy," I tell her. "I'll come home. We both will."

"Yeah, you guys have a pool," Darrin jokes, then reaches out to rub her shoulder.

"Very funny, Darrin Elliott," she scolds.

I glare at him, and he shrugs. Aidan, however, pulls his shoulders back. "I'll make sure they come home, Mrs. Covington. I can promise you."

Mom wipes at her face and notices the black streaks. "I need to freshen up." She sniffles, and I point her toward the bathroom. The woman who's always put together, picks herself up, straightens her shoulders, and walks in that direction.

When the door closes, I hug Darrin. "She was lost. Like me."

Aidan disagrees. "She was protecting you. I can't blame her. I'm never letting you out of my sight."

Darrin pushes me away. "Ew, gag. Stop saying shit like that."

"Darrin, was that a four-letter word I heard out of your mouth?" my mom reprimands from the bathroom, her voice stern again.

"No, Mom," he calls back, giving Aidan the one-finger salute. I have to cover my mouth to keep from laughing.

I don't know what'll happen from here. My mom

might still fight me. She might never accept Aidan. But it feels good to have stood my ground. To have fought for what I think is right. For what I really want.

I take Aidan's hand in mine and squeeze it. Even if my mom comes out of that room and tells me the movers are taking my stuff, if she tells me I have to find my own way, it'll be fine.

Like an adventure.

Being kicked out of this place and losing all my stuff wasn't on my to-do list, but right now, I feel like I could do anything, including starting from nothing.

And I know I wouldn't fail because Aidan promised me forever, and my forever started last night.

27

AIDAN

COACH HANGS UP THE PHONE, and my arm drops. This couldn't come at a worse time. I turn slowly, searching out Bailey.

Seeing her stand up to her mother was inspiring. The fact that it all worked out in my favor? Even better. I capture her gaze and frown. "I hate to do this... That was Coach. He needs me to come in for a meeting."

"Of course," Bailey says, shrugging. "You can meet us at the restaurant after."

A knot forms in my stomach. I really don't like this idea. I eye her mother. She was willing to take the very thing that's giving me life away from me not twenty minutes ago.

I nod toward Bailey's room. "Can I talk to you for a sec?"

"Sure."

She follows me until we're alone, and I wrap my arms around her. "Sorry, Angel. I want to be there for you, but this sounds important."

"Aidan, I'm totally fine. I'm sure you can find a way to make it up to me later. Privately."

The way her eyes shine with mischief nearly undoes me. I grip her cheeks, pulling her in for a kiss. It's short, but I savor the feel of her lips on mine. She's everything to me. "I'm so proud of you." What I saw earlier was a girl turning into a woman. Someone who is taking the reins of her life. Bailey has really stepped into her own.

"I was pretty awesome, wasn't I?"

"I think that's my line."

"Maybe your conceit is rubbing off on me."

I tilt her head down to kiss her forehead. "I know you say it's okay, but I feel like I should be there for you at lunch."

She blinks up at me. "The team is important to you. They're family. I know you would do anything for them."

Her words carve their way into my heart.

When I started telling her about my past last night, it was difficult to explain how I feel about football. I was so inarticulate, but she nailed everything, understanding me in ways I never knew she could.

Family has let me down before. My birth mom never fought for me. But the guys I go out on the field with every practice? Every game? They fight for me every time.

If that's not family, I don't know what is.

"You're going to go, and you're not going to think about me at all," she says, lifting her chin as if I'll just follow her command.

"I'm going to go, but good luck getting me not to think about you."

I kiss her one last time and then lead her out of the room. Darrin and Mrs. Covington are standing near the front door. I give him a bro hug and then shake their mother's hand before excusing myself.

And as for my real family? My parents who took me in when I was left with no one? I'm still trying to navigate the guards I put around my heart so I don't push them away. I have to find a happy medium there somewhere, to deal with the separation in ways other than just not thinking about them. But one thing I know, is that my parents won't give up on me either. They certainly haven't yet.

Considering what we thought could happen today, things couldn't have gone any better. I'm riding out on a high as I exit the house and search the driveway for my car. *Shit, it's at Kenna's.* For a split second, I think about asking Darrin to give me a ride, but I don't want to intrude on their family time. It seems like in the end, Mrs. Covington was only worried about their future and her time with them, so I'm not going to take that away now.

I walk toward Kenna's house, picking up the pace so I don't make Coach wait. When I get there, I slide into the driver's seat of my Charger, start the engine, and take off.

As predicted, I can't keep my mind off Bailey. Even throughout the meeting with Coach, it drifts until I have to make myself focus on what he's saying.

He peers over from behind his desk in his home office. "I've seen great improvement in you, Aidan. You've really turned yourself around."

I take a deep breath and let it out. "That means a lot to me, Coach. I'm sorry I ever disappointed you in the first place. I just got off track."

"I understand being young and dumb. I'm not interested in turning boys into partying NFL players. I'm interested in turning boys into responsible men. You understand?"

I nod.

"I was happy to see your growth and your recommitment to your team and your play over the last couple of weeks. The performance you gave at the last game was beyond stellar."

My heart beats like crazy. "Thank you, Coach. That means so much to me."

"Which is why I'm going to honor you in the

midseason awards with Most Improved Player. You saw your faults, you improved them. I know it's not the award most players want to receive, but this is special. I hope it lights a fire under your ass so you never win most improved again. You deserve all the accolades, son. Your behavior off the field in the fundraiser has been exemplary. Your attitude in front of the other players is second to none. So, I'm also awarding you the midseason Teammate Award."

My heart lurches, and I have to set my jaw so I don't react. *Two awards?* "Coach, I'm honored." My phone starts to vibrate, and I silence it through my jeans, hoping to shut it off before Coach notices.

"I'm glad to be the one to tell you. We're going to give out the midseason awards at the Halloween Ball this year. Let the public see something special." He clears his throat and sets his glasses down. "I hear you and your girlfriend are in a bit of a friendly battle with Kenna and West."

He smirks, and I match it with one of my own. "Yes, sir. We're looking to start dominating soon."

Coach chuckles. "Attaboy. I have no skin in the game other than my wife needs to be completely satisfied with the way everything is going. I'm sure you understand. Happy wife, happy life."

"Completely, sir." My mind drifts to Bails again. I itch to look at my phone to see if it was her.

"Excellent," he says, peering over at his computer. "You can get out of here. I've got other players to see."

I stand. "Yes, sir. See you at practice."

He shakes my hand, and I see myself out of his house. Coach has an open-door policy, so his place is familiar to a lot of us.

When I get to my car, I take my phone out. Bailey's left me a text, so I open it to see where I'm supposed to be meeting them, but instead, a sledgehammer cracks my chest wide open.

> Aidan, I'm sorry, but I left. Please don't contact me again. It's better this way.

28

BAILEY

MOM PULLS her silver Audi into one of the parking spaces on Main Street. She leans over, peering out the windshield with a frown.

Glancing up, I realize we aren't outside the restaurant I put into her GPS. I'd been too busy thinking about Aidan and hoping that his meeting with Coach was going okay to notice where we were. "Why did you stop here? This isn't it."

"We can walk," Darrin suggests from the backseat.

Mom pushes her car door open. "It's not exactly where I'm used to shopping, but the clothes on the mannequin look cute enough."

I side eye her. "You want to go shopping now? I thought we were going to eat."

"I'm not shopping. You are."

I peer up at the window and notice the dresses on the mannequins with the cute flower prints or the styled solid colors. Just the kind of stuff I'm used to wearing before. I give Darrin a quick peek in the backseat, and his jaw is hard, but he looks away when I peer for help.

This is fucking ridiculous, I scream in my head. My temper breaks, like releasing a dam. One step forward, two steps back. "Mom, they're fucking clothes!"

"Manners."

My mouth unhinges. "You have the audacity to say that to me? You're the one telling me I'm not good enough. You're the one shitting on everything I like as a person. I'm not going in there. I'm not buying whatever you think is appropriate. It's lunch. Not a fucking ball."

"No, I've had about enough!" My mother's crazed words chill me, and I seal my lips together. She pinches the bridge of her nose. "I've listened and listened, and you still have yet to give me a good enough reason to change plans. Bailey Marie Covington, I'm ashamed. I really am."

Her words hit me like a punch to the gut.

"Mom," Darrin hedges.

"And I'm disappointed in you, too," she says, whipping her head over her shoulder to look at him. "You should've told me what was going on here. It was your responsibility to look after your sister, and the minute she started acting out, I should have been your first call."

I peer between the two of them. Regulating my breaths is difficult because of the pain slicing through me. Why am I never good enough? Just me?

Darrin hangs his head, and I can't keep my mouth shut. "What changed? Because you were just crying back at the house. I thought you really understood."

She picks lint off her linen pants. "I needed to play along until I removed you from the situation."

"You mean Aidan?"

"I mean that boy and everything else holding you back. The way you have taken the bit of leeway your father and I gave you and have turned it into this is appalling. Your clothes. Your behavior." She swallows. "I found condoms in your nightstand, Bailey."

My stomach clenches. "You went through my things?"

She ignores my question and asks one of her own. "Are you having sex with that boy?"

"Stop calling him that boy! I love Aidan. His name is Aidan."

She scoffs. "This place has brainwashed you. It's exactly what I feared. Indoctrinated you into an ordinary existence. He's going to knock you up before you've even had a chance to live. That's what these... people do. He'll have no chance to take care of you. Or the baby. You'll end up at my doorstep, and if you think I'll help you when you've done nothing but defied me, you're wrong."

"Mom, you're talking about what-ifs that haven't happened." Darrin leans forward, his hand reaching for my mom's shoulder.

She moves just out of reach. "All these people do is have kids and live off the government. I'll be damned if I see it happen to one of my own children."

"But I can go to Carnegie and get knocked up?"

She gasps still but turns up her nose. "At least they could afford to take care of you. Men who come from well-bred families don't shirk their duties."

"You're unbelievable."

Darrin switches his hand to mine and squeezes my shoulder. I take his hint and shut up, wrapping my arms around myself while he attempts to talk to her. "Aidan's one of my good friends. You know that. He's a great guy. At least they're using protection, and Mom, Aidan's going to play for the NFL. If you're worried about Bailey and money, you don't need to."

She rolls her eyes. "The NFL. Please. That's not a career. It's a bunch of men running around playing games."

"Or," I force out. "I can make my own damn money and not put all my hopes and dreams on my future husband because I'm a capable woman who can do shit for herself."

"Or that," Darrin shrugs, slinking away.

"Of course you can do whatever you want, but not

going here." She waves her arms at our surroundings. "In this small town. With an inferior education."

At the same time she says this, a man with a t-shirt and holes in his jeans walks down the sidewalk, and she sneers at him.

"You're so judgmental."

"Am I? Because I've done the comparisons. Have you? Carnegie has a graduation statistic of over ninety percent. Seventy-five percent of its graduates go on to make over half a million per year and most of them make much more than that. Carnegie's graduates are CEO's, CFO's, doctors, engineers, architects. They are the smartest men and women in this entire country."

I wave her away. "Old money always wins."

She shakes her head. "Would you like to hear Warner's statistics? Only sixty percent of its students ever graduate. Half of that statistic is lucky if they make over six figures per year."

"You act like that's terrible. Money doesn't make you happy. Clearly."

Her lips thin. "You're lucky you don't know the stress of being poor."

Uneasiness crawls over me. I understand how fortunate I've been. Truly. But is that the price for freedom? For happiness? Because Aidan isn't at Carnegie, which means my heart—my joy—isn't at Carnegie either. "Even if you had a crystal ball and could tell me all the terrible things that would happen to me by staying at Warner, I wouldn't change my mind."

"You're being naïve."

"I'm being myself."

Mom closes her door. The bang is so loud, I jump in my seat. She immediately puts the car in reverse and squeals out of the parking spot. A car horn blares behind us, and I brace in my seat, expecting a crash that never comes.

Darrin holds on to the two front seats. "What are you doing?"

"It's clear I have to be the parent and make the decision for the both of you."

The restaurant we agreed to eat at is coming up quick on the left. Instead of stopping, she presses harder on the gas. The car jerks all over the road, and I share a look of fear with Darrin.

He sits up straight in his seat, his gaze flicking to hers in the rearview mirror. "I'll drive. I'll take you wherever you want to go."

She glances down at her speedometer, and I take a deep breath as she lets her foot off the gas pedal. "This is what you're going to do, Bailey. You're going to text that boy and tell him that you can't see him anymore and not to contact you again. Cut off all ties."

I press my lips together, tears springing to my eyes. He'll think I abandoned him.

"Do it!"

Her driving becomes erratic again. She misses a stop sign, and the contents of my stomach somersault, sloshing around. She's hit her breaking point, and as much as it angers me, the part of me that knows that this is the mom who cared for me through everything feels terrible to have pushed her to this point. If she wasn't so stubborn.

"Now."

The simple fury in her tone moves me to act. I bring up Aidan's text thread, my fingers hovering over the keyboard. I could tell him Mom's lost it and has taken me hostage, but I don't know what she'll do if she sees I've disobeyed her request.

"You know it's the right thing to do. You're not his type, Bailey."

I squeeze my eyes closed, and with her words, tears run down my cheeks. Quickly, I type out a message and hit send before I even re-read it.

My mom sighs. "Now hand it to your brother."

I slip Darrin my phone. "Make sure she's done it, and then shut her phone off. Shut yours off, too."

After a pause, Darrin murmurs softly, "She did it."

"Are both phones off?"

He nods, and when she peers into the rearview mirror with an arched brow, he says, "Yes," with a definitive crack in his voice.

I reach my right hand behind me, maneuvering between the car and my seat and wiggle my fingers until Darrin clasps my hand in his and gives it a squeeze. More tears slip down my already wet cheeks.

Mom slows the car immediately. We're almost to the end of town, and I can't believe how fond of this place I've become. Its cute shops. The ice cream place. My friends. The sense of community.

A brunette comes walking out of a store, and I immediately look over my shoulder to see if it's Kenna. It isn't, and for some reason, that makes my heart break a little more.

It's not just Aidan that makes me want to stay here. It's his friends on the team that have become my friends. The classes. The way my eyes have been opened. Don't get me wrong, Aidan's my number one reason, but he's not the only thing tethering me here.

Thinking about him makes the longing so much worse though. Like I've ripped off my right arm, and I'm about to leave it in Warner.

The city limit is coming up, and my foot jumps up and down. Mom's obeying all vehicular laws now, but this slow crawl through the last remaining bits of Warner is like the last breaths of a dying person.

Soon, there won't be anything left of me. I might go back to "where I belong" in some people's eyes, but I can't because in my heart, I know I don't belong there anymore. I've found my life. And it might have a terrible graduation rate and a poor job outlook, but goddammit, my place is here. In the arms of the man I love. In the face of being a nobody, I choose to freaking live.

Mom slows for the last stop sign. I press on my seatbelt release as quietly as possible and maneuver it away from me. Swallowing the lump in my throat, I squeeze Darrin's hand and extricate myself from him, hoping he'll forgive me. When she's slowed up enough that I'm seventy-five percent sure I won't die, I force the door open and jump.

29

AIDAN

MY HEART SPEEDS INTO OVERDRIVE. The pulse at my wrist pumps and pumps. The immediate horror that falls over me like a boom of thunder has me rereading the text over and over again.

Aidan, I'm sorry, but I left?

No. This can't be happening.

I type out a response.

> If this is a fucking joke...

I send it, my foot tapping against the floorboards. Externally, I'm peering at my phone and rocking in my car, but internally, a hundred different thoughts are racing through my brain. Her mother convinced her to leave me? I shouldn't have let her out of my sight. As soon as I was gone, she probably told Bailey every reason why she should go to Carnegie, and Bails listened. Of course she did.

Darrin already told me that I was a complication she shouldn't have to deal with.

I spiral deeper and deeper and hit rock bottom when my text comes back as undeliverable.

She turned her fucking phone off? What?

I reverse out of Coach's driveway like a Formula 1 racer and speed all the way back to Bailey's place. Before I even get there, I spot the big truck parked at the curb with guys carrying stuff out the front door. I park, watching them carry out her desk. Next comes her bed.

Slowly, the world starts to rescind. The black edges of my gaze move inward and inward, consuming me. Suffocating me. It's like watching someone literally carry my life away from me, and all of a sudden, I'm that scared five-year-old little boy again who's realizing everything he thought he had was gone.

They left me.

She left me.

Even when she promised she wouldn't.

My heart clenches in my chest as a rip tears down the middle. I'm hollow. Too empty to lash out. Or cry. There's just nothing...

The thrumming of my heart is panic-induced. It beats so fast I gulp in air.

It's as if a typhoon's washed everything away right from under my feet. An hour ago, I had the world.

Now, it's empty.

This is just what happens to me. I love someone so much, but that person doesn't care.

My hands shake. This cruel reality hits like a lineman souped-up on steroids. This is how people act around me. All the accolades in football won't help. They don't matter. Not when things like this go down.

I put the car in Drive, tossing my phone onto the passenger seat. I can't sit here and watch this any longer. Just as I'm about to drive away, my car door yanks open, and a body lands on my lap. "I'm here. I'm here."

Arms move around me, holding me so tight. It takes a moment to realize it's Bailey. The scent of her perfume surrounds us, and her sweet voice is like the purest caress. I shove the car back into Park. "Bails?" I almost can't believe it.

She cups my cheeks like I always do to her and gives me a hard stare. "I didn't want to write that."

"What?" I can barely make my mind catch up. Swimming out of black nothingness is hard. It clings like tar.

Tears track down her cheeks while she looks at me. "Oh, Aidan. I'm so sorry. I jumped out of Mom's car at a stop sign. I ran here. I knew you'd come looking."

"You..." I swallow. "You didn't leave me?"

Her shoulders deflate. "I'm never fucking leaving you. You hear me? For as long as you want me, I'm never leaving you."

Brick by brick, her words build stairs in my mind. Stairs out of the empty dark. I trudge and trudge, fighting my way until I can see more clearly. "Your mom lied?"

She straddles my hips, shaking her head. "She doesn't get it, Aidan. She doesn't get that I'd do anything for you."

"So you were never going to go?"

She laughs. "Did you hit your head, stud? I told you yesterday, I'm in love with you."

I drop my head to her chest, pulling her close. I breathe her in, my viselike grip not letting up. Those few minutes felt like hours. Felt like years. "My brain likes to lie to me."

"We can rewire it together," she says. "You're too pretty to be dumb."

I laugh, the tears that had started to form leaking over now. She kisses them away, and even though I try to fight it—I'm the man, right? I'm supposed to comfort her?—she won't have it. She stays where she is, telling me everything is going to be okay.

Behind her, her whole world is being taken away, yet she's worried about me. "You and me," she promises.

After a few moments, she sighs. "I think I learned a very valuable lesson."

"What's that?" I croak out.

"Family doesn't have to be blood. It's like you with your teammates and your adoptive parents. Sometimes the people you'll give up everything for aren't even related."

She couldn't be more right. Love is when you fight for someone, and my parents have been fighting for me all along. They fought to get me. They fought to keep me happy. My brain doesn't make it easy to let them in, but I can work on that. "You forgot one person," I tell her as that realization sinks in.

"I was implied," she teases. "I jumped out of a moving vehicle for you. I ran Lord knows how many miles in these stupid boat shoes. Remind me to buy sneakers, by the way."

"The car was moving?"

She brings up her hand, pushing her thumb and pointer finger together. "A little, but if I told you it was crawling, it sounds less heroic."

"I'll remind you about the sneakers if you remind me to tell my parents I'm sorry."

A cute wrinkle appears between her brows. "Hopefully one day I can understand the way your brain works."

"If you figure it out before me, will you let me know?"

"You'll be the first." She squeezes me. For a long time, we sit there and hold each other. I take comfort in being this close. I'm never going to take this for granted, I swear. Opening my heart is what brought her to me.

She breathes out, her soft breath a caress on my neck. "Now that that's settled, know anywhere I can stay? Oh, and I might need your help wrestling a few things out of these movers' hands."

I kiss her cheek. "Good thing I'm in the mood to fight."

She untangles herself from me and gets out of the car. Immediately, she reaches back to help me up. Together, we march toward the movers, my arm around her shoulders, like it always was, even when we were "faking" it.

Spoiler alert: I was never faking it.

30

BAILEY

AIDAN GRABS MY THIGH. The black candelabras spread about the room provide the perfect atmosphere for the Halloween Ball. Pumpkin spice permeates the air, skulls and cobwebs line the space, and the deep-orange gown I'm wearing makes me fit right in—if I needed an excuse to fit in, but I don't.

Our table is filled with people I know and care for. The cook from Richie's and his wife, and the little boy and his family from the ASPCA fundraiser. And sitting on the other side of me is someone who's helped me and Aidan so much these past few weeks.

The owner of an apartment complex in town agreed to rent me a room for free for the rest of the semester as long as Aidan would star in their commercial. It was Aidan who arranged it all. He made the calls and pitched his idea, and the couple has turned out to be some of the best people I've ever met. Since the movers wouldn't give me any of my furniture back, they lent me some. Literally, the only thing I walked out of that house with was a box of my "commoner" clothes.

It's amazing how little you need to live the life you want. All I really need is Aidan. Clothes are nice, but— On second thought, would it be so bad to be around him naked 24/7?

Aidan's parents have been great. He sees them more often now, and little by little, their connection grows even stronger the more the armor he placed around his heart dissolves. His mother has become a confidant for me. Someone I turn to when I need advice. We have our own text thread, and I never go more than a few days without writing her.

Darrin, too, made his way back to Warner. He didn't jump out of a moving vehicle to do it—and if you ask me, that's pretty lame—but he made it back, and that's all that matters.

My mom and dad on the other hand? Well, let's just say we're all stubborn, and until they give a little, I'm not going to be the one who does. Healthy boundaries are needed in situations like this. I'm not ready to give up on them, but I don't need to sacrifice myself to rebuild that bridge between us.

Aidan showed me that.

The lights in the room flicker, and Mrs. Thompson climbs the stage steps as the chatter lowers to a hum.

She's dressed in a sensible Bulldog-blue gown. Upon approaching the microphone, she says, "Thank you, everyone, for your donations."

I clap, smiling at the people around our table who paid money to sit with us specifically. They auctioned off seats, all part of their plan to raise more money for the Step-Up Foundation.

"I'm thrilled to inform you of the total amount our fundraising efforts have brought in. With your money or your time, we'll be able to help the less fortunate in our community significantly. From Meals on Wheels to the ASPCA, we all made Warner a more comfortable place to live this year.

"To the donors, I couldn't be happier to call you my neighbors. To the football couples, I'm so thankful my husband gets to tell you what to do so you had no option but to show up."

The crowd laughs.

"But really, I think you all understand what a tremendous thing you've done here for your community. It's because of young people like you that I have so much hope for Warner's future and for society. From the bottom of my heart, thank you."

A round of applause rings from the crowd, and she pauses until it dies back down.

"Now," she says, staring down at a paper on the lectern, "without further ado, I'm so pleased to announce that we've raised over $60,000 in this year's fundraiser!"

My brows shoot up. Some of the football players start chanting "Blue, Blue, Blue!" Aidan joins in, cupping his hands around his mouth.

When I look at him, I can't help but fall in love all over again. I shouldn't be surprised at the way my stomach somersaults. He's been making me feel that way since Darrin brought him to our house all those years ago.

I've never been so sure that fate exists. If he hadn't been the one to show me what a life outside my posh cage would look like, I don't know where I'd be. If he hadn't single-handedly pushed me outside my comfort zone, I wouldn't be at Warner, that's for sure. And likewise, I proved to him that he was worth fighting for. That love is real.

Even when you're faking it.

The chant dissipates, all eyes up on Mrs. Thompson still. "I'm sure you'd all like to hear the football couple winner. The team who single-handedly raised more money than any other couple."

My stomach twists. Aidan keeps telling me he doesn't care if we win, but I hope we do. Plus, the scholarship money would be really handy right now.

College is downright expensive. I've had to apply for loans, and my landlords extended me a part-time position updating their website and social media accounts. I'm able to work on the weekends so it doesn't impact my classes, and it's just enough money to pay for food and the occasional treat now and then.

This money, though, would help me feel more secure. However, we weren't the best at the relationship game we competed in last weekend, much to the crowd's amusement. I have to admit, it was pretty hilarious.

I reach over to grab Aidan's hand, and he squeezes mine.

"And the winner is..." She pauses for good measure, staring out at all the tables. "Clint Barbery and Natalie Simmons!"

Despite the drop in my stomach, I applaud the defensive player and his girlfriend. They totally kicked everyone's ass in the relationship game. When they walk up to the stage to accept their mock crowns, Aidan leans over, still clapping. "Rigged."

I laugh, shaking my head. He always knows how to make me feel better. "Maybe if you knew what my favorite color was, we wouldn't have lost."

"Maybe if you knew I preferred sweet pickles to dill, we wouldn't have lost." He tugs me close, his lips brushing against my ear. "They should've asked us the important stuff. Like, do I think my very real, never fake girlfriend is wearing leggings under her dress? Yes, yes I do."

I nibble on his ear playfully while at the same time

pulling up my dress so he can see he's right. "Plus, the sneakers."

"Always with the sneakers now."

"Well, I never know when I'm going to need to run to you."

His eyes switch from amusement to sincerity. "You're the best thing that's ever happened to me, Bailey Covington, and we'll figure this out."

I'm sure my eyes say the same back because the love I have for him threads through my very being—and I never want it to stop. "Does that mean we can peace out and go to Oral Rock?"

His body locks up. "Troublemaker."

"I think I have some more to-dos to cross off my list."

"I thought we gave up public lewdness." He turns when his teammate starts to give a hilarious acceptance speech.

A rolled-up piece of paper lands in front of him, though, catching his attention. We peer around to see West and Kenna at the table next to us trying not to lose it.

Aidan opens the paper and stifles a laugh. In big block letters reads: *LOSERS*.

I grab a pen from my purse and give it to Aidan who scribbles out, *Right back at ya, bitches*.

He crumples the paper again and tosses it. The misshapen wad soars through the air and lands directly on West's dinner plate. He and Kenna open it, already laughing.

West flips us off while pretending to scratch his cheek.

There are strangers, friends, acquaintances, and loves. There are people you'll go out of your way for and there are people you won't. I'm so happy I learned who my people are.

Clint's speech ends, and Aidan leans over, capturing my lips in a chaste kiss before he says, "Meet me in the bathroom in ten. We can't let our table sponsors down, but that doesn't mean we can't bring Oral Rock here...in private."

I squeeze my thighs together in response to his words. He gets up, walking away casually, and I watch him go with my heart full.

I don't know why my mom is so worried about my future when I couldn't be more sure that it's going to be spectacular. It'll be everything I've dreamed of. Built with love and freedom, we'll bond everything together with laughter and the butterflies he still gives me with one look.

No, I'm not worried about my future at all.

About the Author

E. M. Moore is a USA Today Bestselling author of Contemporary and Paranormal Romance. She's drawn to write within the teen and college-aged years where her characters get knocked on their asses, torn inside out, and put back together again by their first loves. Whether it's in a fantastical setting where human guards protect the creatures of the night or a realistic high school backdrop where social cliques rule the halls, the emotions are the same. Dark. Twisty. Angsty. Raw.

When Erin's not writing, you can find her dreaming up vacations for her family, watching murder mystery shows, or dancing in her kitchen while she pretends to cook.

Made in the USA
Monee, IL
10 January 2025

76537509R00210